The four brutis
the barrel of B

Then they began to march down the corridor toward her.

Should she shoot to wound? Fire a warning shot? Take one of these monsters down?

Caution won out. Brigid aimed above the approaching figures and fired. They slowed momentarily as the blast ripped into the wall in a burst of splintering wood. Then they started moving again, faster this time.

Brigid targeted one of the two in the middle. Aiming for his legs, she sent another bullet hurtling through the air. It struck the thing in his right hip, but Brigid felt little satisfaction as the false man flipped over and dropped to the floor.

His colleagues slowed, but only for an instant. Brigid saw the fallen one roll back up to stand. Her bullet had struck him, but whatever they were made of, it was a lot stronger than human flesh.

"Stay back!" She blasted again, and heard several bullets strike flesh with a familiar dull, wet sound.

And then the first of the monstrous figures was upon her.

Other titles in this series:

James Axler
Outlanders®

COSMIC RIFT

A GOLD EAGLE BOOK FROM

WORLDWIDE®

TORONTO • NEW YORK • LONDON
AMSTERDAM • PARIS • SYDNEY • HAMBURG
STOCKHOLM • ATHENS • TOKYO • MILAN
MADRID • WARSAW • BUDAPEST • AUCKLAND

Recycling programs
for this product may
not exist in your area.

First edition November 2013

ISBN-13: 978-0-373-63880-2

COSMIC RIFT

Copyright © 2013 by Worldwide Library

Special thanks to Rik Hoskin for his contribution to this work.

Printed in U.S.A.

Our knowledge is a receding mirage in an expanding desert of ignorance.

—Will Durant, 1885–1981

The Road to Outlands—
From Secret Government Files to the Future

Almost two hundred years after the global holocaust, Kane, a former Magistrate of Cobaltville, often thought the world had been lucky to survive at all after a nuclear device detonated in the Russian embassy in Washington, D.C. The aftermath—forever known as skydark—reshaped continents and turned civilization into ashes.

Nearly depopulated, America became the Deathlands—poisoned by radiation, home to chaos and mutated life forms. Feudal rule reappeared in the form of baronies, while remote outposts clung to a brutish existence.

What eventually helped shape this wasteland were the redoubts, the secret preholocaust military installations with stores of weapons, and the home of gateways, the locational matter-transfer facilities. Some of the redoubts hid clues that had once fed wild theories of government cover-ups and alien visitations.

Rearmed from redoubt stockpiles, the barons consolidated their power and reclaimed technology for the villes. Their power, supported by some invisible authority, extended beyond their fortified walls to what was now called the Outlands. It was here that the rootstock of humanity survived, living with hellzones and chemical storms, hounded by Magistrates.

In the villes, rigid laws were enforced—to atone for the sins of the past and prepare the way for a better future. That was the barons' public credo and their right-to-rule.

Kane, along with friend and fellow Magistrate Grant, had upheld that claim until a fateful Outlands expedition. A displaced piece of technology…a question to a keeper of the archives…a vague clue about alien masters—and their world shifted radically. Suddenly, Brigid Baptiste, the archivist, faced summary execution, and Grant a quick termination. For Kane there was forgiveness if he pledged his unquestioning allegiance to Baron Cobalt and his unknown masters and abandoned his friends.

But that allegiance would make him support a mysterious and alien power and deny loyalty and friends. Then what else was there?

Kane had been brought up solely to serve the ville. Brigid's only link with her family was her mother's red-gold hair, green eyes and supple form. Grant's clues to his lineage were his ebony skin and powerful physique. But Domi, she of the white hair, was an Outlander pressed into sexual servitude in Cobaltville. She at least knew her roots and was a reminder to the exiles that the outcasts belonged in the human family.

Parents, friends, community—the very rootedness of humanity was denied. With no continuity, there was no forward momentum to the future. And that was the crux—when Kane began to wonder if there was a future.

For Kane, it wouldn't do. So the only way was out—way, way out.

After their escape, they found shelter at the forgotten Cerberus redoubt headed by Lakesh, a scientist, Cobaltville's head archivist, and secret opponent of the barons.

With their past turned into a lie, their future threatened, only one thing was left to give meaning to the outcasts. The hunger for freedom, the will to resist the hostile influences. And perhaps, by opposing, end them.

Prologue

Acre, Haifa Bay, January 1190

The Holy Land looked like hell.

Flecks of ice swirled in the air before settling on the exposed skin of the dead soldiers where they lay in the shadow of the city wall. Their armor was caked with mud so cold it had veins of ice running through it now. Mud and something else—blood, its redness turned brown as its vibrant color rusted in the air, making it almost indistinguishable from the mud that had marred their clothing.

James Henry awoke on that bloody field, dreams of his home hundreds of miles away ebbing from his brain as it tripped back into the waking world. He was cold, his metal-plate armor like a cage of ice around his body, his flesh shivering inside. He still held his sword, his hand cinched around it so tightly that it had frozen in place.

He opened his eyes to the predawn darkness, the sky an eerie shade of blue-black, as if it had been bruised. There was something sticking to his left eye, clamping it so that it wouldn't open properly. He reached up with a hand gloved in metal that made it heavy and hard to manipulate, and wiped at his eye as carefully as he could.

It was sleep. Sleep and blood, crusting over his eyelashes, clinging to them like a film. He swept his fingers over the eye again, rubbing gingerly until the gunk snapped away in red-

and-orange flecks. A moment later, those flecks were lost to the sand, a single grain among a billion others.

There was barely any noise out here, Henry realized. It didn't come as a surprise—he had been here on Richard's pilgrimage for over a year and camped close to the spot outside the walled city of Acre for some four months. The nights were always quiet. What noises they heard came not from the city but from the animals that hid in the daytime, appearing only fleetingly as their night work demanded.

James Henry lay there gathering his wits, striving to recall how he had come to be lying here, facedown in the mud. King Richard had mounted a push against the walls of the city, he recalled, calling all of his knights and soldiers to the battlefield as they pressed against Saladin's forces. Saladin's people had the higher ground here, the high walls of the sand-colored city providing ample defense from their attackers.

They had dropped things on the Faithful of Saint Peter, poured scalding oils that would turn a knight's armor into an oven, roasting him alive before he could remove it. They had used arrows, too, and spears, and they had fought with barely domesticated animals whose training had extended only so far as to make their targets those chosen by man rather than those they would choose themselves—though that difference was negligible.

And then the soldiers had come, pouring from the city in a great flood tide, swords held high in cruel warning. James had been struck by the colors as he always was, the brightly colored robes these locals wore as they came to meet their Christian visitors.

They had fought like mad things, swords cleaving the air with sunlight flashes, men crying in exertion and desperation and pain. The Lord was watching and the pilgrimage was a just one, a need to secure the corner of Earth where everything of value had begun.

The battle had started in the early afternoon and had continued long into the night, as wave after wave of soldiers from both sides had joined the fray. Richard's prestige forces all bore the red cross on their tabards, his soldiers bearing the same on their dirt-encrusted clothes; Saladin's army wore the colors of the East, bright in the sun of the late afternoon, dulling to a uniform gray-indigo as it set.

Now, with dawn nudging toward the horizon, James Henry found himself sprawled in the mud beyond the city walls, his body cold, his head heavy. Around him there were bodies; some were men he knew. He could not remember being struck, and he could feel no wound, no tell-tale warm dampness where blood had gathered about his body. He had fallen from exhaustion, then, unwounded but tired beyond comprehension, lugging a suit of metal on his body like a snail carrying its shell.

He had imagined that the Holy Land would be warm, a place of sunlight and tranquility, of green plants and singing birds. But it wasn't. The plants offered sparse cover when you were at war with the locals, and any singing birds had long since departed the battlefields for fear of getting caught in the crossfire or, more likely, eaten by the invading pilgrims who craved sustenance in this little corner of hell. It could get stupidly hot by the afternoon, but it was beastly cold once the sun set.

Henry clambered to his feet, rising from the ground like a felled English oak in reverse, struggling to move in the metal suit. Normally he would have an aide to help him with such maneuvers, but there was no one else about, only dead men lying in blood that had long since mingled to become one mighty crimson smear on the land.

He stood at last, his movements in the armor like those of a ridiculously heavy mannequin given the semblance of life by a puppeteer. He used his sword, the one he had never relinquished, even in sleep, to help him stand, leaning his weight against it, its tip pressed into the mud. There was ice on the mud, a thin film that cracked as the sword touched it.

Henry looked at the sleeping city, then turned his attention to the sky. The sun had not yet risen but it would, and soon. Already he could see that blush of orange suffused with white where the sun played the last seconds of hide-and-seek with the horizon, waiting to reveal itself.

He watched the sky for a few moments, gathering his wits. And as he stood there, the knight in mud-caked armor saw something flicker on the horizon. It was gold, like that fabled star over Bethlehem, shimmering in the predawn light. It was shaped like a star, too, but one that had been cut in half across its horizontal, leaving only the points that stuck up to the heavens, a flat base all that was left below.

Henry blinked, feeling the tiredness in his muscles, wondering if he was still half-asleep. The star flickered again, twinkling on the horizon, swimming in and out of existence as if it was not quite solid.

"What are you—?" Henry muttered, crossing himself as he had when he had pledged his allegiance to King Richard and made the vow that would only be fulfilled when they reached Jerusalem.

The strange star shimmered, the reaching rays of the rising sun catching its edges, lighting the flat line that formed its base in fiery gold and brass.

Momentarily the knight looked away, scanning the debris of the battlefield where a half-dozen soldiers lay, Muslims and Christians both. He was the only one who had survived, and he dared not call to the city and alert them to his presence, no matter how much he desired to share this experience and confirm it was truly happening. Men saw strange things when they were dying, he knew, and he feared blood loss was causing this vision of the rushing star.

The half star winked one last time before fading from his view like a painting seen only through steam, gone again forever.

James Henry watched the spot in the sky where the thing had been, his breathing slow and deep, waiting for it to re-appear. But it did not. Closing his eyes, the lids heavy with sleep and cold, the Englishman turned away from the sky and began his long trek back to camp where Richard's forces would welcome him with open arms with warm food and with the safety of numbers he needed to rest his tired body.

But it was only natural that he turn back, just once, just to be sure that the bisected star was no longer there. So he turned his head, peering over his shoulder, and he saw the second miracle, just as in the tales he had heard in church. There was a second star now, smaller but shining with the same golden intensity, standing in the sky where the first had been. The first star, the one that was abbreviated on its center line, had not reappeared, but this smaller one seemed to be waiting in the same place and growing larger.

No, Henry realized, it wasn't growing larger—it was coming closer. Painted the gold of the sun's rays, the star shot across the heavens like a streak of light, its shape ill-defined, the sunlight twinkling across its surface in ever-changing patterns.

The knight watched as the star became bigger, bigger still. It was accompanied now by a noise like galloping horses, like one hundred hooves drumming across the heavens in perfect unison. The star tore across the sky and clipped low over the sandy-colored buildings of Acre, hurtling over Henry's head. The noise became louder as it shot directly overhead, as though mighty steeds had been unleashed, and he could feel the heat emanating from it even down here, two hundred feet below. Around him, the flecks of ice that were swirling in the morning air rose, lifted up as if by a magnet, drawn to the passing star as it blasted across the sky. The star continued on, rushing toward the camp where his fellow pilgrims slept.

The thought struck Henry out of nowhere: it will kill us should it strike at such speed. The magic of the whole moment had gone; now all he cared about was his brethren down by the coast.

Henry ran, or ran as best he could in the heavy armor, metal plates clanking like the sounds from a smithy's shop.

The star continued to grow, igniting the heavens with a trail of fire the way oil can be set alight and sent on a hurried race across a tabletop. The trail waited above him, burning in the heavens before ebbing to a spark as the star continued its trip. James had never seen its like before, but he could see where it was heading now, and he could estimate that it would land with some force on the ground, a shooting star brought down by its weight.

The star trailed across the sky in a burning streak for another three seconds…four…five…before plummeting behind a ridge where Henry could no longer see it. He continued hurrying toward it, driving his aching body on, unable to truly run in the suit of armor.

A moment later, the sound of drumming hoofbeats stopped, and James watched the overhead path of flame flicker and die, the sky just the sky once more. Behind him, his own hurried footprints sat like hammer indentations in the icy mud, the flecks of frost still batting about in the wind.

Over the ridge. James Henry was breathless now, his skin ruddy with sweat, the cold flakes of ice melting as they touched his exposed face. He stood at the crest of the ridge, sword before him, blade tip in the dirt to steady his weary body. The star waited on the other side, its body glowing yellow-gold as flames. It was smaller than he had imagined, but it was still large, the size of a farmer's cottage or a stable back home. As he looked at it, he saw that the fiery yellow was marred with blocks of black in geometric shapes, squares and oblongs, the lines perfectly straight.

The star had left a trail in the dirt, the mud turned to water in a line where it had touched down, a long streak of puddle cloudy with soil.

The camp was not far from here. A mile maybe? Not even that. The star had missed it but it had been close by the reckoning of cosmic things.

Henry drew his sword from the dirt and stepped closer, trekking down the muddy bank, walking sideways to keep his balance. Closer, the star did not look so much like a star as a pebble, smooth and oval with those black shapes drawn flat on the surface. The glow of the star was ebbing as Henry watched, its lightning color turning the rich golden of burnished brass, then darkening further as he watched until it reminded him of caramelized sugar or the crust of freshly baked bread.

Something hissed as the surface darkened and Henry watched as one of those black forms bowed out and upward, revealing a trapezoid shape in the surface of the star. The top and bottom lines of the trapezoid were parallel, but the bottom was much wider than the top. It was dark, but there was light there, too, small traces of light in colored lines.

Henry watched, knowing not what it was he was looking at. He had come to the Holy Land to secure access to Jerusalem; he did not want for bravery. But this—this was beyond his comprehension, a star fallen from heaven, waiting on the outskirts of his camp.

Then a figure appeared, framed in the trapezoid, which Henry realized was a door—a door into a star. It was a man, white skinned and dressed in armor the like of which Henry had never seen. The figure had a beard like his, but where Henry's was a muddy brown the stranger's was blond as the sun's rays. The figure carried a weapon, too, though it took

Henry a moment to recognize it; it looked like a sickle but it was longer and it glowed the green and gold of the ocean's surface catching sunlight.

Henry looked at the figure as it emerged from the star, a cloak billowing behind it as it stepped on Earth soil. It was then that Henry knew just what he had to do. He sank to his knees—graceless in the restraints of the armor—and bowed his head. Henry was a knight for Richard the Lionheart, and had willingly joined him on this pilgrimage to safeguard the Holy Land. He knew a savior when he saw one.

Chapter 1

Serra do Norte, Brazil, July 2204

It was always hot in Brazil, and in July it was hotter, Domi reflected as she took another sip from her water bottle.

"Careful with that," Mariah Falk recommended, peering up from her equipment. "Controlled sips, or you'll start to feel bloated."

"I've done this before," Domi replied irritably and made a show of smacking her lips. Dammit, that woman has the hearing of a bat, Domi cursed to herself. Mariah's warning was sound advice, and reminding even a seasoned field agent like Domi was never something to regret. But it annoyed the heck out of Domi because Mariah tended to speak to her as if she were a child.

It was understandable that she did, however. Domi was waiflike in appearance, her small frame more like that of a teenage girl than a grown woman. Furthermore, she dressed like a child, as well, favoring short, sleeveless tops that barely covered her small, pert breasts and cutoffs that left her thin legs bare. While slim, her legs and arms were still muscular, her physique reminiscent of an acrobat or a ballet dancer, all coiled sinew waiting to spring. Domi also preferred to go barefoot, whatever the terrain she found herself in; right now she was especially enjoying the way the tufts of grass that grew tenaciously from the sandy soil of the riverbank tickled her pale toes.

"Pale" being the operative word, of course; Domi was an albino, skin chalk-white with hair to match, cut in a pixie-ish bob that framed her sharp features. Within that sharp face it was the eyes that drew attention—two pools of ruby-redness like congealing blood. In a simpler time she might have been mistaken for a devil or sprite and burned at the stake.

Domi was a field agent for the Cerberus operation, a set-up based in North America that had dedicated itself to the protection of mankind from the dangerous forces that threatened it. The reason that sounded like a pretty weighty remit was because it was—Cerberus had fought with alien races bent on the destruction of humanity, battled creatures in other dimensions and even fought with world machines that had been programmed to bring forth Armageddon.

Domi had grown up far away from the technological hub that was the Cerberus headquarters, a military redoubt built in the twentieth century that had been secured by her lover, Mohandas Lakesh Singh, the contentious leader of the Cerberus team. Domi had, instead, been born in the Outlands beyond the reach of the walled villes that dominated the North American landscape, and while she had witnessed and been a part of a great many lifestyles since then, she remained an outlander at heart, a wild free spirit with a quick temper and a keen survival instinct.

Domi wore the bare minimum of clothing for decency and she wore something else, too—two weapons that she did not leave the Cerberus redoubt without. The first was a combat knife with a cruel, nine-inch serrated edge, cinched to her ankle in an undecorated sleeve. She had once used this blade on her ex-master, Guana Teague, when she had been indoctrinated into his cruel regime as a sex slave, and its value to her was incalculable.

The second item, unholstered but slipped through her belt at the small of her back, was a Detonics Combat Master

.45 pistol with a dull finish. While Domi might get more personal satisfaction from using the blade on an enemy, she was also a crack shot and wouldn't hesitate to use the weapon if danger called.

Domi's companion was unlike her in almost every way. Mariah Falk had been born in the twentieth century and had trained to be a geologist before enlisting in a government research project that had placed her on the moon. While there, Mariah had been put into suspended animation and had missed the most significant event of the twenty-first century—the nuclear holocaust that had rewritten the maps and left civilized society as little more than a memory smoldering in the ashes.

That was two hundred years ago, and since then, the world had moved on quite a bit. Mariah had been awakened in the twenty-third century, along with a number of fellow experts, when a Cerberus exploratory team had ventured to the Manitius Base on the moon, and she had soon been invited to lend her services to Cerberus for the betterment of mankind.

Mariah was a woman in her late forties, relatively speaking, with a narrow frame and a thin face. Her short, chestnut hair was streaked with white here and there, and there were lines around her eyes that spoke of her easy nature and ready smile. Though perhaps not conventionally pretty, Mariah was genial and a natural at putting people at ease.

Most people, that was—she and Domi had a little history dating back to when Domi had been forced to shoot her in the leg to prevent her from moving. While the shot had saved Mariah's life, it still rankled that Domi hadn't found a less aggressive way to save her skin. When it was cold—which, thankfully, Brazil wasn't just now—the ghost of that bullet still caused her leg to ache as if the devil himself was inside it, strumming on the bone like it was a tea-chest bass in one of those old skiffle bands her dad had liked to listen to.

Unlike Domi, Mariah was dressed conservatively in a white jumpsuit twinned with a simple jacket, the latter doubling as a hold-all with voluminous pockets across the chest and arms. Mariah carried no weapons; she had been trained in basic firearm use like all Cerberus personnel, but she remained uncomfortable around guns and considered them very definitely a last resort. Which was why Domi was here with her—while Mariah employed her expertise as a geologist to scrutinize the immediate area, Domi assumed the role of bodyguard.

Domi was an odd choice, perhaps, to an outsider, but her keen senses, determination and combat prowess, not to mention a somewhat fiery temper, made her every bit as protective and dangerous as a well-trained bullmastiff.

Mariah was here—"here" being a secluded delta of the Juruena River a good seventy miles from the nearest human habitation—taking rock samples and testing the soil composition via a portable spectroscope attached to her laptop computer. The Cerberus mainframe, a database tuned to numerous remote sensors and satellite relays, had detected something out of the ordinary in the radiation content of the region.

"Find anything?" Domi asked, her shrill voice breaking into Mariah's thoughts.

"It's too soon to say," Mariah responded automatically. She had always been methodical rather than prone to great leaps of intuition—her would-be lover, Clem Bryant, had been the intuitive one, and all that had ultimately gotten him was killed. "Radioactivity is certainly higher than we'd expect for this kind of area," she confirmed, gesturing vaguely around her.

The area was overgrown, with trees bending down toward the river under the weight of their leaves, and mossy grass vying for space along the banks. Colorful birds flitted be-

tween the trees, small as a child's hand, their shrill calls joining the incessant insect buzz that hummed in the air.

The area was the very definition of remote. If there had
once been human habitation anywhere nearby it had almost
certainly been exterminated by the nuclear exchange that had
almost destroyed the northern part of the American continent. South America had, by contrast, gotten off lightly, but
still the population had been culled to perhaps fifteen percent
of what it had once been, and the rise in base-level radioactivity had left many people sterile, resulting in a fall in the
birthrate and a concurrent rise in the appearance of "mutie"
babies, creatures who had perhaps started life as human but
whose DNA had become so mangled that they now resembled nothing short of monsters. They had been strange days
indeed, those that had followed the nukecaust.

Despite its remoteness, Domi and Mariah had had little
trouble getting here from their base in the Bitterroot Mountains of Montana in North America. They had traveled via
an instrument called the interphaser, a portable teleportation
device that tapped the quantum pathways between spaces to
move people and objects instantaneously all over the world
and beyond. The interphaser relied on fixed-point locations
to transmit its passengers, utilizing an ancient connected web
that underlay the structure of Earth itself. These locations
were called parallax points and many of them had become
sites of worship to primitive cultures, when men were more
in tune with the planet and aware of the vortices that flowed
around these strange places.

"'Hot' or 'hot hot'?" Domi asked, taking in the forest with
her gaze.

"Welllll…" Mariah said, stretching out the word. "The
plant life is certainly flourishing. As are the birds and whatever passes for the other local fauna, too."

"'Fauna'?" Domi queried before Mariah could continue.

Mariah had forgotten that Domi was a child of the Outlands, and that sometimes she didn't know what their colleagues might call the ten-dollar words for things.

"Animals," Mariah clarified. "The strange part is, while the soil is showing a lot of radioactivity, it's not leaked into the rocks."

"Meaning?" Domi prodded. The albino was a woman of few words.

"Whatever caused this is most likely a recent phenomenon," Mariah mused, "which may also explain why it didn't appear on our previous sweeps of the area. My computer is doing a spectral analysis, which should bring us closer to an answer."

"How long?" Domi asked, eyeing the area warily.

Mariah checked the flip-open screen of the laptop where she had placed it on a large, flat rock at the edge of the river bank. "Eight minutes."

"Hah," Domi sneered. "Computers don't know everything." With that, she padded barefoot into the forest, brushing a low-hanging branch aside.

Mariah eyed the computer screen again before watching Domi trudge through the trees. A countdown on the screen assured her that the spectral analysis would be complete in seven minutes and forty-nine seconds, which to a geologist used to dealing with rocks that may have been formed over thousands or even millions of years, didn't seem a very long time to wait. But Domi was impatient, and Mariah couldn't help but admire her blind determination to make something happen, even if she was one hundred percent certain that nothing would.

"Hold up," Mariah called to Domi. "I'm coming with you."

Domi turned her head and slowed for a moment, granting Mariah an eerie smile, white teeth gleaming between white lips. It was the most unsettling thing the geologist had seen today.

Pushing her sweat-damp hair from her face, Mariah walked deeper into the forest after Domi. It took just fifteen paces to completely lose sight of the river, such was the density of the foliage here. Up ahead, however, Domi was always visible, a streak of white amid the green.

A few steps farther and Domi stopped. She stood there, in the space between the trees, her nose twitching as she sniffed the air.

"What are you looking for?" Mariah asked as she came alongside her colleague.

"Something's not right," Domi said, pitching her voice low.

Mariah knew better than to argue with the albino warrior. While Domi may seem primitive in her outlook, and more than a little eccentric, she was notoriously in tune with her senses.

After a moment, Domi reached forward and grasped the leaves of a fern that had grown to waist height. "The plants," she said, studying the leaves. "They're not…"

Mariah waited for the other woman to finish the statement, and when she didn't she looked at her with furrowed brow. "Not what?" she asked.

Mariah watched Domi lean down and pull the plant stem closer, sniffing at its leaves. After a moment the albino girl shook her head.

"Well?" Mariah prompted, not bothering to hide her irritability.

"They don't come from here," Domi replied, letting go of the fern and reaching up for a strange-looking fruit dangling from a nearby tree.

Mariah wasn't sure what the fruit was, but its glossy skin was a purple so dark it was almost blue-black. "What is that?" she asked.

Domi looked up, fixing Mariah with her eerie stare. "Was hoping you'd know. Not from around here, either."

Mariah was a geologist not a horticulturalist, but she knew enough about plants to recognize more than just the basic types. That knowledge could be invaluable sometimes when she was looking at certain land types, and it had acted as a pointer to discovery on more than one field trip. "Yes, you're right," she said, nodding gently. "I don't recognize that…"

"Recognize any?" Domi asked. Her words were clipped now, syntax fractured, the way the Outlanders spoke. The woman would slip into this dialect now and again in times of anxiety.

Mariah peered around warily, looking at the leaves on the trees, the fronds that stood out from the bushes close to her hips. "I…don't." Suddenly, Mariah was feeling decidedly unsettled. "Do you think…? *What* do you think?" she finally managed to ask.

"Alien," Domi replied matter-of-factly.

"This area," Domi indicated. "Twenty feet square. Everything here doesn't belong."

"Then we tell Cerberus," Mariah insisted, but Domi was moving once again. This time the chalk-skinned warrior was reaching for the roots of a tree, plucking at them as if to reach beneath. "Domi? What are you doing?"

"Investigating," Domi replied, and she produced her knife from its sheath at her ankle. In another second she was working the knife at the tree roots where they protruded from the soil, scoring the earth beneath. "Something down here," she said.

Mariah watched with a sense of foreboding as the smaller woman went to work on the ground with her knife. "Do you really think it's alien?" she heard herself ask. She had experienced alien things before, most significantly when she had been indoctrinated into the prototype version of a cult led by

Ullikummis; the deranged monster who had killed her love. That was when Domi had had to shoot her in the leg. Mariah didn't like alien stuff one bit; she would much rather leave that aspect of Cerberus's work to her colleagues.

Domi worked her hands into the soil, scraping now and then with the knife as she worked stones loose. She didn't seem like a woman in those moments; she was more like an animal burying food.

"Domi?"

Clink!

The noise came from the tip of Domi's knife as it struck something hard under the ground. It was right beneath the surface.

Warily, Mariah stepped closer, peering down at the parted earth. There, smeared with loosened dirt, she could see what appeared to be a pale blue metal plate. It was not a painted blue but rather it was metallic, like the oily sheen on chrome. She felt goose bumps rise on her arms, despite the heat. It was hard to explain, but looking at it felt—well, it just felt *wrong* somehow to Mariah. "What is that?" she asked.

"Not sure yet," Domi replied, getting back to her feet. "Guessing it's the source of all your radioactive."

"Radioactivity," Mariah corrected automatically, muttering the word.

Domi walked a circuit around the tight confines of the forest clearing, sweeping overhanging fronds away with her feet, dragging her toes through the dirt as if feeling for something. "It's buried all about," she explained. "Not very big."

"Is it one thing or lots of things?" Mariah asked.

"I think it's just one thing," Domi said. "Big as a Sandcat." A Sandcat was a multipassenger assault vehicle, roughly the size of a small truck or an old army tank.

"A…spaceship?" Mariah asked, hardly believing she was saying the word.

Domi nodded. "Small one," she said "Maybe one-man. But yes, probably. It's not from around here anyway."

Chapter 2

Domi and Mariah set to work searching the area close to the Juruena River for more clues about what was buried beneath the soil. At some point, Mariah's laptop announced the completion of its spectroscopic analysis with a ping, but Mariah was too keyed up to notice. Instead, she stuck close to Domi, trusting in that old adage of safety in numbers.

She need not have worried. Whatever it was that had been buried under the ground had been there a while, and while the local flora had been "infected," for want of a better description, there was no indication that the object itself had any semblance of life, either its own or any life form operating in tandem with it. In fact, the whole area remained just as remote and forgotten by intelligent life as it had when Mariah and Domi had arrived.

It took forty minutes to find a way down to the thing, one that was larger than the hole Domi was capable of digging with her limited tools. Mariah had brought a survey kit with her that included a small trowel, which proved better suited to digging, though progress was slow.

In a quarter hour the albino woman had uncovered a great swath of metal sheeting before revealing the edges of what appeared to be a door.

"Got lucky," Domi said with a smile.

Mariah wasn't so sure. "I'm going to speak to Cerberus," she said. "Bring them up-to-date with what we've found here."

"Good idea," Domi said as she worked her fingers around the groove of the door, mapping its edge.

The Cerberus people had seen a lot of alien artifacts since they had set themselves as guardians of Earth. Some had been majestic feats of technology that hung outside the atmosphere with an almost impossible beauty. Others had been ancient beyond imagining and had been on Earth for so long that they had come to be incorporated into the locals' way of life, worshipped as sights of great spiritual interest or esoteric knowledge.

For a spaceship to be hidden so shallowly below the surface told the geologist two things. One, it hadn't been intended to be hidden here, or if it had, it was done in a hurry; and two, it had not been here very long. In simple terms, the earth shifts over things that are buried, sinking them slowly deeper as more detritus covers them. That's why, when people went looking for them, the skeletons of dinosaurs weren't sitting plumb on the surface of the ground where the carcasses had rotted.

So, given that the artifact had not sunk very far below the surface, Mariah would guess it either got here recently enough to just barely start to be covered—which didn't seem right, since the plant life over its resting place had been altered—or…?

"It crash-landed?" Mariah whispered as she reached her laptop on the rock overlooking the river. "Wow."

Mariah was a scientist first and foremost, and she respected and employed the scientific method in her investigations. Which meant she wasn't about to turn a little educated guesswork into a statement of fact just like that. She would ask Cerberus for advice and then she and Domi would proceed from there. *Quod erat demonstrandum,* as Clem Bryant was wont to say.

Mariah automatically glanced over the laptop's screen,

nudging the touchpad to bring it back to life from sleep mode. It showed the results of the spectrographic analysis. There was a charge to the soil, and it had a higher level of radiation than it should. Furthermore, the soil was much more alkaline than Mariah would expect, although that hadn't seemed to have any negative effect on the flora growing here. "Domi said the plants were alien," Mariah reminded herself.

The Annunaki, a bored alien race who had interfered with man since the days when he was still cowering in trees from saber-toothed tigers, had been a thorn in the side of Cerberus for a long time. Highly advanced, Annunaki technology was characterized by a melding of semiliving traits, something expressed most obviously in their sentient womb-ship, *Tiamat*.

Tiamat had been destroyed over a year ago, committing a kind of honorable suicide while still in orbit around Earth following the disastrous rebirth of her offspring. Parts of *Tiamat* had survived, however, and a great chunk of the ruined spaceship had literally regrown as the Dragon City, an uninhabited settlement on the banks of the Euphrates River.

The strange plants that had sprung up on this site might have a similar origin, Mariah theorized, peering back into the forest. Could the plants be some kind of alien technology? A warning system, perhaps?

Placing a radio mic/earpiece over her left ear, Mariah tapped a code into the laptop and boosted a radio signal to the Cerberus redoubt back in Montana. "Hello, Cerberus?"

There was a pause of a few seconds while the signal was bounced off a satellite before a familiar voice answered.

"Hello, Mariah," Donald Bry began cheerily from the Cerberus comm desk. "How are things in Brazil?"

"Hot," Mariah said as she wiped sweat from her damp hands on the legs of her pants.

"I hear they have an awful lot of coffee in Brazil," Bry taunted, recalling the words of an ancient song.

"We've not drunk any so far," Mariah replied. "But we've found something here that'll keep us awake at night, Donald. What appears to be a spaceship, alien in design, is buried a little way back from the Juruena River at our current location."

There was no need for Mariah to give the specific location; all Cerberus personnel were surgically fitted with a transponder that broadcast their location, as well as details on their health such as heart rate and brain activity, back to the home base in real time. The transponder was a harmless nano-engineered attachment that was filtered into the bloodstream, making it near impossible to remove or disrupt. Back in the Cerberus operations room, Donald Bry would already be looking at a triangulation of Mariah and Domi's position on his computer monitor.

The radio communication itself was achieved via the Commtact, a top-of-the-line communication system discovered by Cerberus personnel among the artifacts of Redoubt Yankee a few years earlier. The Commtacts bounced a signal from the Keyhole Comsat satellite, which had been accessed by Cerberus for such a purpose, providing near real-time communication no matter what location the Cerberus field personnel wound up in. As a rule, field personnel had the Commtact surgically embedded beneath the skin behind an ear, where the unit could be activated at will. However, following some recent problems with the Cerberus base, Mariah had opted for a handheld version. It was another reminder that she wasn't a true field agent, she was a scientist. Exploring buried spaceships was well outside of her comfort zone.

"How large is this spaceship?" Bry asked. He made the question sound ordinary, though it was clearly anything but.

"It's still buried, so we can't be sure," Mariah replied. "Domi estimates it's roughly the size of a Sandcat."

"And where is Domi now?" Bry asked after a moment's consideration. Naturally, he could pinpoint her location accurately using the transponder, but that wouldn't tell him anywhere near as much as the eyeball report of a person on the ground.

"Still investigating the ship," Mariah said.

At the other end of the communication, Mariah heard Donald Bry's sharp intake of breath. "Is that wise?" he asked.

"I have full monitoring equipment here," Mariah reassured him. "And I'm just activating the camera unit now. There's no sign of hostile life, just some rather beautiful plants."

"Okay," Bry replied. "Keep me apprised."

"Will do."

Mariah closed down the communication with Cerberus and reached into her rucksack for the portable video camera she had brought. The unit was roughly the size of her balled fist and fit snugly into the palm of her hand. Its carrying strap doubled as a handle, so that all she needed do was point and shoot. She flipped open the screen and checked the battery life—it was fine, there was plenty of recording space in the little unit, more than enough to film the inside of a Sandcat, or something of equivalent size.

Leaving her laptop, Mariah began to march back to the clearing where she had left Domi.

BY USING THE TROWEL, Domi had worked her way around the edge of the hatch in the spaceship's skin. Revealed, it was three feet wide and just a little more than that high. She figured that whoever used it was either very short or they were used to ducking.

There was no sign of a handle or door lock of any kind; both the surface of the door and its surrounds were smooth. In fact, had it not been for the way the specks of dirt had become lodged in the seal, Domi might not have noticed the hatch at all.

Gingerly, she worked the head of the trowel around the

hatch's edge again, using both hands to wiggle it here and
there as she sought a way in. When she reached one of the
shorter edges—the one she had come to think of as the top
edge, even though the hatch plate was actually lying parallel to the ground right now—Domi felt something begin to
give. She wiggled the trowel again, scraping it back and forth
along the lip until she located what seemed to be a catch. The
blade of the trowel was too thick to hook beneath the catch,
so Domi placed it to her side and drew her knife once more.

In less than a minute, Domi had her knife under the part
of the hatch she had snagged, and she felt something pop as
she placed pressure there. There was a gasp of release as the
hatch popped open, and Domi rolled back as the door pulled
away on sliders, disappearing into the body of the ship. She
smelled the trace of stale air as it dissipated around her.

Domi peered into the hatch, her free hand reaching automatically for the pistol she had tucked into her waistband. The
hatch appeared dark and empty, the only illumination coming
from the sun's rays filtering down through the tree canopy.

Domi took a step forward, scenting the air for danger.
Unlike Mariah, Domi's Commtact was embedded beneath
her skin, giving her immediate access to her communications. The radio communications device traced the line of
her mastoid bone.

Like Domi, most of the members of the Cerberus field
teams had a Commtact surgically embedded beneath their
skin. The subdermal device operated via sensor circuitry,
incorporating an analog-to-digital voice encoder that was
implanted in each subject's mastoid bone. Once the pintels
made contact, transmissions were picked up by the wearer's
auditory canals. Dermal sensors transmitted the electronic
signals directly through the skull casing, vibrating the ear
canal. In theory, even if a user went completely deaf they

would still be able to hear normally, in a fashion, courtesy of the Commtact device.

Commtacts also functioned as real-time translation devices, providing they had enough raw vocabulary from a language programmed into their processors. Furthermore, because they were directly connected to the body of the user, they could amplify speech no matter how quiet. For a moment, Domi wondered if she should radio back for advice… but where was the fun in that?

Her mouth set in a grim smile, Domi climbed into the rectangular hole and dropped down. Inside, the ship smelled musty, the faint aroma of sweat—or perhaps it was pheromones—on the air.

Out of the sun's glare, Domi waited for her keen eyes to adjust. Unlike the hull exterior, the inside walls were soft. Domi stepped closer, pressing her hand against one wall. It was covered in some kind of padding; small roundels of cushioning bubbled across the surface like the grips on a sneaker shoe.

She moved away from the wall, stepping deeper into the interior. It took a moment to work out what she was looking at—not because it was alien but because, Domi realized, the ship was upside down. She was standing on the ceiling in what amounted to a small cabin that might fit four people comfortably, six if they squeezed. The cabin was empty and there was a viewport on the far wall through which she could only see darkness—the soil that the ship had sunk into.

In front of the viewport was a desk-like series of controls arranged in a graceful arc. Despite the controls, there was no sign of a pilot's chair—instead, there was a simple bench arranged to either side of the control board, running the length of the walls and large enough to seat two adults each.

Between the two benches was a square block that—reversing it in her mind's eye—Domi guessed would touch as high as her belly. The square unit was decorated with cuneiform patterns and looked damaged by smoke, a watery gray-black streak marring most of its surface. Though she shouldn't understand them, Domi thought she recognized the patterns—they looked a lot like the writing she'd seen on Annunaki objects.

"Damn snake-faces," Domi growled as she padded across the ceiling to get a closer look at the box unit that dominated the cabin.

"DOMI? ARE YOU THERE?"

Standing at the clearing, Mariah saw immediately what had happened. The top of the space vehicle was exposed, showing a five-foot tract of uncovered metal where Domi had worked at the earth. Even here it was barely twelve inches below the surface, just enough to hide it from prying eyes.

Mariah stepped closer, feeling the hairs on the back of her neck rise. "Domi?" she called again, raising the camera to shoulder height.

She saw the hatch then, a dark square in the ground. "Domi?"

Domi's voice came back a moment later, echoing in the cavern of the ship's cabin. "Down here," she said. "Just taking a look around."

Mariah toggled the switch on the side of the camera and set it to record, using the eyepiece to frame up a clean shot of the open hatch. "Time now is 11:45," she began, before giving the date and location. "Domi and I have found what appears to be an alien spaceship, which I speculate may have crash-landed here within sight of the river."

Mariah took a step back, belatedly deciding to get a full shot of the area, as well as a wider view of the exposed hull of the spacecraft and the open hatch. As she did, she became aware of a noise that she had not noticed before. It sounded like the old stable her uncle used to keep, the sound of agitated horses as they stomped their hooves on the ground.

Mariah stopped to listen, still holding the camera up at head height. The sound was distant but it was getting louder, which meant it was coming nearer.

"What the heck is that?" Mariah muttered, peering up at the sky.

For a moment there was nothing, just the clear blue sky peeking through the green canopy of the forest. Then a flock of birds took flight from the trees all around her—and she saw *it* for the first time. It was a golden streak in the sky, like a falling star.

"What is that?" Mariah repeated, tilting the camera up to capture what she had just seen. But now there was nothing; whatever it was had moved past her field of vision.

But the noise was even louder now, like a hundred horses galloping by overhead.

"Domi!" Mariah called, stepping back away from the buried spaceship. "Something's happening out here."

"What?" Domi's voice came back to her, barely audible now over the sound of the rushing hooves.

Overhead, a second golden light streaked high over the trees, scoring a line of fire in its wake. As Mariah watched, the light returned, zipping across the open space between the tree cover like a shooting star.

"I think we may have company up here," Mariah shouted, raising her voice above the strange drumming.

WITHIN THE BURIED SPACESHIP, Domi felt something shift beneath her and she found herself tumbling to the left. Domi was incredibly agile and had a sense of balance that would make a gyroscope blush, but she found herself slamming into the bulkhead with a gasp of surprise, taking the brunt of the blow on her left shoulder.

"Dammit!" Domi snarled as she righted herself.

The spaceship seemed to be moving but there was no sense of power inside, no familiar shudder of an engine starting up. Perhaps it was being dragged then, pulled by something.

Domi used the bobbled walls to pull herself up along the tiny boxlike lobby that led from the cabin to the hatchway through which she had entered. "Mariah?" she called as she moved. "What's happening out there?"

Before Mariah answered, the spaceship lunged again and Domi found herself stumbling backward and into the cabin once more.

THE NOISE OF thundering hooves had peaked and dropped, becoming more like a gentle simmer that rumbled through the air.

Mariah watched as the twin points of gold seemed to hover in the sky. They were both visible through the gaps in the leaves almost directly overhead. For a moment, Mariah watched them, transfixed. Then she remembered the video camera she was holding and she raised it to her eye, turning the lens on the two golden shapes and adjusting the focus.

They looked like pebbles—sleek ovoids in a rich buttery-yellow that shone like the sun. They were so bright that the camera kept dimming the image, trying to make sense of it without burning out.

"Domi," Mariah called again without taking her eye from the camera. "You need to see this. Get up here."

There was a noise from behind Mariah at that moment—the noise of a great weight of earth being moved. Mariah spun around and the image seen through the camera lens turned to a blur of foliage, and then ground, as she tried to keep things in focus.

The earth where the spaceship had been buried was shifting, soil tumbling aside as a great chasm opened up.

"Domi!" Mariah called, not taking her eye from the camera viewfinder.

The soil tumbled from the hull of the buried starship as it ascended to the surface. It waited there, shaped like an elongated letter D, its hull a gleaming blue metal resembling oil on water. It was a little longer and a little taller than a family sedan and, inappropriately given what was happening at that moment, Mariah smiled as she realized how close Domi's estimate of its size had been.

Mariah filmed as the revealed spaceship shook in place, rising higher until its lowest point was a foot above the ground. Domi was still inside there, she knew. She had to do something.

"Domi, get out now," Mariah said, pulling the camera from her eye. She stepped closer to the hovering craft, seeing it shake just slightly in place as though caught in a subtle breeze.

And then it shook more definitely, shrugging earth from its back and sending a cloud of dislodged soil up around it. Mariah staggered back, choking on the lungful of earth she had unwittingly breathed in.

"Domi—" She could hardly speak for coughing. "Domi, get out—" she called between gasps "—out of there!"

Before she could say anything else the blue starship rose higher into the air, passing the overhanging trees before nudging up above the highest of their number, shaking in place high above Mariah's head. Grains of soil tumbled down from the ship like a waterfall, smothering the nearby plants with dirt.

INSIDE THE ALIEN artifact, Domi had made her way back to the hatch only to find it had sealed shut. The cabin was brighter now that the soil no longer obscured the viewport, and she could see a series of hinged panels or small cupboards running the length of the bobbled wall close to the hatch. They reminded her of the wall cupboards in the science labs at the Cerberus redoubt, doors for little glass beakers and Bunsen burners.

Swiftly, Domi's pale fingers worked at the panels to the side, opening each as she sought some kind of release button. Behind the fourth door she found a lever that seemed to be the equivalent of the bar on a fire door, yanked it once, twice, until it moved. Lights came on in the cabin and the lobby area, casting the interior in a soft blue light, but the door stayed resolutely closed.

"Mariah?" Domi called, engaging her hidden Commtact. "Mariah, can you hear me?"

Mariah didn't answer and Domi cursed, recalling that the woman relied on the archaic handheld version of the personal radio system. This was one of those times where linked implants would have been ideal.

Try someone else, then.

"Cerberus, come in, Cerberus," Domi called, shouting to be heard over the screech of metal all around her as the ship took flight. "This is Domi. Come in, Cerberus."

"Domi?" The comm officer replied. "Where—?"

But before Domi could reply, the spaceship lurched violently and she found herself hurtling toward the decking that had been above her just a moment before. Her skull slammed against the metal-plate flooring with a resounding clang, ensuring that, whatever happened next, Domi would not be conscious to witness it.

MARIAH WATCHED AS two streaks of golden lightning soared across the sky, pulling the blue metal spacecraft with them as they disappeared from view.

"Domi," she gasped, watching the empty section of sky that was all she could see through the canopy.

The horse drumbeats continued loudly overhead, then dimmed over the next few minutes until finally, they could no longer be heard.

Chapter 3

Bitterroot Mountains, Montana, United States, post-holocaust

By the time Mariah Falk arrived back at Cerberus headquarters in North America, the operations room was already abuzz.

She arrived in the mat-trans chamber that dominated one corner of the ops room, appearing from a multicolored whirlpool that had suddenly materialized inside the protective armaglass walls of the chamber. The whirlpool contained every color of the rainbow, and it seemed to spread upward from the floor in a conical shape and then down into the floor itself in a reflection of that fantastical cone.

Within those cones, streaks of lightning charged across the impossible depths like witch fire as the interphaser unit cut a path through the quantum ether. This was the visual effect of the interphaser, a teleportation device designed by the Cerberus personnel, allowing them to cross great distances in the blink of an eye by tapping into the quantum pathways that were accessed by what were known as parallax points.

The compact interphaser, just one foot in height, appeared at Mariah's feet as she emerged inside the mat-trans chamber.

"Where exactly was Domi when you last saw her?" Lakesh asked Mariah as she stepped from the mat-trans chamber. Mariah had sent a report ahead of her through the Commtact, outlining exactly what had happened before her eyes up to the point where the two golden lights had retreated, along with the spaceship with Domi still inside.

Once she had finished her report, Mariah had requested advice from Cerberus and it was decided that she wait in place for a half hour in case the mysterious sky craft returned. She had anxiously done so, reporting in every five minutes to confirm there had been no change. In all that time, Domi had failed to respond to any hail from the Cerberus comm desk.

Once the thirty minutes had passed, Mariah had been instructed to return to Cerberus headquarters, and she arrived ten minutes after that, utilizing the nearest parallax point in the Brazilian forest.

Lakesh met her as she exited the mat-trans, and his face was a picture of worry. Lakesh—more properly, Dr. Mohandas Lakesh Singh—was the founder and leader of the Cerberus operation, although the latter title had occasionally been a contentious one.

A dusky-skinned man apparently in his fifties, Lakesh had unusual blue eyes and jet-black hair that was swept back from his forehead with a few streaks of white apparent above the ears. He had an aquiline nose and a refined mouth, and his gaze invariably gave the uncanny impression that he was thinking very deep thoughts. Lakesh wore a white jumpsuit with a blue vertical zipper that was the standard uniform of all Cerberus operations staff. Lakesh looked anxiously at Mariah as she emerged from the chamber, and his words tumbled out in a rush.

"What state was she in? Was she hurt?"

Mariah held up her free hand—the other was weighed down with the interphaser unit—to halt Lakesh's stream of questions. "Whoa, Doctor," she said. "Let a girl catch her breath already."

"I-I-I'm terribly sorry, my dear," Lakesh stuttered with

evident embarrassment. "I quite forgot my manners. How are you? Are you hurt?"

Mariah stepped across to the polished table in the anteroom beyond the mat-trans chamber door and placed the interphaser upon it. The interphaser looked innocuous enough—just a one foot high, one foot wide, square-based pyramid-shaped device made of a gleaming metal that had odd reflections on its surface.

However, its design had been refined by Lakesh himself to access preexisting quantum gateways that provided a reliable means of teleportation. It wasn't Lakesh's first experimentation into teleports. He had been one of the designers of the original mat-trans system employed by the United States military toward the end of the twentieth century, before the nuclear exchange had brought civilization to an abrupt halt. Lakesh and his creation had survived that terrible onslaught—he by cryogenic suspended animation, his mat-trans device held safely in one of the protective military redoubts that were scattered across North America and beyond.

"I'm fine," Mariah confirmed. "A little shook up and a little dusty, but I didn't sustain any damage."

"And how about my dear Domi?" Lakesh wanted to know. It was only natural that he would be the first to ask about Domi, Mariah thought. Although physically her senior by at least thirty years—and actually over two centuries older—Lakesh was in a long-term relationship with Domi. The two of them were very different—he a scientist and what they used to call an egghead in Mariah's day, she an almost-feral, self-sufficient survivor from the barely civilized areas of the postnukecaust landscape. Still, they seemed happy together and their relationship had stood the test of time so far. Perhaps it was true what they said, Mariah reflected—opposites did attract.

Lakesh was still looking at her intensely as he waited for her to answer his barrage of questions.

"She was fine when I last saw her, which was just before she entered the ship," Mariah confirmed. "That was before the golden shapes appeared in the sky," she added by way of clarification, "and she certainly gave me no indication that she had become wounded in the meantime. Once the ship took off, I lost whatever contact I had, however."

"We've had no success hailing her at this end," Lakesh reported sourly. "She's not responding to attempts to contact her via the Commtact."

"What about her transponder?" Mariah asked.

Lakesh shook his head. "Negative. Donald traced her movement for approximately two miles before she and the ship disappeared from all tracking devices. It's as if the transponder simply cut out."

"Any—" Mariah began to ask, then thought better of how to phrase her question. "Was there any indication that she had suffered in any way at that point?"

"No, thank goodness," Lakesh said firmly. "Her heart rate had initially increased, naturally enough, but there was no other significant change."

"What about the craft she was in?" Mariah asked.

Lakesh looked frustrated. "We've tracked back via the Vela satellite but there's simply no sign of it. Wherever it went, we lost it."

"Same for the two visitors?" Mariah queried.

"I'm afraid so," Lakesh confirmed. "Which puts us soundly back at square one, doesn't it?"

"I'm not sure," Mariah said, slowly shaking her head. "I've been thinking about this while I was prepping for the journey back—"

"After you filed your last report?" Lakesh clarified.

"Exactly. There was no engine noise from the vehicle that

Domi was abducted in, and she entered it of her own voli-
tion," Mariah said. "If it was meant as a trap, it was a very
elaborate trap. I think those other two vehicles I saw—the
streaks of gold that hovered briefly in place overhead—came
and took the ship with Domi on it."

"Like some sort of…cosmic tow trucks?" Lakesh asked,
trying to get his head around the idea.

"Something like that," Mariah confirmed, her easy smile
showing once more. "I figure if it had been capable of moving under its own steam, it would have."

Lakesh rubbed at his long nose in thought. "Quite the proposition," he mused. "You mentioned in your report about a
film recording of the event?"

Mariah was impressed; following his initial outburst of
emotional concern, Lakesh was already back to professional
mode, approaching this logically and methodically.

DRESSED IN A one-piece swimsuit that left her back exposed,
Brigid Baptiste stood before the swimming pool in the Cerberus compound and took a deep breath, reveling in the sterile smell of chlorine. She was alone, just the way she liked
it. The pool was an adjunct of the gymnasium facilities that
had been set up here back in the twentieth century when this
base had been built for the United States Army.

The Cerberus headquarters had been constructed within
a hollowed-out mountain in the Bitterroot range, where it
had remained hidden from view for over two hundred years.
In the years since the nukecaust, a peculiar mythology had
grown up around the mountains with their dark, foreboding
forests and seemingly bottomless ravines, and the Cerberus
installation itself had remained untouched until Lakesh had
repurposed it for his own use some years ago. The wilder-
ness surrounding the redoubt was virtually unpopulated; the
nearest settlement could be found in the flatlands some miles

away and consisted of a small band of Indians, Sioux and Cheyenne, led by a shaman named Sky Dog.

Though the redoubt was well hidden, it had not escaped the attention of Cerberus's most relentless foe, the would-be god prince called Ullikummis. With his army of devoted followers, Ullikummis had stormed the redoubt several months ago and left the facility spoiled to such an extent that much of it had been considered unusable. It was only in the past three days that the swimming pool had finally been reopened, considered, as it was, a nonessential part of the facility.

Brigid Baptiste did not consider it nonessential, however. While many of her colleagues might argue that the postnuke-caust world provided more than enough workouts, Brigid had always enjoyed the calming effects of the pool.

Brigid was a beautiful woman in her late twenties, with the trim figure of an athlete and a cascade of sunset-red curls falling to midway down her back. Her skin was flawless and naturally pale, and she had vivid emerald eyes that shone with curiosity. Her high forehead suggested intelligence, while her full lips implied a more sensuous side; in reality she was both of these aspects and many more, besides.

Brigid had grown up in Cobaltville, one of nine walled cities that had controlled the postapocalypse United States mainland for almost her whole life. She had worked as an archivist in the Historical Division until she became embroiled in a conspiracy, her knowledge of which had threatened to expose Cobaltville's leader for the manipulative nonhuman he really was.

Forced into exile, Brigid had found a home in the Cerberus redoubt with her fellow exiles Kane, Grant, Lakesh and Domi. Together, the five of them—along with other recruits who joined over the months that followed—had become a potent force for good in a world full of evil.

The main reason that Brigid was considered such a threat

to Cobaltville and the baronies was that her photographic—or, more properly, eidetic—memory enabled her to perfectly recall anything she had seen. Coupled with her competence in combat and her near-superhuman intuition, Brigid was one of the most fearsome members of the Cerberus team.

Brigid paced over to the diving podium and climbed the ladder. Her movements were swift and economical, lithe muscles working effortlessly as she ascended. In a moment she was standing atop the high board, taking in another calming breath and tasting the acid tang of chlorine at the back of her throat. She did not notice the other person who had entered the pool room as she was clambering up the ladder, and she remained oblivious as he stood close to the doors, watching her in silence.

Brigid padded to the edge of the diving board and looked down, judging the height that she perfectly recalled from the last time she had done this, months ago. It was two inches less than ten feet from the water, same as she remembered, same as it had been before Ullikummis had wrecked this place. Then Brigid took one single step back from the edge, thrust her arms out wide and straight, and sprang from the diving board.

She leaped high in the air, using the springboard to throw herself up another six feet before flipping her body in a complicated X-Y axis spin, thrusting her arms out before her to part the water as she began to drop. As she did so, the other figure in the room called out a single word, loud and echoing through the pool room.

"Shark!"

Brigid's body slipped into the water with perfect precision, casting barely a ripple as she disappeared beneath the surface.

When she emerged the other figure in the room was applauding, a wicked grin on his face.

"Now," said Kane, "that's just showing off, Baptiste."

Brigid scowled at him until he stopped applauding. "I didn't hear you come in," she said, and it was clear from her tone that she thought he had rather enjoyed sneaking up on her.

Kane's smile remained in place. He was a tall, muscular man in his early thirties with broad shoulders and long, rangy limbs. His tousled hair was cut short in something like a military fashion, dark brown with hints of lightness where he had caught the sun. He stood in a pair of swimming trunks that left most of his muscular body on show, and there could be no escaping the scar tissue that crisscrossed his flesh. Kane was a fighter, once a Magistrate for Cobaltville until his exile in the same conspiracy that had seen Brigid expelled. Since then, he'd enforced a different type of law—the law that assured mankind's survival against the most lethal of threats.

As well as fighting on the same side, he and Brigid shared a very special link known simply as the *anam chara* bond, which translated as "soul friends." As they understood it, this meant that, like it or not, Kane and Brigid were tied throughout eternity, to always watch over each other and protect the other from harm.

Brigid was still glaring at Kane as he paced over to the edge of the pool to join her. "Well? Don't you have anything to say for yourself, sneaking up on me like that?" she demanded.

Kane shrugged. "Hey, I didn't want to interrupt you while you were gathering your mojo or whatever it is you do when you're up there on the board."

Snarling, Brigid clenched her fists. "I'll gather *your* mojo in a minute."

Kane simply laughed. "My mojo's too big for one person to gather," he told her. "Way, way too big. I have *mucho mojo* as Rosalia would say."

Brigid shook her head in despair. "What are you doing following me anyway?"

Kane looked mock offended. "I came for a swim, same thing you did. Great minds think alike, right?"

"So I heard," Brigid deadpanned.

Kane looked up, judging the length of the pool. It was designed to Olympic specifications, back when that had still had meaning in the world, with plenty of space for them both. "You want a race?" he suggested.

Brigid tsked. "It's always a competition with you, isn't it?"

"It's kept me alive so far," Kane responded. "So, what about it?"

Without a word, Brigid turned her back on Kane and kicked off, intentionally splashing him as she did so. "See you at the other side, slowpoke!" she taunted.

Kane took a moment to watch the red-haired woman as she began to swim toward the distant side of the pool. Despite their outward antagonism, they had shared a lot, the two of them, adventures and downtime, becoming as close as siblings and maybe even lovers, though their relationship remained purely platonic.

She was beautiful, Kane thought; there was no question of that. But as he watched, his keen eye noticed something as Brigid retreated: a white scar that ran between her shoulder blades at the top of her spine. Usually that scar was covered by her long hair, he guessed, but just now her wet hair had fallen to one side. The scar had come from an assault Brigid had suffered at the hands of Ullikummis, who had reached inside her and disrupted the transponder that ran inside her bloodstream. The transponder had since been reengaged, but for a while Brigid—his friend, his *anam chara*—had been lost.

"Never again," Kane muttered, as he dived into the pool.

THE REDOUBT'S OPERATIONS room was a vast space dominated on one wall by a Mercator map that showed Earth crisscrossed with colored lines and illuminated spots. A little like a flight map, the spots represented the known mat-trans points across the globe, while the lines that joined them showed the various paths one could travel when using them. The Cerberus redoubt had been dedicated to propagating and exploring the limits of the then-nascent teleportation network, and to a certain extent it was still involved in that endeavor, albeit with an emphasis shift to the Parallax Points Program discovered in an ancient military database.

The room itself featured twin aisles of computer terminals where a number of personnel took shifts monitoring the input from sensor equipment and satellite feeds, scanning for new discoveries and potential new threats.

The redoubt was manned by a full complement of staff, fifty in total, the vast majority of whom were cryogenic "freezies" from the twentieth century who, like Mariah, had been discovered in suspended animation in the Manitius Moon Base and many of whom were experts in their chosen fields of study.

Tucked beneath camouflage netting, hidden away within the rocky clefts of the mountain range, concealed uplinks chattered continuously with two orbiting satellites that provided much of the empirical data for the Cerberus analysis software. Gaining access to the satellites had taken long hours of intense trial-and-error work by many of the top scientists on hand at the mountain base. Now, the Cerberus staff could draw on live feeds from the orbiting Vela-class reconnaissance satellite and the Keyhole Comsat at any hour of the day. This arrangement gave the resident staff an almost limitless stream of data about the surface of Earth, as well as providing near-instantaneous communication with field teams across the globe.

Mariah and Lakesh had taken up a position at his desk, set at the back of the room and overlooking the twin aisles of computers. There, Mariah had connected her compact video camera to the computer monitor and played back the recording she made of the buried spaceship and its subsequent disappearance so that Lakesh and his team could watch.

The recording was crude, often out of focus and slipping into a blur of incomprehensible colors as each new event caught Mariah by surprise when she was wielding the camera. But she had secured a good visual record of the original starcraft that had been buried close to the river and had caught several respectable shots of the twin lights that moved above in the sky, including an extended view of them leaving with the fully revealed spacecraft.

There were eight staff working the desks during that shift, and each one came over to view the footage, watching as Lakesh and Mariah paused and rewound the pertinent sections relating to Domi's kidnapping. Everybody had ideas about what could have happened, but of course no one knew for sure.

"What we may conclude," Lakesh proclaimed as he studied the footage in slow motion for the umpteenth time, "is that the golden lights are craft of some description. They may be spacecraft or merely aircraft, and we cannot rule out the possibility that they had no prior connection to the buried artifact that you and Domi uncovered this morning." He paused the image with a keystroke, leaving it locked on blue sky where the two golden lights hovered in the heavens.

"So, you think they didn't come to tow it back home," Mariah clarified, "but maybe just to steal it?"

Lakesh nodded. "That's a distinct possibility," he said. "The designs of the two visitors' ships—at least, from what we can make out—are quite different. There's no obvious uniformity there.

"The item you initially found looks distinctly Annunaki in form, but these two—" Lakesh tapped the screen where the golden craft were framed in midair, bright specks on blue "—are sleeker in style."

"Could they be older versions of the same craft?" Donald Bry suggested from where he had perched on the edge of Lakesh's desk. He was a nervous-looking man with an unruly mop of copper-colored curls and the fretful appearance of a nocturnal animal caught outside its burrow in the daytime. Bry acted as Lakesh's lieutenant and right-hand man, taking the unofficial role of second in command of the Cerberus organization. "Or newer?"

Lakesh rubbed at his tired eyes, trying to make sense out of the static image on-screen. "We could speculate, Donald, but it would be just that—speculation. What we need is a plan of action, a way to locate and retrieve our dear Domi." Lakesh raised his voice and called over to the redoubt physician. "Reba? Has there been any reappearance of the transponder?"

Reba DeFore, a buxom woman with tanned bronze skin and ash-blond hair that she had weaved in an elaborate braid, shook her head sorrowfully from where she sat at a monitoring desk. "Donald might be able to tease something out of the computer tracking, but I certainly can't. Just now, the system's showing nothing for Domi whatsoever."

"And with no transponder signal," Donald added, "we have no way to track her."

"Would you be so good as to look into this, my friend?" Lakesh asked distractedly.

Bry nodded. "Brewster's been trying to recalibrate the unit remotely with no success, but I'll see if I can add anything."

Lakesh nodded in gratitude, the fierce fires of determination burning behind his clear blue eyes. "Call Kane, Brigid and Grant—assemble CAT Team Alpha," he said. "If we can't do anything here, then we'll do something there."

So Donald Bry sent out a request on the internal communications system for the three members of the CAT Alpha field team, and by the time Brigid and Kane appeared in the operations room less than ten minutes later, Grant was already waiting for them.

"What took you two so long?" Grant asked. He was a huge man with skin like polished mahogany and bulging muscles across his mighty frame that strained at the blue T-shirt and olive combat pants he wore. His head was shaved and he had recently affected a goatee-style beard that circled his mouth in a narrow black line. A little older than Kane, Grant had partnered the man back when they were both Magistrates in Cobaltville, and the two shared a connection that made them seem like brothers, despite their physical differences. Grant's voice was a rumble like thunder when he spoke, but despite how threatening he seemed, Kane knew when he was just kidding.

Kane brushed back his tousled hair, which was still a little damp from swimming. "Nothing," he assured his friend with a wicked smile. "I was just showing Baptiste here what a magnanimous winner I could be."

Brigid shot Kane a look, her eyes narrowed in annoyance. "I think you'll find I was faster than you in every length we raced."

"Faster, yes, but look at you," Kane teased. "You're exhausted."

He was wrong, of course. Both of them were at the peak of physical fitness, and a few lengths of the swimming pool were hardly enough to get Brigid warmed up. In fact, had Bry's request not come through she would have spent the rest of the afternoon there, challenging herself to be faster, to swim farther and to hold her breath longer. You never knew when such endurance would come in handy.

Brigid had dressed in a loose shirt over a sleeveless black top and dark pants. The shirt went some way to hide the curves of her figure, but she had still turned heads in the operations room when she entered. Without the time to dry her long hair, Brigid had tied it in a scarf for now.

Kane had dressed in a pale shirt that was open at the collar and casual pants tucked into a pair of scuffed combat boots. The boots were a carryover from his days as a Magistrate, similar to the ones he had worn when on patrol.

"It's good of you all to come so swiftly," Lakesh said, beckoning the three of them over to his desk. The video camera was still attached there, and Mariah took a few minutes bringing them up to speed on what had happened out near the Juruena River before Lakesh outlined what he had in mind.

"Working on the assumption that the golden aircraft arrived to acquire the buried spaceship," Lakesh said, "I propose we put something out there that will encourage them to come back."

"You mean bait?" Grant asked.

Lakesh smiled. "Precisely! We have several alien vehicles in our possession. If we can leave one on show, perhaps drawing attention to it, our scavengers—if that's what they are—might come to take a look."

"That's a big 'if,'" Kane groused. "How were you thinking we might draw attention to this if we were to follow through on your plan?"

"Well, I'll leave the mechanics up to you," Lakesh admitted drily. "But my thought was we could stage some kind of elaborate—I don't know—crash-landing spectacle that might draw the attention of the kind of people who come to pluck buried Annunaki spaceships out of the ground."

"Crash landing, huh?" Grant asked dubiously. "We try to avoid those."

"Hence *elaborately staged*," Lakesh reminded the larger man.

"And if we do bring your golden visitors back?" Brigid asked. "What then?"

"Ah," Lakesh said, "I was rather hoping you'd be able to… um…work on the fly at that point and see where the situation takes you."

"You want us to follow them?" Kane asked.

"Just to get Domi back," Lakesh told him. "I don't want you to put yourselves in unnecessary jeopardy."

"Fake a crash landing," Kane grumbled, ticking off the points on his fingers, "deceive the well-armed strangers, and free the companion we don't know for sure has been kidnapped."

"Nobody said they were well armed," Lakesh complained.

"Nobody said they weren't!" Kane, Brigid and Grant responded in unison.

Chapter 4

Serra do Norte, Brazil

Eighteen hours later, two slope-winged aircraft shot across the skies over the Juruena River, vying for position in the cloudless sky.

Identical in appearance, the aircraft were constructed from a bronze-hued metal that glimmered in the early-morning sunlight. Their graceful designs consisted of flattened wedges with swooping wings curving out to either side in mimicry of the seagoing manta ray, which was why they were called Mantas. Each Manta's wingspan was twenty yards, and its body length was almost fifteen feet. The entire surface of each vehicle was decorated with curious geometric designs: elaborate cuneiform markings, swirling glyphs and cup-and-spiral symbols. Aerodynamically flat in design, each vehicle featured an elongated hump in the center of the body, which provided the only indication of a cockpit.

Graceful as they appeared, right now the two craft were involved in what appeared to be deadly combat. The lead vehicle swept dangerously low over the canopy of trees, kicking up leaves in its wake. Its trailing companion followed it move for move, nose cannon spitting a steady stream of bullets as its pilot sought to knock it out of the skies.

Inside the lead vehicle, Grant jerked the joystick to the left, sending his craft away to port in a turn so sharp that the Manta appeared to stand on one wing for a moment. He wore an all-encompassing helmet, colored bronze like the craft and locked into the back of the pilot's seat. A small oxygen supply was attached to it.

Grant was also dressed in a shadow suit, a body glove made from an incredibly durable fabric that acted as armor without hindering movement in the slightest. The shadow suit could deflect knife blades and redistribute kinetic impact. Microfilaments in the weave regulated the wearer's body temperature to keep the wearer comfortable in extremes of temperature, and the shadow suit also offered protection from environmental threats. Grant had augmented the shadow suit with camo pants and he had also brought a long duster coat, which was folded on the backseat in the two-man cockpit.

With a growl, Grant yanked at the joystick again, reeling as a series of bullets from his pursuer kicked against the back fins with a rattle like dice on a craps table.

"Son of a…" he spat out. "Give me some space to climb already."

Grant's pursuer didn't hear the instruction, though if he had there was a reasonable chance he would have ignored him. Evidently, he was set on bringing Grant's craft down, preferably as a fireball.

Grant urged more power to the engine as he pulled back on the stick, sending his Manta up in a near-vertical climb, grimacing at the sudden increase in g-forces inside the cockpit. Internal gravity compensators would kick in in a moment, he knew, but for the next few seconds he would feel as if he weighed as much as a blue whale.

"The next time Shizuka tells me she's worried about her weight," Grant muttered to himself, "she's going up in one of these things."

INSIDE THE TRAILING VEHICLE, Kane tapped something on the control board, cutting his speed to a whisker below 100 miles per hour, allowing Grant breathing space to gain a little extra distance as he stood his Manta on its tail.

"You go for it, pal," Kane muttered. "Keep running—let's make it look good."

Kane was also dressed in a shadow suit, to which he had added a simple denim jacket and camo pants.

The Mantas were very ancient and they had been in use when the Annunaki had first invaded Earth many millennia ago. The two that now flew in an elaborate game of cat and mouse over the Brazilian countryside had been acquired by the Cerberus team for long-range missions after being discovered where they had been left discarded on Earth thousands of years before. They'd be found by CAT Team Alpha during one of their exploratory missions. Capable of both transatmospheric and subspace flight, the adaptable vehicles were largely employed for long-range and specific edge-of-atmosphere work, including satellite maintenance.

Like Grant, Kane also wore a bulbous pilot's helmet, which entirely covered his skull. The helmets had come as a part of the recovered vehicles and were wired into the cockpits, operating on a swivel system that plugged them into the back of each pilot's seat.

Inside the helmet, the relatively simple cockpit controls were augmented by a detailed heads-up display that responded to the pilot's eye movements. When Kane focused on the tail of Grant's Manta, the display system automatically gave a detailed summary of the craft's speed, trajectory and many other factors, including a full analysis of the vehicle's armament. A slight movement of Kane's pupils and the display would magnify the view of the vehicle, singling it out and running infrared, ultraviolet and various other analyses, all in the literal blink of an eye.

Anxiously, Kane kicked the Manta back to full speed once

more, shooting upward, chasing the bronze tail of his partner's vehicle.

Seated directly behind Kane in the tight cockpit of the Manta, Brigid Baptiste was watching everything through the hidden viewports of the craft. She, too, had dressed in a shadow suit, adding a lightweight jacket and belt, along with a pair of boots with low heels. The boots were unnecessary—the shadow suits had flexible soles built in, but Brigid preferred the added comfort the boots gave, plus they drew attention away from the strange glove-like fit of the suits themselves.

Brigid eyed the skies warily, scanning for signs of other vehicles.

"We have anything yet, Baptiste?" Kane asked, raising his voice over the noise of rushing wind streaking past the Manta's cockpit.

"Negative," Brigid replied. "Clear skies so far."

Kane tapped the trigger controls again, sending another flurry of bullets at the aft of Grant's rapidly retreating Manta. The bullets cut the air around the Manta, a handful striking the metal hull with another rattle of impacts. They were 9 mm bullets and wouldn't hurt the Manta, Kane knew, not at this distance, anyway. The whole thing was just for show, trying to convince anyone who might be watching that they were engaged in a running battle in the sky.

WHILE TIME WAS of the essence with Domi missing, there were other considerations that had to be factored into a sting operation. That was why it had taken eighteen hours to move from theory, in the Cerberus ops room, to execution, here over the rushing waters of the Juruena.

Grant flip-flopped his Manta in a spiraling turn, spinning the giant bronze shape through its y-axis as another burst of bullets cut the air from behind.

The Juruena was below him now, a trailing silvery snake

amid the green as he whipped high in the air over it, aircraft upside down, cockpit turned toward the ground. Behind him, Kane was bringing his own Manta in a banking turn, nose gun blazing.

Calmly, Grant moved the joystick fractionally, sending his Manta in a slow turn that would bring it around again, as well as setting it back to right side up.

"Come on, Kane," he muttered. "Don't make it look too easy."

Kane's Manta tracked the move, cutting across the wide arc of Grant's craft and powering toward him at a sharp angle. Grant pitched and yawed, shaking his craft in place as Kane sent another burst of fire in his direction.

"Steady," Grant reminded himself as bullets thudded against the armored hull. "Steady."

There was a patch of open ground below them now, a small clearing set a little way back from the riverbank. It was maybe twenty-five yards at its longest side, half that at its shortest. At the speed they were traveling it would be a tight landing, but with the Manta's Vertical Take Off and Landing, or VTOL, capacity, it shouldn't be too hard to hit the target. Rather, it was just a question of whether they could convince an outsider that it was unintentional. Grant figured it was the best they were going to find at such notice, which meant it would have to do.

Grant waggled his wings for a second, rolling in place as Kane lined up another shot.

"I hope you saw that, Kane," he muttered, inwardly cursing that they had been forced to maintain radio silence for the duration of the sting. It wouldn't do for someone to overhear these two "enemies" sharing tactics over their Commtacts.

KANE WAS WATCHING Grant's Manta like a hawk, and so he saw the wing tips briefly waggle as the aircraft cut across the skies to the east of the river.

"It's on," Kane told Brigid, and he watched Grant swoop into a trajectory that would take him much lower. "We have an audience yet?"

"Still nothing," Brigid replied, trying to keep the frustration out of her voice. "We're putting Grant in a lot of danger with this plan," she reminded Kane.

"Danger's just a vacation spot to Grant," Kane snapped back. "It's his favorite place to visit."

They were not far from where Mariah and Domi had found the starcraft, just four miles from the burial site. The idea was that they would stage this dogfight in the vicinity of the previous appearance of the golden ships. Hopefully those same people would track this activity, and when Grant's Manta went down in an apparent crash landing, they would come out of the woodwork to investigate.

It was a long shot, but right now—with no way of tracing Domi and no indication of where she was being held—it was all they had.

Flipping a switch on the joystick, Kane engaged an incendiary missile. It locked in place in the firing bay, waiting for the command to launch. Up ahead, Grant was bringing his Manta around in a long arc that would ultimately place him in line with the open landing area he had identified. Kane urged more power from the air pulse engines of the Manta, waiting for the target reticle to switch from green to red on his heads-up display. The moment it did, his thumb stroked the trigger and the missile launched, whipping ahead of his Manta in a streak of white smoke.

Kane watched the missile go, trusting that those extra hours at the redoubt would pay off now. The tech boys there had retrofitted one of his missiles with a false charge, all noise and light but no explosive—which meant it wouldn't do much more than dirty the shell of Grant's Manta when it struck. To be doubly sure, the missile had been primed to go off a few feet before reaching the target, meaning that—to the naked eye, at least—it would still look as if all that fire and noise was coming from a point of impact at the rear of Grant's wounded Manta.

"I hope if they're watching, they ain't watching too close," Kane muttered to himself as the missile streaked away with a shriek of burning air.

GRANT'S TACTICAL DISPLAY had switched to alert mode, informing him that someone had his ship in a target lock, and furthermore, that there was a missile cutting its way toward his rear even as he continued on the path toward the clearing.

"Beginning evasive maneuvers," Grant said lackadaisically, rolling the Manta over as the missile howled toward it.

The Manta flipped over twice as the missile neared, and the missile adjusted its course in response, getting closer with every passing microsecond.

Twenty feet.

Ten feet.

Five feet.

Now.

Grant's left palm slapped against the newly added bulge on the side of the control board, feeling the button there depress. It was big so that he wouldn't miss it, since most flying skill is instinct, and trying to add an extra feature to a fighter jet—especially an alien one like this—involved hours of training to get the pilot used to it.

Grant didn't have the time for hours of training and so the Cerberus techs had settled on a very big, bright red button as the best chance of his hitting the right control when he was thinking at one hundred feet up while traveling at close to a hundred and eighty miles per hour over the rainforest.

There was a fraction of second's delay—made infinitely longer in Grant's mind as he worried about something going wrong. Then he felt the back of the Manta kick like a mule as the explosive charge hidden beneath the plating went off, sending a stream of thick black smoke and small debris up into the air behind him. At roughly the same moment, Kane's missile detonated, sending a burst of light coupled with the sound of an explosion out in all directions, giving the illusion that the missile had hit.

"And after that apparent pain in the aft, boys and girls," Grant said, "it's time to crash this bird and crash it good."

Grant eased back on the throttle and sent the hurtling Manta in a plummeting spiral toward the ground, keeping the tract of open land in his viewport as best as he could without making it too obvious that he was still in control. He was going too fast, he knew, could feel the air buffet his wings as the Manta rocketed earthward, the shriek of engine strain loud to his ears.

Grant's heads-up display was going crazy, alerting him that he was moving toward the ground too fast and that he needed to pull up now.

"Yeah, I hear ya," Grant growled to the navigation system. "I just don't plan on paying any attention."

A moment later, the tallest of the trees came rushing into view and Grant gritted his teeth. This was what it all came down to, audience or no audience.

KANE WINCED AS Grant's Manta dipped beneath the tree line, the trail of dark smoke marking its passage.

"I hope you're okay in there, buddy," he said as the Manta dropped out of view.

A moment later, the trees below shook and a flock of startled birds took to the sky, cawing angrily to one another as they hurried from the crash site.

"Still nothing, Kane," Brigid confirmed before he had time to ask.

"Roger," Kane acknowledged automatically. "Time we blew this mutie-chomp stand."

With that, Kane engaged the full force of the pulse engine, sweeping over the crash site of Grant's Manta as if to eyeball it before roaring away through the cerulean skies. His vehicle notched up to two hundred miles per hour in a second, was closer to three hundred by the time his shadow had crossed over the crash site below.

In five seconds, Kane's Manta was gone, and the only evidence of its passing was the smoking shell of the identical craft it had apparently brought down.

Chapter 5

Strapped tightly into the acceleration couch of the felled Manta, Grant strained to peer out of the viewport and into the skies above. He watched for a moment as Kane's aircraft hurried away from the scene, the imaging software in the heads-up display picking out highlights and focusing on the air trail it left long after the craft itself had disappeared from view.

"I hope you caught all that, bad guys," Grant said, settling back down into the pilot's seat. "Because I'd hate to have to put on an evening show, having already used up all our best tricks for the matinee."

Grant pushed back the helmet and took a breath of unfiltered air before adjusting the straps that held him in place. There was nothing out there now, just the trees—which he had deftly managed to avoid in his faked crash—and the empty, cloudless sky hanging above him like a brushstroke of blue paint. He could be here awhile, he knew, and he had come prepared.

First, however, he checked the hand weapons he had brought with him. There was his Sin Eater pistol, which clipped neatly into a holster that attached to Grant's wrist. The weapon retracted out of sight while not in use, its butt folding over the top of the barrel to reduce its stored length to just ten inches.

The Sin Eater was the official side arm of the Magistrate Division, a compact 9 mm automatic that both Grant and Kane favored from their days as Magistrates. The holster operated by a specific flinch of the wrist tendon, powering the blaster straight into the user's hand.

The weapon's trigger had no guard; the necessity for one had never been foreseen since the Magistrates were believed to be infallible. Hence, if the wielder's index finger was bent at the time the weapon reached it, the pistol would begin firing automatically. The blaster was a reminder of who Grant had been, and its weight felt natural on his wrist the same way a wristwatch seems natural to the wearer.

His other weapon of choice was a Copperhead assault rifle, an abbreviated subgun that was less than two feet in length. The Copperhead's extended magazine contained thirty-five 4.85 mm rounds that could be fired—or perhaps *unleashed* was a better term—at a rate of 700 rounds per minute.

The grip and trigger were set in front of the breech in a bullpup design, allowing for one-handed use, and the weapon's low recoil permitted devastating full-auto bursts, chewing up anything that came into its path. A scope with laser autotarget facility was mounted on the top of the gun, but Grant's hand-eye coordination was refined enough to operate the weapon without the autotarget feature.

Grant slipped the Copperhead down beside the pilot's seat, the safety on and grip within easy reach. If anyone tried to pry open the cockpit without warning, they'd get a face full of lead for their troubles.

Certain that his weapons were primed, Grant reached into the storage pouch at his left and pulled out the book that his girlfriend, Shizuka, had loaned him. It was an ancient and well-thumbed copy of *Family Traditions on the Art of War* by Yagyu Munenori, a samurai treatise from the sixteenth century. He could be in for a long wait.

FOUR HOURS PASSED without incident. Kane had taken his Manta away to the north, settling down by a clump of trees in the densely forested Serra do Norte three miles from where Grant had set down. He left his engines powered down but idling, ready to reignite at any moment, should Grant patch an alert to him.

"This is taking too long," Kane grumbled as the clock ticked into the start of their fifth hour hiding in the forest. "I'm going to call Grant and let him know it's a bust."

"Don't," Brigid replied from the seat behind his. She sounded sleepy, as if she had been dozing when she had first heard him speak. "Give it time."

"How much time?" Kane asked, a note of challenge in his voice. "We're going to start getting old if these twerps don't show up soon. More to the point, my stomach tells me it's lunchtime."

"Then eat," Brigid told him calmly. "You have ration bars there, don't you?"

"Yeah," Kane grumbled and he reached into a storage pouch located beside his right knee and pulled out one of the foil-wrapped bars. He unwrapped it and took a bite, his nose wrinkling in disgust as he was reminded why he hadn't eaten them earlier. "This ain't food. These things look like cardboard, smell like cardboard and taste like cardboard."

"Quit complaining and eat your lunch," Brigid chided, closing her eyes again as she settled back into a light doze.

BY THE SIXTH HOUR, Grant was more familiar with the philosophical musings of Yagyu Munenori than he would have wanted to get in one sitting, and the straps of the pilot's couch were chafing him no matter which way he sat. His Manta had long since cooled down, and the plume of smoke that might have acted as a location marker to any passing scavengers or cosmic tow trucks had long since faded.

Putting the book down, folded open and resting on one knee, Grant leaned forward and glanced through the canopy once more. The skies remained clear. The trees were sway-ing with the breeze and, as he watched, tiny, brightly colored birds flitted between branches, dining on berries or aphids, whatever it was that they were finding up there that was good enough to eat. Watching them, Grant remembered the ration bars he had in one of the storage pouches in the cockpit and pulled a face. "May as well eat cardboard," he muttered, re-calling their taste.

As he leaned forward, the book began to slip from Grant's leg and he reached for it in a rush of limbs, bashing his right elbow against the side of the cockpit as he tried to stop the book from disappearing into the foot well. He snared it with two fingers, pressing it against the lower part of his leg to stop it dropping until he could get a better grip.

"Dang!"

Knowing Shizuka, Grant guessed the book had been in her family since her great-great-great grandfather—some all-wise samurai or other—had gone to a book signing in 1640. He could just imagine what she'd say if he managed to step on it while it rattled around in the crashed Manta's foot well. "You stepped on the most precious and most sacred tome, which has guided my family for a thousand years, Grant-san. You have dishonored my ancestors with your big feet."

"My big feet won't be dishonoring anyone's ancestors today," Grant muttered as he brought the book back from the brink. As he did so, something whipped past the corner of his eye, and he looked up, peering into the cockpit viewport.

Blue sky. Empty.

Grant kept watching, folding Shizuka's book closed as he scanned the skies. He couldn't see anything different—but he could hear something. It sounded like a distant stampede.

"What is that?" Grant muttered, eyeing the sky.

Blue. Empty.

The noise was growing louder, which usually meant whatever was making it was getting closer. Grant took a moment to return the book to the storage webbing by his leg before pulling the flight helmet back over his head. The heads-up display automatically reengaged, sensors scanning where he looked, picking out details of the trees and the birds as they tracked into view.

"Come on, twitchy," Grant muttered to himself.

Blue. Empty.

Then came that irritating moment of self-doubt, when Grant felt sure he had seen something but started to wonder if he had just imagined it. He ran his tongue along his teeth, counting the seconds, waiting for something to happen.

The Manta's sensors caught it first, circling and highlighting it on the multicolored heads-up display. It appeared from the edge of the tree cover, traveling high and fast. Grant focused automatically, and the display focused with him, zooming in on the speck of light as it shot across the sky like a streak of lightning. The image magnified, magnified, magnified—and then whatever it was had passed, leaving only a ghost image in its wake. Specifications ran down the side of the display, giving Grant an estimation of its velocity and a bearing on its direction.

A moment later it was back, and the thundering horse hooves were suddenly much louder in his ears. This time, the Manta's software caught it, bringing up a close-up still overlay image of the aircraft—and it *was* an aircraft—alongside the real-time moving speck, running down the full specifications including an analysis of its armor shielding.

It was light on armor, Grant saw, which made it fast. That was the classic trade-off with fighter jets—the more armor you carried, the more weight you needed to propel and the slower you became.

Grant reached forward for the control panel, his fingers

drumming against it as he pondered whether or not to start up his engine.

Then a second craft appeared in the sky, this one much, much closer and accompanied by the deafening noise of galloping horses. Grant watched as it circled overhead before plummeting toward him, its shell gleaming like liquid gold. Before Grant could think, the Manta began to shake around him, and he felt himself being drawn up into the air.

Chapter 6

Kane was sitting in the cockpit of his own vehicle watching the skies, three miles from where the twin golden craft were circling the crashed Manta.

"Hey, Baptiste? You see that?"

When Brigid didn't answer, Kane raised his voice and tried again.

"Hey, wake up, Baptiste!"

"I wasn't asleep," Brigid insisted, brushing a stray lock of red-gold hair from her eyes. "Just resting my eyes."

"I hope you rested them good," Kane snapped, "because I'm going to need a second opinion. You see that?"

He pointed through the viewport and Brigid looked where he was indicating.

"What am I looking for?" she asked.

"A flash in the sky, some kind of light or something," Kane told her, reaching for his flight helmet.

"You think it's…?" Brigid began.

"Let me see if I can get a better visual," Kane cut in. If the force that had abducted Domi was here, Kane didn't want to move too soon and scare it away. He slipped the flight helmet over his head. Its bronze-colored faceplate covered his features entirely, granting him complete access to the Manta's sensor technology in its colorful heads-up display. Numbers raced before his eyes as he searched for the flash he had seen a moment ago.

GRANT FELT AS if something was tugging at his whole body, like a magnet lifting the bones through his skin.

Around him, the Manta shuddered as it was lifted from the ground by some invisible force. There was no hook that Grant could see, no beam showing in the visible spectrum.

He screwed up his eyes for a moment, forcing himself to look beyond the sensation. When he opened them again, he saw the trees appear to descend around him as he rose gently in the cockpit of the ascending Manta. Up above, two bright gold aircraft were poised in place roughly a hundred and fifty feet above the ground. The vehicles were ovoid and looked smooth all over, like a pebble washed by the sea. They glimmered a brilliant gold, bright as the sun's rays, which they reflected. But Grant could see something else within that gold—dark patches forming lines and shapes across the flawless shells. They hadn't moved for the last thirty seconds, just waited there as Grant's Manta was gradually drawn up toward them.

With a mental command, Grant ordered the sensor array to give him a full analysis of the hovering craft. There was no further data than that he had already seen, so he blinked rapidly, commanding a full spectral analysis, jumping from gamma to X-rays before slipping over to the other side of visibility: infrared, terahertz, microwaves. The rapidly changing views on his HUD were gaudy as an old black-light picture, but only the ultraviolet scan gave any notable information. The ultraviolet spectrum is where electromagnetic radiation is visible, and the display showed an inverted pyramid, its walls insubstantial, the points of the base corresponding with the two golden aircraft that hovered above.

The Manta was the third corner of the triangle, Grant realized, picturing it in two dimensions in his mind's eye. He was in some kind of magnetic beam, he concluded, and it was pulling his craft up into the sky as if it were a great claw. The beam was being projected somehow from the two golden aircraft hovering above him, but how they were doing it and what interaction was necessary to create the beam itself he couldn't know.

As he ascended above the level of the highest tree branch, Grant leaned back in his pilot's seat and continued playing possum. Let them think he had died in the crash—it might be the only way to find out where they had taken Domi.

GRANT'S MANTA WAS automatically tagged on Kane's display and Kane watched as it ascended above the tree line, a yellow reticle identifying it as friendly. Kane's eyes were narrowed as he observed through the magnifying software of the Manta's sensors. The mysterious visitors hovered in place as Grant's Manta was lifted into the air.

"Looks like we hooked our fish," Kane said, bringing the Manta back to life. "Or maybe they hooked Grant."

"Kane, wait," Brigid instructed, slapping her palm against the back of his pilot's seat.

"What?" Kane responded irritably, still holding the joystick as he got ready to leave their hiding place amidst the trees.

"Don't move too soon," Brigid reminded. "You'll scare them off."

"Grant's in danger," Kane snapped.

"And aren't you the one who told me that that was his favorite place to be?" Brigid snapped back.

Kane snarled something incomprehensible in reply, but he eased his grip on the stick. Brigid was right. "If he gets killed and haunts me, I'm telling him this was your idea," he growled.

"Let's just see where they're going first," Brigid said, ignoring Kane's jibe. "We don't want to blow our chance to get Domi back."

Arranged in a loose triangular formation, the two ovoid vehicles turned northward, pulling Grant's Manta along behind them. All three aircraft began to accelerate and then, without warning, disappeared entirely from Kane's scopes.

"What the—?" Kane growled.

In the seat behind him, Brigid felt her stomach sink. Please don't lose him, she thought.

WITHIN THE TIGHT cockpit of his Manta, Grant found himself jostled around as his aircraft was yanked away at high speed from the crash site. His muscles and flesh seemed to be pulled back as he was slammed against the acceleration couch, and it felt as it his bones were being yanked through his skin. He had never known such speed—certainly not in an atmospheric vehicle.

The sensor displays in his helmet were going wild, colored symbols flashing in quick succession as the Manta warned its pilot that they were out of control with the engines still powered down.

"I know," Grant growled as his head slammed into the starboard viewport. He cursed as he tasted blood in his mouth. His eyes teared and he blinked the tears away, struggling to see through the blur. Then he realized it wasn't the tears that were making his vision blurry—through the viewport all that could be see was a green-again, blue-again blur where the trees and sky rolled past at incredible speed. The Manta was spinning, Grant realized, rapidly rotating on its y-axis so that it went upside down and right-side up, over and over. Grant cursed again, wishing he could check on Kane, speak to him via their Commtacts.

Up ahead, Grant saw the two fixed spots where the golden

aircraft towed him through the air on their magnetic beam. For now, he was at their mercy.

"I only hope Kane's keeping up," he muttered.

KANE WAS NOT keeping up. His heart was drumming against his chest as he fed full power to the Manta, speeding to the site of their last visual. The air was clear, and a quick run-through of the sensor feeds showed no evidence of where the three aircraft had disappeared to.

"He's gone," Kane spat. "No energy signature, no trail. We've lost him."

Brigid eyed the empty sky from the rear seat. "There has to be some way to track him," she insisted. "Think…think…"

"Cerberus!" Brigid and Kane exclaimed together.

Brigid started running a full-scope analysis on the data the Manta had amassed, while Kane hailed Cerberus over his Commtact. He was relieved when Lakesh's eager tones filled his ears.

"We've lost Grant," Kane explained, cutting to the chase.

Lakesh sounded astonished. "Lost how?" he asked.

"His Manta was there and then it wasn't," Kane summarized. "Last visual, he was being towed by two aircraft that matched the description Falk gave us. Headed on a northeast bearing and just disappeared before my eyes."

"And you didn't go with him?" Lakesh began, then corrected himself. "Of course you didn't. You wouldn't be contacting us if you had. What do you need me to do, my friend?"

"Sensors picked up some data that Baptiste is running through as fast as she can," Kane explained. "But we need a position for Grant's transponder. Plus anything you can add from the Keyhole sat."

"The instruments are showing a significant cation trail, positively charged," Brigid added.

SITTING AT A DESK in the Cerberus ops room, Lakesh listened over the earpiece as Kane read out the specific figures relating to the cation trail. Domi had been missing for thirty-two hours now and Lakesh had enlisted most of the Cerberus personnel to cover for this sting op, placing himself at the heart of the communications network so that he could field any messages that came through.

"You heard Baptiste. That all mean anything to you?" Kane finished.

Lakesh nodded, concern etched on his face. He had been a physicist of significant renown in his day. He could already visualize the data in his mind's eye and see how it related to what had happened in the skies over Brazil. "Kane, what you've recorded there is an ion transfer," Lakesh stated.

"Say again?" Kane requested. "In English."

"An ion transfer," Lakesh explained, "is the process wherein electrostatic acceleration of charged positive ions is generated to release incredible amounts of energy. In the twentieth century, rocket engines employed this system to achieve liftoff."

"So, we're looking at a rocket trail?" Kane asked.

"The application of an ion engine would suggest as much," Lakesh confirmed. "Did you see anything take off?"

"No, we were still a couple of miles out when it happened," Kane clarified. "Didn't wanna spook them. Looked to me like Grant and his new friends just—pop!—winked out of existence."

Two desks away from Lakesh, staff physician Reba De-Fore tilted her computer monitor toward him and called for his attention.

"One moment, my friend," Lakesh told Kane before examining DeFore's screen. "Yes, Reba—what do we have?"

"Grant's transponder data," Reba explained, indicating one of three sets of data that showed on her screen. There, three lines were glowing in different colors alongside a numerical display for his blood pressure. The numbers looked normal enough, but as Lakesh watched, they cut abruptly before reappearing a second or two later. The other two displays remained rock solid.

"What is that?" Lakesh asked her. "What's happening?"

"We're losing the data in a fixed three-quarter-time pattern," DeFore said. "Kane and Brigid are still in place—" she indicated the other two data feeds "—but Grant's has been glitching like this for the past fifty seconds."

"As though our equipment can't fix on the transponder signal," Lakesh mused. He was already turning to Donald Bry, where the copper-headed man sat at another terminal analyzing geographic data. "Donald? What do you have for me?"

"We can still pinpoint Grant's position," Bry said with his usual concerned expression. "But the transponder signal is getting weaker. He's moving fast—by my estimate he's traveling at six hundred miles per hour, although I'd need to run through the figures properly to…"

"Yes, yes," Lakesh quieted the man. "Kane, we have a fix on Grant and he's moving fast."

"HOW FAST?" KANE ASKED, sweat-slick grip still locked on the Manta's joystick.

"Six hundred miles per hour on a bearing of north-northeast," Lakesh replied. "He's showing as twenty-four miles from your position with the distance increasing rapidly."

"On it," Kane snapped back, adjusting the trajectory of his Manta and kicking in full power. Engines roared as Kane ramped up the acceleration.

"Distance now is twenty-five miles," Lakesh confirmed.

Kane's Manta swooped over the trees, speeding on a north-northeast bearing.

Lakesh's voice came over the Commtact again. "Twenty-six."

Brigid gasped. "Kane—we'll never catch him at this rate. It's not possible."

Kane shook his head, the bulky bronze helmet shaking. "Gotta be a way," he muttered, peering through the sensors at empty sky. He wasn't going to lose his partner, no way.

"Twenty-seven," Lakesh's voice chimed emotionlessly.

In that instant, Kane made a decision, pulling back on the joystick and tipping the Manta up on its tail. "Hang on to something," he told Brigid somewhat belatedly as the g-forces drove them both back into their seats.

Mantas were capable of operating inside the atmosphere and outside of it, Kane recalled, but space travel required a whole different set of principles for its execution—which meant that the Manta utilized an entirely different system to achieve it. He checked the altimeter as his craft climbed to thirty-four thousand feet in ninety seconds. A little higher and they would move out of the troposphere and the pressure would drop. The Manta's air pulse engines roared as it hurtled straight up in a vertical climb to the very limits of the atmosphere.

Brigid felt herself being dragged back in her seat as the incredible craft hit Mach 1.

GRANT'S SENSES WERE reeling but he was beginning to get the hang of things again. He was being pulled at incredible speed toward their mystery destination.

The sensors informed Grant that he had moved thirty-two miles already, and there was no sign of slowing down. The twin golden craft continued hurtling ahead of him, visible in the viewport as they dragged him onward. They were moving so fast that Grant wondered if they would leave Brazilian air space before much longer.

Then something caught Grant's eye, shining in the distance like a golden aberration in the cloudless blue blanket of the sky. It shimmered into place like a rising flame splitting from a fire, ebbing and sparkling as he tried to see just what it was.

Below, trees were hurtling past as all three vehicles continued to speed toward that distant speck in the sky. It hovered a mile and a half above the ground, static and serene, with a strange waver to its appearance that reminded him of heat haze. As if it was not fully there, Grant realized, like a hologram or an object seen in those confused seconds between dreaming and full wakefulness.

At the speed they were traveling, the speck became a circle in just a few moments, and Grant could begin to make out some details. His first thought was that it was a star, but as he neared he saw that the thing was unbalanced. Yes, it resembled a star, but one that had been cut in half along its horizontal midpoint, the lower section discarded. The jagged top glowed like a miniature sun while its base was entirely missing in a straight-line cut.

"What have we here?" Grant muttered as he peered at the strange star through the magnification sensors of the Manta's heads-up display. The lenses sought to get closer, dimming and filtering the brightness of the distant object to prevent the pilot from being dazzled. Strangely, the sensors could not seem to lock on to the object—each time they got close, the view would shimmer and the image would be lost, causing them to reset and begin the process again.

"Darn thing isn't solid," Grant realized, shutting down the sensor scan.

Details continued to pan across his field of vision in colored numerals, but the stuttered magnification ceased, and with it Grant's sense of disorientation.

Grant waited impatiently, wishing he could contact Kane, wishing he could find out where it was he was being taken. Up ahead, the golden half star resolved itself into something more solid, and Grant could make out its details properly for the first time. It wasn't a star; it was a city, gold as the sun's rays, floating above the ground, its towering buildings thrust up into the blue sky.

"Well, that gives a while new meaning to the term *skyscrapers*," Grant muttered incredulously.

Elsewhere

THE BUILDING LOOKED like an anvil cast in copper, with a mighty waterfall running down one of its two-hundred-foot-high walls. The waterfall fed a deep stream that surrounded the building entirely and was filled with genetically modified piranha, fast and hungry, ensuring that no one could get in or out without the express permission of the king.

One man, however, came and went as he pleased: the guards merely waved Ronald through the security, for he was above reproach. He glided past the main desk in his sleek-sided motion chair, moving into an elevator that worked via the principles of compressed air, like the internal postal system in old buildings of the 1930s. A moment later he was sitting before the incarceration complex where the building's lone guest was held. The interior walls here were clear, so that the guest's every action could be observed.

The single inhabitant was called Wertham the Strange, and he sat cross-legged atop a table he had pulled up to one of the transparent walls, staring down at his visitor across its transparent barricade. Wertham's face was sunken, hungry, and the whites of his eyes had taken on a yellow cast like egg yolks, dark pupils watching from their midst. His hair— brown with flecks of gray like steel wool—was cut in an unflattering basin style from which it had begun to grow free, the tangles curling up from his scalp as if they were rising flames. He wore the simple clothes of a prisoner, a cotton shirt and pants dyed the bright green of freshly mown grass.

"I tire of waiting," Wertham said in a voice like nails down a blackboard. "Tell me you have news."

Ronald turned to the guards and instructed them to leave with the slightest incline of his head. He was a neat man in middle age, wearing flexible indigo armor and a skullcap. He sat in the confines of the motion chair, his legs unmoving. The chair was metallic red with twin hornlike struts towering behind it similar to upturned elephant's tusks. "Your pleas are heard in the royal court each week," he assured Wertham, "and each week a new reason is found to hold you longer."

"They think me strange," Wertham said. "Wertham the Strange. Because my ideas are too wild for them."

Ronald nodded. "You see things differently from the norm," he said. "It can be hard for others to accept that. Fear guides their hearts at each clemency hearing."

Wertham nodded. It was true. Even now, he could see the shapes that hid themselves from human eyes. No amount of jailing would cleanse that from his system.

"Plead my case, Doctor," Wertham urged as the last guard shuffled out.

Ronald looked down at his legs where they were held in the motion chair, and when he looked back at Wertham his face had taken on a bitter aspect. "They won't listen. They look at me as if I am worthless because of my injury."

"They think the same of me because I dared to think further than merely technology, brother," Wertham agreed.

"I'm not your brother, Wertham."

"But we share the same goal—to see Authentiville's stagnating regime overthrown. The same goal and the same hate."

Ronald looked down at his legs again before shaking his head. "You can stop the pain? You can make me walk?"

"A king stands proudly above his subjects," Wertham

hissed. "Have faith, brother. Am I not the master of all things strange and all things wonderful?"

Dr. Ronald nodded solemnly. "You have so much to teach," he said. "If only they would listen."

"They will, brother," Wertham assured him. "They will."

Chapter 7

Kane's Manta rocketed straight up, crossing the faint blue line that marked the edge of the atmosphere and plunged onward toward the cold vacuum of space.

"Kane," Brigid gasped through clenched teeth, "what… are…you…?"

"Al…most…there," Kane replied, struggling to speak as the press of gravity pushed down hard against his chest. Even the g-compensator of the Manta was not capable of alleviating the change in pressure at this climb speed; it required time to catch up—time Kane didn't have to spare.

The curvature of Earth was visible through the side viewports of the Manta. It was like looking down at a blue-white marble from very close, the great line of the horizon curving away into the distance.

Kane didn't take much notice of the view. His mind was focused on the sensor display, where the Manta continued to track the movement of Grant's transponder, blipping in and out of reception. The sensors didn't tell him much; he only hoped it was enough to track Grant before he disappeared entirely, the same way Domi had.

Kane gritted his teeth as the Manta sped beyond gravity's reach.

The Manta was burning through the last vestiges of the atmosphere now, hurtling up past its blue limit. Up ahead in the viewport, the blackness of space was becoming more pronounced as they reached the very edge of the atmosphere.

"What…do…you…plan to…do?" Brigid asked, every word a struggle as the gravity compensators in the Manta strove to keep up with the crushing pressure of the g-forces.

"Turn…around," Kane bit out, "and catch…Grant…on the…flip side."

Brigid was not certain what that meant, but it was too much effort to ask. She sat back in the acceleration couch behind Kane's seat, clinging to its sides with a death grip.

Lakesh's voice came over the Commtact at that moment, his concern clear. "Kane? Your transponder is showing some incredible physical strain, as is Brigid's. Where are you? What's going on?"

"Backing…my partner…up," Kane replied, his eyes locked on the blurring numbers racking up on the altimeter where it was displayed on his heads-up software. They were beyond the limit of the atmosphere now, where the Manta would engage a secondary propulsion system.

Wind drag cut abruptly and Kane felt the Manta lurch forward as it was freed from the grip of gravity. Kane felt the ramjet cut out as the solid-fuel pulse detonation rockets kicked in, blasting the Manta out into the void. Below them, Earth turned very slowly, and Kane counted equally slowly in his head, trying not to rush. In his mind, he had counted to three, but it felt like forever knowing that Grant was in danger. A moment later, Kane flipped the Manta, cutting a tight arc around, bringing the beautiful craft almost a full 180 degrees until it began to hurtle back toward Earth. Behind him, the Manta left a streak of flame as the solid fuel blasted from its rear.

GRANT'S MANTA CONTINUED coasting toward the city in the sky, caught up in the magnetic net cast by the golden air vehicles. The city hung a mile and a half above Earth's surface, moving at a swift pace over the lush greenery of the Brazilian rain forest. As Grant tried to focus on it, it seemed to flicker in and out of the air, its golden spires and minarets wavering into view like a mirage.

Grant studied the there-again-gone-again buildings that covered its surface. There were mighty towers that shot high into the sky, many as tall as forty stories or more. There was also an abrupt line beneath the city, a straight plain like a flat disc on which the whole thing rested. The floating spectacle was big as a ville; in fact, it reminded him a little of Cobaltville, where he had grown up. Grant estimated it was larger than Cobaltville, though it was hard to be sure from this distance and with the flicker.

Grant refocused his eyes, scanning the two craft ahead of him as they drew him closer to the city in the sky.

"Come on, Kane," he muttered to himself. "Wherever you are—get back here quick."

As Grant watched through the viewport, the air below seemed to shimmer with new energy, and he saw something burst from the floating city like the beam of a powerful searchlight. It could only be described as a wide track hanging in the sky, its lines straight and parallel. It glistened there like a river surface catching the moonlight.

Grant's heads-up display analyzed the new data, detecting powerful ion energy. The thick line of energy wavered into place as if it were a waterfall catching the sunlight. The beam appeared to be stretching out from the mirage city, reaching out toward his Manta and its silent escorts.

Grant felt something lock on to his craft with an abrupt shunt, saw the twin golden pebbles similarly locked in place as they were caught within the twinkling beam. The Manta rattled as it was pulled on a new vector toward the city in the sky. But where was Kane?

"KEEP…HOLDING ON TO…something," Kane advised Brigid as they slammed back into the atmosphere with a red scar of reentry heat.

His crazed maneuver had cut a tiny corner from the journey, using Earth's rotation to boost Kane's craft forward, as if it were a skipping stone bouncing on the planet's atmosphere. Both engines were working to power the ship back to the ground, driving the Manta ahead at a breathtaking velocity, gravity adding even more urgency to the descent.

The sense of speed was incredible—at this distance, their eyes told them that they were hardly moving at all, and yet their bodies could feel the velocity in every organ, every bone.

"Kane, I can't see anything down there," Brigid admitted as she tried to spot Grant far below them.

"He's there," Kane insisted. "He's got to be."

Kane scanned the ground as it loomed into view. At first there was simply the rich darkness of the foliage like a splash of green paint. And then Kane identified the Juruena River, a snaking line cutting through the green, while his heads-up display gave him a location update so that he could get his bearings.

A moment later, Grant and his unwanted wingmen came into view on Kane's scanner, still just pinprick dots in the distance, Grant's ship automatically tagged by the Manta's unique software.

There was something else there, too, Kane saw: a shimmering line, a quarter mile long and fifty feet in width, streaking across the sky above the dense forest.

"What th—?" Kane muttered as he pulled his Manta out of its dive, wrestling it toward the streak of light.

From this angle, the beam of light hung in the air like a sunbeam catching dust motes before disappearing in a broken, fading line.

"What is that?" Brigid asked from behind Kane's ear. She still sounded breathless.

"I don't know, Baptiste," Kane admitted, "but Grant's heading right for it.

Kane's heads-up display informed him of the increased ionic activity, just as Grant's sensors had done seconds earlier. Kane remembered what Lakesh had told him about the ion transfer, how its energy had been used to power rocket ships in the twentieth century.

"They're boosting Grant's Manta using an ion beam," Kane realized. "Piggybacking him on its energy trail to shunt him to wherever it is they're going."

The Manta was closer now, whipping through the sky and leaving a double sonic boom in its wake. Below, Grant and his mysterious companions seemed to be stretching across the farthest end of the ion beam, pulling away into infinity.

"They're disappearing," Brigid gasped. "What can we do?"

"Keep your fingers crossed," Kane told her. "Maybe your legs and your eyes crossed, too. I'm going in."

With that, Kane ignored the straining engines of the Manta and entered the glistening beam of light as Grant's Manta began to flicker and fade from its far end.

Kane watched as Grant's Manta seemed to evaporate before his eyes. Without conscious thought, he pressed hard on the accelerator, willing the twin engine systems of his own Manta to catch its disappearing twin.

There was a flicker of light as Kane struck the space where the three aircraft had been just moments before. And then— nothing.

AN IMPOSSIBLE INSTANT PASSED, a swirl of colors racing before their eyes as Kane and Brigid hurtled tangentially across infinity.

The lush green canopy of Serra do Norte had disappeared.

The blue sky had also been replaced, too, a slowly changing kaleidoscope of color taking its place, one shade flowing into the next, no one point remaining the same. Ahead of that, Kane and Brigid saw the golden city for the first time where it rested on its disclike base, hovering in multicolored limbo.

"It's beautiful," Brigid said as she craned her neck to peer through the viewport.

"It's dangerous," Kane spat in response. "Remember that—always."

Unseen by Kane, Brigid nodded, checking the sidearm she had holstered at her hip. It was a TP-9 semiautomatic, a bulky hand pistol with a covered targeting scope across the top, finished in molded matte black. The grip was set just off center beneath the barrel so that, when removed from the holster, it created a lopsided square with the user's hand and wrist forming the final side and corner.

In the pilot's chair, Kane hailed Cerberus but received no answer. Wherever they were, their communications with the outside world had been blocked.

Before him, the two ovoid vehicles were descending toward the city, dragging Grant's unpowered Manta behind them. Wouldn't they be surprised to learn the Manta was undamaged! Kane spotted a landing strip ahead, a golden-butter color, jutting out from the side of the flying city.

"What have we stumbled on to this time?" he muttered incredulously. Kane had seen a lot of strange things in his time with the Cerberus organization. He had visited the city of Agartha hidden beneath the surface of Earth and fought running battles on the Annunaki mothership, *Tiamat,* as she coasted Earth's atmosphere. But this golden city was something new, a settlement hidden…where?

"What is this place?" Kane wondered. "The gold at the end of the rainbow?"

"No, Kane," Brigid said. "Look again. Don't the colors remind you of anything?"

Kane eyed the rainbow display that painted the heavens before them. The constant flux was reminiscent of the blossom of force exuded by the interphaser, a portable teleportation device that Cerberus had made use of on countless occasions. That projection included not only a swirl of color but streaks of lightning that would crackle like witch fire when the quantum portal was opened for a teleportational jump. "The interphaser," he replied. "But where's the lightning?"

"Below us," Brigid said, and Kane peered down at the ion stream that shimmered with white streaks.

"The stream—it's lightning?" he said in stunned astonishment.

Brigid nodded. "Great gouts of it arranged in parallel, like a colossal circuit board."

"Then we're jumping parallax points?" Kane guessed uncertainly.

"I think we're in some kind of cosmic rift between dimensions," Brigid suggested, "with the positive charge of the ion stream boosting us toward our destination."

"The ville," Kane finished.

They continued on toward the butter-colored airstrip, carving a path through a space that didn't seem to exist.

Within seconds, all four vehicles were brought down to the surface, executing smooth landings arrayed in a diamond shape on the landing strip. Neither Kane nor Grant had had to do anything to land their Mantas; instead, there appeared to be an automated system in place that guided the air vehicles down to the required point from the ion stream.

"Pretty smooth," Kane muttered, watching the landing area through the sensor mask of the Manta.

The Manta's engines were powering down automatically,

even though Kane had sent no command for them to do so. It made him suspicious.

"Keep your eyes open, Baptiste," he instructed. "I don't like it when someone else starts calling the shots."

They waited for the better part of a minute while the lead vehicles went through their postlanding sequence. Then their smooth exteriors buckled momentarily and a trapezoid door appeared in both, through which the interior of each craft could be seen. Their insides looked dark, with a smattering of glowing streaks in green and red.

Moments later, the pilots stepped out. They were clearly humanoid, and they were dressed in what appeared to be sleek, form-fitting armor that featured illuminated strips running across the torso and up and down the limbs.

One pilot's armor was blue, while his companion's was a rich purple that shimmered in the light like shot silk. Their flight helmets looked like upside-down buckets with stylized wings retreating back from just above the ears, running six inches behind them in a polished metal that might have been silver. The metal helmets covered the top half of each pilot's face and included a molded pair of goggles with tinted black lenses, leaving the mouth, chin and the bottom of the nose exposed.

The analysis software in Kane's heads-up display was feeding him conflicting reports on the composition of the armor, as if it was unable to scan it properly. Kane pushed back the visor, shaking his head. "Giving me a headache," he muttered, wishing once again that he could break radio silence.

The pilots turned to the grounded Mantas and acknowledged them with a curt nod. It looked a lot like a warning. Then they turned in unison and marched toward a low building that crouched at the side of the airfield. Similarly armored figures waited there, poised behind large shieldlike plates with transparent windows.

The Cerberus warriors watched as the pilots disappeared into the building. The building had gold walls with vertical strips of light running up its surface, reaching from ground to roof in a line no wider than a man's hand. Above, the sky swirled with a rainbow mix of color, reds and yellows colliding to form new shades of orange, blues meeting the reds in rich shades of violet.

Kane, Brigid and Grant were left idling on the airstrip, waiting in readiness.

"They're going to kill us," Kane muttered.

"Optimist!" Brigid chided, but she wondered if he might be right.

Chapter 8

Bitterroot Mountains, Montana

It had been ninety seconds since Kane's Manta had disappeared from sight, following Grant's own disappearance scant seconds before.

In the operations center of the Cerberus redoubt, Brewster Philboyd breathed deeply as he studied the satellite image over the Serra do Norte region of Brazil, trying to settle his racing heart. The feed was live, albeit with a momentary delay as the signal was bounced back down to the redoubt's pickups and translated into an overhead image from high in the air. The satellite could be trained on specific sites as required, and Brewster had directed it to the area in Brazil by Lakesh's command.

Another freezie exile from the Manitius Moon Base, Philboyd was a highly adept astrophysicist whose problem-solving abilities and general computer know-how put him at the core of a very small group of Cerberus personnel who might genuinely be described as irreplaceable. A tall man with a gaunt face and lanky frame that seemed just a little too long for the desks and chairs of the ops room, Philboyd had blond hair that was swept back from a high forehead and his cheeks bore evidence of acne scars from his teenage years. Besides the uniform white jumpsuit of all personnel, Philboyd wore a pair of black-framed eyeglasses that could make his blue-eyed gaze seem rather challenging.

"We've lost them," he announced, not quite believing the words himself. "Am initiating a full sweep of the area to see if we've missed anything."

Lakesh was pensively watching the same feed from the comm desk. He had felt the same sense of unreality when he saw Kane's Manta wink out of the picture and desperately hoped he hadn't lost his field team on a fool's errand the same way he had lost Domi. "Check the satellite feed, Mr. Philboyd," he commanded automatically before switching to the Commtact receiver without taking breath. "Kane? Do you read me, Kane? We have lost visual and I have received no response to my summons. I repeat—we have lost visual. Do you read? Please come in. Brigid? Grant?"

Lakesh waited for any response, but none came. Just the same as nothing had come over the Commtact for the past two minutes.

Two and a half minutes.

The clock in the corner of Lakesh's monitor screen was relentless.

"We've lost their transponder signals," Donald Bry reported, calling the information across the busy ops room. "Checked twice now, including full system analysis."

"Confirmed," Reba DeFore said grimly from her seat at the medical monitoring station. "Their lights went out three minutes ago. I can't home in on anything."

Lakesh looked plaintively at his colleagues, then turned back to the satellite feed where it showed on his screen. "Mr. Philboyd, do we have anything?"

"Feed is still live, Dr. Singh," Brewster said, using Lakesh's formal title for a change. It seemed appropriate somehow, in a situation like this, when the chips were down. "Lot of trees still there, but no sign of the Mantas or the other two. Wide scan shows nothing, no evidence of their passage."

Lakesh nodded solemnly, still listening with dwindling

hope to the static over the Commtact headset. Three minutes had passed already since their last contact, longer by far than CAT Alpha should have been out of touch. As he waited, Lakesh felt his heart sink. This was how they had lost Domi, only that time he had not even had a satellite in place to watch her.

Lakesh pressed his fingers to the sides of his nose in frustration, tweaking it with pressure. You foolish, foolish man, he cursed himself. First you lose the beacon of your life, then your most trusted allies.

He had sent them into this trap, planned it and briefed the crew who had prepped the Mantas for the ruse. And now he had lost them all and they were nowhere nearer learning where Domi had gone. He had lost everything.

"Keep scanning," Lakesh told Philboyd. "Donald, I want a full report on the transponder signals, triangulation with prospected movement based on last known point of contact, speed, trajectory—the works. We follow that through to the ultimate end point, and I want a field team ready to scramble to that position in ten minutes. Call Edwards, Sinclair— whoever is available from R and D."

Bry nodded, his fingers already working his keyboard.

"Reba," Lakesh continued, turning to the stocky ash-blond physician, "I want a full report of the search team's health at the moment of their disappearance, as well as constant monitoring for if—for *when*—the signals return."

The clock showed six minutes since last contact. Already Lakesh felt sure the elapsed time was too long. Six minutes was plenty enough time to die.

Chapter 9

Location unknown

In the Manta's rear seat, Brigid Baptiste smiled as she watched the sky change color. "I can't get over this place," she said. It had been five minutes since the armored pilots had disappeared and CAT Alpha remained waiting on the airstrip.

"We should get out," Kane told her.

"Not yet," Brigid insisted. "They know we're here. They'll come to us when they're ready."

"I still say we should get out and speak to them," Kane growled.

"And say what?" Brigid challenged. "'Hi, we didn't invade your airspace in heavily armed vehicles to cause any harm'? The weight of human history says otherwise—don't be too surprised if they shoot you on the spot."

"Humph," Kane snorted. "I just don't like waiting."

"No one likes waiting, Kane," Brigid assured him. "But most of us learn patience by the time we're ten."

"Humph," Kane snorted again.

Eventually, more figures emerged from the low building. There were five in all, including the two pilots. The pilots had removed their flight helmets and to Kane's relief looked entirely normal—and human—beneath. Both were clean-shaven, Caucasian males with neatly cropped hair, one blond and one black haired.

The pilots led the way, escorting a man in what Kane took

at first to be a single-person conveyance. The chair had no discernible means of propulsion yet moved across the airstrip with remarkable grace. A line of lights ran up its exterior in a pattern of bright white circlets, and the vehicle was colored a reflective red like tinted metal. It featured two great struts running above it like an elephant's tusks, towering over the heads of its lone rider's standing companions. The rider wore a pair of dark goggles over his eyes and a skullcap that entirely hid his hair—assuming he had any—along with an indigo uniform that buttoned up tight to his neck and covered his seated body in one piece.

Besides the man in the conveyance and the pilots, there were two other figures, a man and woman. Both were young and wore armorlike suits similar to the pilots but with their heads uncovered. They carried boxed equipment belted to their hips. Although they didn't have helmets on, both of them wore headbands that encircled their foreheads with narrow metal strips. The strips were of a multicolored, mirrored material, glinting as they caught the swirling sky.

"Looks like the party's starting," Kane muttered as the strange figures neared.

The others held back while the man and woman approached. They first stood before Grant's Manta and touched their fingertips to their headbands, closing their eyes. In the cockpit, Grant was overcome by a strange sensation, a feeling of vertigo, and the inside of his skull seemed to itch. He reached down for the handgrip of the Copperhead subgun where it waited in the foot well, but after a few seconds the vertiginous sensation passed.

He watched through the viewport as the man and woman turned away and reported to the man in the strange conveyance. Once they had, they strode across to Kane's Manta farther down the landing strip. Grant could not hear what was being said, but reading the strangers' expressions he detected no hostility or alarm.

The two strangely garbed figures halted before Kane's Manta and performed the same routine. Sitting in the pilot's seat, Kane grumbled something to Brigid, expressing his loathing for mind readers.

"I think we have to trust them," Brigid told him. "At least for now."

In a moment, the weird sensation had passed, and once the two had reported to the rider of the red chairlike conveyance, they took up positions behind him while he approached the Mantas.

The seated man motioned, his fingers spread wide. Grant took this to be a signal to open up, and he popped the canopy of the Manta and let it glide back on its runners, his free hand grasping the Copperhead subgun.

"Welcome, traveler," the seated man announced in a loud voice. "There's no need to be shy."

Grant raised himself in his seat until he could be clearly seen over the lip of the open cockpit. "Howdy," he said.

"Let me introduce myself," the seated spokesman said as his companions waited at his side. "My name is Ronald and I'm here to welcome you to Authentiville. I must apologize for the manner in which you and your companions arrived— our scouts had not realized that your conveyance was occupied when we snagged it, and once they were made aware of the error it seemed prudent to bring you here to explain their oversight."

"Is there just one of you in that craft?"

"Yes, sir," Grant confirmed.

"And the other one? Your companion? Two inside, I am told."

"Yeah, two," Grant confirmed. "Pilot and, um, teammate." He didn't like giving information so freely, but these people seemed to be a step ahead of them right now. He guessed that the itchy experience he had felt in his skull had been some kind of mental scan—he had experienced similar before, most recently at the hands of a group of deranged immortals known as Dorians. He didn't like it. However, Grant had detected no outward signs of aggression from these people—in fact, they didn't even appear armed, although he guessed the odd vehicle that their leader utilized might have some armament. For now, at least, they weren't pointing anything obviously in his direction.

"Please—come down," Ronald encouraged. "Join us." As he spoke, his companions made their way over to Kane's Manta.

Carefully, Grant flipped the Copperhead's safety back on and slipped the weapon into a hidden sleeve in the inner lining of the Kevlar duster he sported. Then, with the weapon concealed, he lifted himself from the cockpit and clambered down the wing to join Ronald and the others on the landing strip.

Thirty feet behind him, Kane and Brigid were just exiting their own Manta at the request of the other local reps.

"I hope you'll forgive my not standing," Ronald began as Kane and Brigid joined them. "Unfortunately, destiny has decreed that I not perform such feats."

Grant realized then that the strange conveyance was a wheelchair, though it was one unlike any he had seen before. "You called this place—Authentiville?" Grant asked to cover his embarrassment.

"That's correct," Ronald said, nodding eagerly.

"Can I ask where we are, exactly?" Brigid asked.

As they spoke, the group passed through the doors of the golden tower and found themselves standing in a grand lobby. The lobby had eighteen-foot-high ceilings and featured towering machinery set at the sides of the vast space to leave a spacious, open floor area. To Brigid's trained eye, the machinery looked like something medieval, and yet it glowed with modern illumination.

"Authentiville is an independent city state," Ronald continued as he glided across the room. "Our contact with other territories is of a limited nature."

"We're searching for a friend who went missing," Kane stated.

"Missing friend?" Ronald repeated, confused.

"Pale girl by the name of Domi," Kane told him. "Pure white skin and hair, red eyes. There's no mistaking her. We think a couple of your flyboys picked her up yesterday morning."

Ronald offered Kane a sincere smile. "I know Domi—and I assure you that she's quite safe. I'll send word ahead and see that she knows you're here. May I enquire as to your names?"

"Kane," Kane told him. "And you've already met Grant, and this is Baptiste."

"Brigid," the distaff member of the Cerberus group corrected automatically. Kane had an irritating habit of using only her surname.

They passed through another set of doors and into a corridor lit by long horizontal streaks running along the walls. The illumination was a soft yellow color, like sunset in the tropics. Ronald glided alongside Kane, discussing Domi further and deflecting questions adroitly. His conveyance moved with almost total silence, only the very faint whir of its energy source humming at the periphery of hearing.

The two pilots took time to welcome Grant, apologizing for the way in which he had been brought here and complimenting his piloting skills.

"Your conveyance is Annunaki in origin, did you know that?" the dark-haired one asked.

Grant's eyebrows rose in surprise at the query, but he

covered it swiftly. "Yeah, me and Kane came across these two while we were doing a little exploring. Liked the way they handled and decided to keep them."

"They're fine vehicles," the blond pilot agreed with a curt nod. "Safe skies to you."

The two pilots disappeared through a door to the side of the corridor, leaving the Cerberus team, Ronald and his two assistants alone.

The corridor ended with a circular seal made up of four interlocked panels that peeled back like the petals of a flower. Kane, Grant and Brigid watched as the sections parted, revealing a long platform that jutted outward from the building. They could see now that the platform was arranged high above street level and it contained enough free space to hold a dozen or more people with ease. Beyond the platform, the colossal towers of Authentiville waited like golden monoliths, forming a skyline that looked like the pipes of a church organ.

"Our steed will be here in a moment," Ronald assured the Cerberus visitors as they halted at the end of the corridor.

It took only a few seconds before their promised "steed" arrived, a broad-faced mechanical vehicle that traveled along what appeared to be a projected beam of light. The vehicle was a wine-red color with rounded sides and an arched roof, a continuous broad golden metal bumper running along its sides at waist height. The vehicle approached with a *whsk-whsk* sound like a desk fan before pulling to a halt at the platform edge.

In a moment, the sides of the vehicle retreated into their casings, granting a wide entrance through which passengers could enter. There were no seats inside, and nothing to hold on to while the vehicle was in transit. There was also no driver, just a box of lights located at the rear of the cabin that flickered different colors while the group stepped aboard.

Ronald assumed a position at the center rear of the vehicle, while his assistants, still wearing their mirrored headbands, took up their posts immediately beside him, hands folded behind their backs. The Cerberus team were encouraged to join them.

The interior of the "steed," as Ronald had called it, was very plain, with strip lighting set in the curved walls and ceiling to illuminate the interior. There were windows on all sides, running the whole length of the vehicle. The windows reached up to the ceiling and down to Brigid's kneecaps, granting the passengers a panoramic view of the city beyond the airfield. There were separate window panes set in the roof and a circular one in the center of the floor, beneath which the empty drop beyond the platform's edge could be seen in all its breathtaking glory.

Kane ran his fingertips along one of the windows, feeling the smooth surface. It did not seem to be glass, but neither did it have the warmth of plastic. In fact, it felt more like crystal.

Once everyone was aboard, the side of the vehicle shuttered closed and it began to move noiselessly along the beam of light, picking up speed as it made its passage across the rooftops and between buildings, running on the narrow beam of light.

"What powers this vehicle?" Brigid wondered, addressing her question to Ronald.

"I can't say," Ronald replied with a shrug. "I didn't build it."

Brigid laughed at that, realizing it was like asking someone the principles behind the mat-trans simply because they could operate the teleportational system by punching in the right transmit code.

While Brigid had their host's attention, Kane turned his back and surreptitiously activated his Commtact. Because the remarkable communication devices were surgically implanted into the user's skull, they could pick up subvocalized speech as well as words said aloud. Thus, not using his voice, Kane called for Domi.

"Domi, this is Kane. Please respond."

Kane waited a few seconds as the strange steed powered away from the airfield, weaving a path through the buildings as it followed its single, shimmering rail. There was no response. It appeared that, wherever they had landed, the Commtacts didn't work.

Through the windows, the buildings were set in clumps of varying styles. It took Brigid a moment to recognize that they were flying over an industrial area, by-product pouring from high golden funnels in clouds of multicolored mist. Seen from above, the factories were shaped like gigantic cogs, giving the appearance of the workings of a bank-vault door. Steam dissipated above the buildings, and the steed cut a path through its fog. From inside, the steam appeared washed through with colors in the whiteness, pale blues, pinks and greens hanging there in pastel shimmers. It looked like cotton candy, pollution turned into art.

"What do you think this train runs on?" Grant asked Kane as they peered from one of the windows at the strange rail of light. He pitched his voice low, not trusting these strangers.

The rail seemed to be forming just a few feet ahead of them, giving the impression that it materialized as needed and changed route as required.

"It looks like a rail," Kane said, "but not like one I've ever seen before."

Despite the sudden appearance of the rail just a few feet ahead, the journey was exceptionally smooth.

As they traveled, Brigid spied someone flying past the window panes.

"Look!" Brigid called as she spotted the figure.

He was a young man in his early twenties wearing a blue jumpsuit. He had a luxurious mane of long red hair and a set of honest-to-gosh wings strapped to his back. The wings looked to be made of molded plastic with a hinge attachment at the midpoint. They did not flap, but seemed to glide, finding passage between buildings. The Cerberus team watched dumbfounded as the man landed on a building rooftop and the wings folded in on themselves as his feet touched solid ground.

As they watched the emerging vista around them the Cerberus teammates spotted more of the flying figures in ones and twos. Their dress varied, and so did the color of their wings, but they all traveled through the air in a similar manner.

"What are those things?" Brigid asked. "How do they do that?"

Ronald smiled amiably. "Pegasuits," he said. "They gift the user with the power of flight—it's very simple. Of course, it's easy to forget how little you have down on the surface."

They continued past the industrial area and crossed over green fields where cows and sheep grazed. The fields were arranged in steps that ran across the tops of buildings, fences of hard light penning the animals in place.

In total, the journey took ninety seconds. Soon they were approaching a colossal building that dominated the center of the city. The building reached not just upward but outward, spanning hundreds of acres. Its roof was curved in a graceful arc resembling a wave, rolling from west to east in a golden curl. Beneath this, the building's facade was decorated with huge pillars and columns, each one more than a thousand feet high and as wide as ten men. The windows were vast, too, panes of colored glass as tall as redwood trees, grand figures etched into them that twinkled like cut crystal.

"Where are you taking us?" Kane asked as the strange conveyance shuttled toward the colossal building.

"Where all visitors to Authentiville go," Ronald replied. "The court of Jack the King."

It looked like a palace made for gods.

Chapter 10

King Jack's court was as impressive from the inside as it had been on the outside. The first room the Cerberus crew entered was wide as a football field, with a ceiling so high that birds flew up there, nesting in the distant rafters. The floor was polished onyx that caught every highlight and reflected back the faces of Kane, Brigid and Grant when they peered into it.

There were statues to each side of the vast room, human figures dressed in elaborate armor, carved to three times life-size so that they towered over anyone who entered. The twin statues at either end of the room wielded spears the size of saplings, which they aimed at each other, creating a make-shift arch over the two doorways of the room.

"This sure is one *big* room," Grant muttered as he saw its proportions for the first time.

Ronald led the way through the room in respectful silence. The Cerberus warriors followed while Ronald's two psychic readers brought up the rear, their shiny headbands catching the light. Brigid had been thinking about the mind scan that they had performed, concluding that it was mechanically enabled somehow, utilizing some function of the headbands coupled with the equipment they wore at their belts. She peeked surreptitiously at said equipment but it gave away no secrets, its appearance a blank-faced box with a series of small, diodelike lights running up one edge.

Grant stopped before one of the towering statues, brushing a hand across his shaved scalp. "I wonder who she is," he said.

The statue was of a woman wearing a stylized breastplate, metal skirt and long boots with spiked heels and spurs. A helmet covered her face, leaving only her ruby lips on show. The sculptor had gone to great lengths to elaborate on her cloak, a fan of feathers that flowed down to her ankles, billowing out behind her like the rising tide.

"Looks like an old girlfriend of mine," Kane said with a chuckle.

A few paces ahead of them, Ronald pulled his chair to a halt and turned back. "This way, please," he instructed, his voice barely above a whisper.

Laughing like schoolboys, Kane and Grant followed the wheelchair-bound man with Brigid and the mind readers striding behind. As he approached the far door where the twin spear-carrier statues waited, Ronald said a word that none of the Cerberus warriors recognized. The spears in the statues' hands glowed momentarily and then the double doors opened inward, granting entry into a second room.

"Through here," Ronald encouraged, leading the way.

Through the doors, the Cerberus warriors found they had entered an even larger room. Its floor was made of translucent red-and-green strips like polished ruby and emerald, while its rafters were so high that clouds had formed beneath the distant ceiling. Birds sang as they flew through those clouds, alighting on huge constructs that depended from the ceiling in odd shapes, each one made from purest gold. This was the court of King Jack.

"I take back what I previously said," Grant muttered. "Now, *this* is a big room."

Kane nodded, eyeing the surrounds with amazement. There were no statues in this room, but there were towering pillars that stretched up until they were lost in the wispy clouds. People worked at desks placed at the edges of the room, great rows of them wired into the desk machinery, eyes enshrouded in goggles that plugged directly into their desks.

Other figures moved about the room on wheeled vehicles, single-person conveyances made of a short strut on which the user stood, with a control stick poised in a graceful curve that belled out from the front of the vehicle, enabling them to be operated one-handed.

"Y'know," Kane commented drily, "I think I've seen countries smaller than this room."

As the Cerberus rebels entered the room, one group of vehicle drivers settled into position at their flanks, accompanying them as they strode across the vast space toward the thrones that stood in the room's center. The escort riders were dressed in matching uniforms—and they clearly were uniforms—with ear protectors and dark goggles that hid their eyes. They wore the fixed expressions of bored soldiers the world over, using their strange conveyances to keep pace with Ronald and his entourage as they crossed the red-and-green floor to the raised dais where the thrones stood.

There were two thrones, both elaborate with high gold backs and an abundance of gemstone decorations. The backs of the thrones stretched thirty feet into the air, and colorful birds settled on their high tops, singing delightedly as Grant, Kane and Brigid approached. At a glance, the thrones appeared to be constructed from many parts, giving the impression of something industrial or mechanical rather than designed for comfort. Sitting on the thrones were two figures—a man and a woman—with a glowing shaft of energy sparking between them, lancing from the floor to the height of their seats.

The man was dressed in golden armor that had been polished to mirror brilliance and was decorated with a bright red sash that covered one shoulder and hung down past his waist like a cape. The armor featured a golden kilt and a high collar that sat snugly to his neck, above which his face had been left unadorned.

It was the face of an old man, square and strong, and above it grew wiry gray hair that showed no sign of receding. Kane guessed the man was in his sixties but he was a young sixty, still tough-looking with the steely determination of an experienced magistrate or military man.

This was King Jack. His eyes smiled as Kane and his companions approached the thrones, and Ronald instructed them to wait.

Beside the golden king sat his queen, a striking woman with dark eyes and long hair that was colored neon-blue with a brilliance that glowed. Her hair was held back with a dark-colored tiara that reflected the changing vibrancy of the hair. Like her husband, the queen wore armor, hers dark and flexible with a low cut that was reminiscent of a ball gown, and with a beaded necklace on her bare décolletage.

Between the two thrones was a low, circular unit made of burnished golden metal. Roughly fourteen inches across, the unit was formed of concentric rings, each one detailed with carved letters and glyphs eerily similar to those found on the wings of the Mantas. Each ring was slightly higher than its larger predecessor, creating a mound effect that peaked just a few inches from the floor. Within this mound, a golden rod had been placed, fourteen inches long and held firmly by the center circle. The rod crackled with barely restrained energies that flickered around it in a halo, glinting from a rubylike jewel embedded at its crown. This was the strange lancelike source of the crackling energy.

"My lord, my lady," Ronald announced as they reached the podium containing the thrones. "May I present our guests from the surface clan called Cerberus." Then he turned to Kane, Grant and Brigid. "Cerberus visitors, this is King Jack and his wife, the Queen Rosalind."

There were an awkward few seconds in which none of the Cerberus team knew quite what was expected of them. And then Brigid took the initiative, curtseying separately before both the king and the queen and hissing to her companions to do likewise. Feeling self-conscious, Kane and Grant bowed before the royal couple.

"It is an honor to meet you both," Brigid announced, taking the lead. "I am Brigid Baptiste."

"The honor's probably ours, lady," King Jack replied with a dismissive wave of his hand. "We don't get many surface folk coming up here these days." Strangely, he didn't sound regal at all—in fact, he sounded decidedly ordinary.

"You pledge fealty to the Cerberus clan?" Queen Rosalind asked. "Is that correct?"

"It is, Your Highness," Brigid confirmed.

"Then we have another of your people here, don't we, my dear?" She consulted her husband. "An entrancing and delightful young waif by the name of Domi."

"That's why we came here," Kane began, stepping forward to get closer to the beautiful queen on her throne. As he did so, the guards on their mechanical sleds whirred nearer, as if in warning that Kane should not get too close. Kane noticed that none of them wore weapons and he automatically wondered if he and Grant could take them with their hidden blasters should the need arise. Neither Kane nor Grant ever traveled far without their sleeved Sin Eaters.

"That's all right," the king said, waving the sentries back. "These folks aren't here to hurt us, are you?"

"No, sir, that's not our intention," Kane confirmed. "We lost Domi about thirty-six hours ago in the same region where you picked up my friend Grant, here."

"Grant, is it?" King Jack asked, looking at the dark-skinned ex-Magistrate. "What about the rest of you? You know me and Roz—you folks have names, I take it?"

"Kane," Kane told him before gesturing to Brigid. "And you already met Bap—"

"Brigid," Brigid interrupted as Kane started to say her surname.

"Brigid, yes," the golden-armored Jack repeated, rolling the name around his mouth as if he was sampling a fine wine. "So you're the *bridge* between these two, is that it?"

Brigid blushed. "Well, I never really thought of it like that, Your Highness. If I am, then it's just a coincidence."

"Names can hide a lot, young lady," King Jack assured her. "You'd be surprised how much of our destinies are decided on the day we're named.

"Anyway, I'm talking here like you kids don't have some place to be. You came looking for your friend, Domi, is that it?"

"It is, Your Highness," Kane agreed.

Before either the king or the queen could respond, Ronald spoke up. "I've already placed a summons for her, my lord. She will be with us presently."

For a moment, the conversation cooled while King Jack discussed the matter with Ronald. The chair-bound man appeared to be some kind of aide and was clearly well thought of by both the royals.

Waiting in silence, Kane felt strange standing in this vast room before this couple. He was more used to combat than he was to negotiation, and making a good impression didn't come naturally to him. He was still trying to put together the puzzle of what had happened.

From what Brigid had suggested, they were in a city that was locked inside the quantum fold of a teleport jump, hidden in nonlinear space. The glistening ion stream had been a kind of docking system that drew the Mantas and their escorts here. As if that wasn't unbelievable enough, the technology that was casually on show was incredible.

Reaching for the crackling shaft of energy, King Jack caught Kane's eye and smiled, and he spoke almost as if he had read Kane's mind. "I guess you kids have a lot of questions you want to ask. Why don't we get out of here and you can join us for a little bite to eat. You will eat, I take it?"

Kane nodded. "Right now, I'd eat anything you put before me, Your Majesty." His companions agreed. Too long waiting around in the Mantas' enclosed cockpits had left them all ravenous.

King Jack stood, plucking the energy lance from its holding pen in the circular construct between the thrones. Beside him, the neon-haired Queen Rosalind also stood. As Jack pulled loose the energy shaft, hidden lights in the room seemed to dim, switching the bright daylight feel of the vast throne room to a kind of evening warmth.

Together, the royal couple, Ronald and the Cerberus warriors made their way toward one of the imposing exits. It was located between two towering pillars, the door so well camouflaged that it looked as though the room continued behind it.

Perhaps it does, Kane thought, still trying to process the concept that they were within a quantum wormhole.

"So, you're technologists?" Kane asked as he blew on his soup to cool it. The soup smelled kind of like duck, but Kane could not identify the spices that had been employed to flavor it.

The banquet hall was, if anything, even more impressive than the throne room, despite its smaller proportions. The walls were carved from wood in such a way that they looked like a forest, each carved tree trunk placed in line one after another. Leaves fluttered constantly through the air as if on an autumn breeze, but on closer inspection, each leaf turned out to be a holographic image, allowing diners to see through them when peering across the table to address their fellow guests.

The table itself was constructed in three joined circles, the largest of which was fifteen feet in diameter and placed in the center where it held various dishes that had been prepared for the occasion, despite the lack of warning. The other tables were ten feet across and constructed in such a manner that they appeared to almost bud from the first, joined to their central companion along one smooth edge to allow the food to be brought and served easily.

The room's centerpiece was a circular fire with a ruby-red flame that seemed able to dance in upon itself in the way a fire spirals under a strong draft. It gave off no heat, and the Cerberus teammates realized that, like the falling autumn leaves, it was holographic and designed solely for decoration.

King Jack sat beside Queen Rosalind at one of the smaller tables, assuring his guests that he liked to be well placed to see what was being served next. He seemed friendly, his manner unthreatening, and Kane felt his guard begin to drop as he spoke with the man.

Jack had invited the Cerberus companions to take up places next to him and his wife. "We can all share one table," he said. "There's plenty of room and it saves on too much shouting to be heard."

Ronald declined the offer to join the king, retreating from the room but leaving his two companions to enjoy the monarch's company. They remained standing while the food was served, taking up positions at the back wall overlooking the table, their expressions fixed in studied disinterest.

Kane noticed that Jack had brought the strange golden rod with him, and he had placed it in a slot similar to the circular design on throne room's floor, this one a pace behind the treelike seat in which Jack sat. The rod appeared to be held by some kind of magnetic field, Kane saw, not clamped in place as he had first assumed, and it stood upright, fixed in position and sparkling with unknown energies.

The guests were brought drinks of iced water and some fruit juice that had a sweet tang before being served soup by the palace staff. The staff had lusterless skin and wore blank expressions, and they shuffled as if they had little energy. Their presence made Brigid uncomfortable, reminding her of corpses, and she asked about them.

"Don't let the Gene-agers worry you," Queen Rosalind told her, patting her hand over Brigid's on the table. "They have no desires of their own, other than to serve us. They won't hurt you."

That was when Kane had posed his question about King Jack and his people being technologists.

"Not really," the king told him. "Although I can see that it may look that way to an outsider. We're really just searchers—what you see here is the application of technology we've scouted for across the globe."

"I suspect you're being coy, Your Highness," Brigid said as she took soup onto her spoon. "We've never seen anything like this. It's very advanced."

King Jack laughed. "We employ what we find in a number of ways. We've been…fortunate."

"What you 'find'?" Kane inquired, placing special emphasis on the word.

"Let me ask you this, Kane," Jack began. "How did you get here? Where did your air vehicles come from? You didn't develop them, I can tell you that. They're found technology. And that's what we have here—found technology. Do you see?"

Kane nodded as he swallowed a mouthful of the soup. He was beginning to understand what was behind this city of miracles. Found technology, much of it alien, the detritus of numerous alien excursions onto planet Earth.

The Cerberus team had spent most of its existence repelling the plans of an alien race called the Annunaki who had been manipulating mankind since the very dawn of recorded time, posing as their gods when the human race was very young. There had been others, too—the Tuatha de Danaan, a peaceful race who had emphasized the spiritual in their music and their art, and who had supplied the Annunaki with much of their more elaborate machinery; the Archons, or First Folk, a race derived from the Tuatha de Danaan and the Annunaki as a bridging gesture between the species, and of whom Cerberus's ally Balam was the very last.

There were doubtless others, too, like the Naga, whose role in the development of human society might only have been tangential and whose place remained in the shadows even now. For the people here in this hidden city to pillage and reuse that tech was both incredible and logical.

It was like a cargo cult from olden days, where the inhabitants of a remote island would come to rely upon and worship the strange artifacts that were washed ashore from passing ships in error, and later dropped from the air during periods of strife such as the Second World War. Primitive islanders in New Guinea and Micronesian societies had formed whole religious rituals around the acquisition and safekeeping of such objects from the more technologically advanced quarters of the world, believing them to be gifts from the gods themselves.

The people of Authentiville seemed likewise enamored of the forbidden tech of alien visitors, and they were employing it in a far more sophisticated way than the usual cargo cult society.

"I thought I recognized the matter-transfer system as an adaptation of something we're…familiar with," Brigid said, but Kane shot her a warning look. He was unsure how much to tell these people, despite their apparent friendliness.

"You mean the Ion Bridge?" Jack laughed. "I haven't been on that in a long time." As he spoke, he finished the last mouthful of his soup and smiled, delicately wiping his mouth with a napkin.

"You seem to know a lot about us," Grant said, gently replacing his spoon in his empty bowl. "Where are you guys from?"

Rosalind snickered. "Oh, Earth—like you. Only it was a long time ago. So long, I can scarcely remember how it looked."

"How long, exactly?" Kane pressed.

The queen shook her head, the rays of blue neon swinging to and fro like sunlight seen from beneath the ocean. "Time is…" she began, then changed tack. "The years flow by and none of us are bothered by their passage. Isn't that right, darling?" she said, locking eyes with her husband. There was love there, Kane could see—genuine human emotion, despite the strange clothes and trappings of these people. Clothes maketh the man, perhaps, but love gave his life purpose.

"I supposed that once our son, Neal, settled, our need to go surface-side became less pressing," said Jack wistfully, and his eyes took on a faraway look. Then he peered around the table at his guests and smiled that broad, engaging smile he had first shown them when they had entered his throne room. "My son hasn't walked these halls in many years now. You'll forgive an old, old man his reminiscences."

The Cerberus team waited while the main course, which consisted of some kind of meat and vegetables, was served by the emotionless waiting staff that Rosalind had called Gene-agers. They were thorough, performing their functions without a word.

As the staff filed out, a young woman dressed in a long dress of metallic purple that clung to her slim figure like paint hurried into the room and spoke discreetly with the royal couple. King Jack dismissed her and addressed his guests as she hurried out of the room.

"My newfound friends," he said, "you came here seeking your companion. Ursula tells me she's just entered the building and will be with us momentarily."

The Cerberus field team looked at one another with surprise. They had become so used to things being difficult in their travels that to meet someone so genuinely engaging and helpful was…well, unsettling.

A few minutes and a mouthful of food later, Domi entered, accompanied by a posse of sentries dressed in the same manner as the ones who had kept pace with Kane's team in the throne room. She wore supple armorlike clothing in a dark jade that covered her torso, arms and legs, leaving only her pale hands and face uncovered. Her usually bone-white hair had been streaked with highlights of purple and, for once, she wore boots on her feet. She also wore a pair of artificial wings on her back, folded in on themselves now but of the same type that Ronald had called pegasuits. Strangest of all, she was wearing an expression of absolute bliss.

Chapter 11

Elsewhere

Even now, Wertham could see the shapes that hid themselves from human eyes: alien geometry, dazzling in its brilliance.

Wertham the Strange was in the brightly lit bedchamber of his cell, sitting hunched over on the bed. They called it a cell, but it was more like an apartment, albeit one with no doors. The walls were clear, and highly advanced monitoring systems functioned to keep tabs on his movements even when his guards weren't watching. It didn't matter to Wertham. He had had a long time to figure out the angles of the cell, a long time to apply his "strange view" to this tiny corner of the world.

There were places, even here, that were hidden from view if only one knew how to find them. The shadows in the cup of a man's hand never went away; they could always be drawn upon to hide small items like the ones Wertham worked with now. There were two items there, each no larger than a penny.

One was a capsule with a colored strip across its center, one end green and one end white.

The other was flatter, square in shape with rounded corners and roughly the size of a man's fingernail. The flat item was colored the dull brown of worn copper and had a streak of bright gold running down its center. This split at one edge to form a fork pattern. This was a miniaturized circuit.

Wertham manipulated his thumb joint, rolling the circuit

over to study its reverse. Ronald had passed this to him in one of his meals some weeks before, and he had searched his stools until he located it, away from the probing eyes of the guards who were understandably repulsed by such behavior. Once he had found it, Wertham had hidden it, sticking the circuit to the flesh of his chest where sweat and a fold of material held it in place until it was required.

He had always sought knowledge, and as he had matured he had placed fewer restrictions on what that term should encompass. He had been an engineer once, and he had been highly regarded in the court of King Jack. Latterly, he had worked not with physical objects but with the human mind, applying alien substances to alter a man's perceptions and change his potential.

There were numerous alien substances out there, foods and drugs and things that had been grown. The Annunaki, for example, employed a kind of organic engineering in much of their technology, which, in the hands of a skilled horticulturalist, could be grown and manipulated to achieve staggering results.

To many, Wertham's greatest achievement was his work on the Chalice of Rebirth. Wertham had broken down the formula and figured out a way to reproduce its effects. Furthermore, he had manipulated it for human usage, so that it did not simply repair damage but retarded ageing, the one great battle that, it was thought, no man could avoid losing. The whole of Authentiville relied on that advance now; without his insights they would be a city of old men languishing in the crawl space between worlds.

But it had just been a task to Wertham, another assignment, a puzzle to solve. In the years after that, with the residents of Authentiville safe in their near-immortal lives, Wertham had looked at what the limits were on the human condition. He had experimented with drugs, alien substances that had acted to expand a man's primate mind, others that could tap the vestigial reptile responses that still remained hidden in the human soul. At first, Wertham had used the Gene-agers and their ilk for his experiments, but that could only show so much. Ultimately, his thirst for knowledge had driven him further, and he had turned those drugs on himself and seen the world in a whole new way.

The good people of Authentiville had locked him away for what he saw, unable to share in his colossal vision. Not at first, of course. At first, people had been drawn to him, an innovator, an imaginaut exploring the realms of possibility, just as the city's founder, King Jack, had explored and created new paths in reality.

Wertham was second generation. He had been born within the embrace of Authentiville itself, back when it had still been just a village really, a village that popped into and out of phase with reality as the general populace understood it, peeking out from the quantum ether. Jack had discovered the parallax system, utilized it at first to hide his horde of treasure, and later to build his own kingdom, far from the envious eyes of lesser men. Wertham had been born here, long after Jack's ascension to the throne, long after godhood had been imparted to him in the form of a crown—a crown made of nothing more than ideas. Wertham understood that, saw how ideas flourished here, how the scavenged alien detritus could be retooled into greater and greater shapes. The drugs had shown him shapes that men were never meant to see.

When Wertham had come out with his ideas, some had believed him to be a visionary. All had believed he was harmless; even Jack and Rosalind had welcomed his ideas in the early days. It was only later, when the fallout from the Titan suit had hit a whole nursery of newborns—only when that the high-ranking officials of King Jack's court had seen the results, the deaths, *the twists*—that Wertham had been branded "the Strange."

Incarceration followed. Ironically, this was the strangest thing of all that had happened to Wertham the Strange, for Authentiville was a society without prisons. Until that moment, the need had never arisen to lock a man away. King Jack had feared that Wertham's ideas might seduce the innocent. Perhaps they had already begun to do so. That was why he had to be locked away by a society that had never had a prison.

On pronouncing sentence, Jack had assured Wertham that no harm would come to him, that he would be treated fairly and well, that he would live in comfort, albeit in solitude. That had been seven hundred years ago.

DOMI GRABBED BRIGID around the shoulders and hugged her close.

"Brigid! You're here," she cried. "You're all here. You made it."

The sentries accompanying Domi into the room hurried to keep pace, discreetly remaining a few steps from the triple table.

"Domi, it *is* you," Brigid replied, emotion welling within her.

Domi was the most sensitive of the Cerberus team, and she was easily riled by changes in temperature or atmospheric pressure. She was also highly alert to dangers that other people missed, in the same way that animals can sense an eclipse or a storm before it occurs. Many of the more scientifically minded personnel at the Cerberus redoubt considered Domi more animal than human, and they kept their distance unless specifically ordered to work with her.

Brigid, Kane and Grant didn't think of Domi that way, although they all knew how uncannily aware of her surroundings she was. In fact, they'd had that alertness to thank on a number of occasions for saving their lives. As such, seeing her so at ease—so downright happy—here in this ville tucked in a quantum pocket both pleased and amazed them.

"Hey, Domi," Grant said as the albino woman reached across to hug him. "How have they been treating you here?"

"Just wonderfully," Domi sang. "They have so much here you wouldn't believe. I flew—on my own! In the air! Oh, Grant, it's so good to see you."

They had a history these two. Back when he had been a Magistrate in Cobaltville and Domi had been Guana Teague's sex slave, Grant was instrumental in securing Domi's freedom and protecting her life. Domi had nursed an infatuation for Grant for a long time because of that, seeing him as her knight in shining armor, the great hero who had freed her from her life of servitude and misery.

That had just been one part of the series of events that had led both Grant and Kane, along with Brigid Baptiste, to leave the ville and become outlanders, people with no ville to call home. It had also been the start of their alliance as the organization that had grown into the Cerberus of today, and Domi had joined them, albeit as an outsider.

As her relationship with Lakesh matured, so had her respect for Grant as a person, rather than some idol to be worshipped. For his part, Grant had taken Domi under his wing a little, looking out for her and doing whatever he could to help her adjust to life in what was, at heart, a military operation, although one that played by its own rules. While he considered Kane a brother and respected Brigid as a comrade in arms, Domi would always seem the little sister of their strange family, wayward and a little unpredictable, but loyal to a fault.

Grant smiled, hugging Domi back with just a smidgeon of his exceptional strength. Who, he wondered, would ever have thought I'd be putting my neck on the line and scouring infinity for this girl?

Kane eyed her for a moment, appreciating the cut of the armor and the way it was molded to her delicate frame. Kane had never seen her look so formal. She looked resplendent. "You look…all right," was all he could think to say.

Domi laughed as she hugged him. "Thanks, Kane. I still can't believe you guys came. Have you seen this place?"

"Briefly," Brigid told her.

The albino woman was so full of life, it had taken everyone aback.

"We came over here via some kind of…monorail, I guess it was," Grant explained.

"Never mind that," Kane butted in. "What about you? How did you come to be here? Mariah was pretty frantic when you disappeared—what happened?"

"I was exploring that spaceship," Domi began. "She tell you that? Well, turned out it was an Annunaki lifeboat—the guys here think it may have jettisoned from *Tiamat* back when she blew up while in orbit."

Kane, Grant and Brigid all remembered the incident well. They had been battling with the deranged dark goddess, Lilitu, aboard the Annunaki mother ship when the self-destruct sequence had been initiated. They had barely escaped the ship in time, and they had watched from Earth orbit as *Tiamat* exploded in the heavens. Kane could still feel the pinch of Lilitu's claws on his throat as she had tried to prevent him from leaving the doomed mother ship.

"They guess it got buried," Domi continued. "Must have been there quite a while, too. But it turned out the Authentiville scouts had spotted it in one of their sweeps and were set to hoist it up to their storage and analysis facilities when I happened aboard.

"Basically, your standard case of bad timing on my part," she concluded, rolling her eyes expressively.

"So, what do you do once you have this alien tech in your possession?" Brigid asked, addressing the question to King Jack.

"Our scientists, like Dr. Ronald, whom you've met, break it down into its component parts and then they begin to analyze the various applications to which it might be put," the king explained.

"You make it sound easy," Kane said with frank disbelief.

"My boy," Jack said, "we have been doing this for a very long time. Far longer than you've been on the planet, I assure you."

Kane believed him, though he couldn't say why. There was something in the king's nature that implied honesty, and while Kane couldn't put his finger on it, he knew enough to trust his instincts.

"Once we've finished our meal here I'll show you the Happening," King Jack concluded. "That will help make everything clearer."

As the king spoke, his blue-haired wife beckoned Domi over and insisted that she join them for the rest of their repast, apologizing for not waiting for her arrival. Domi readily accepted. It wasn't often that she found such welcoming hosts—she could count on the fingers of one chalk-white hand the number of times "normals" had invited her to a meal.

Elsewhere

WERTHAM THE STRANGE looked at the items hidden in the shadows of his hand and saw the shapes forming, the ones no one else could see. He had waited seven hundred years in this enclosed apartment space, seven hundred years of never seeing past the walls of his prison. Not, at least, in any conventional sense. The time was now.

"Guard," Wertham pronounced, not bothering to even raise his voice. He knew they were monitoring him, knew that they would hear him. "Guard, I feel faint. Dizzy." He sagged to the bed, palming the twin items away as he listened for the clattering feet of the guards.

It would not be long now. Placing the capsule on his tongue, Wertham closed his eyes and entered the fight trance, letting the sense of serenity wash over him, the ultimate calmness of the faux death. Hidden in the shadow of his cupped hand, the circuit clicked and shimmered and buzzed and burrowed into Wertham's palm, disappearing in the folds between the flesh where the drug had made it supple.

Eyes closed, Wertham listened as his guards hurried to see what had happened. He counted three of them moving, discussing what to do.

"He's collapsed," one was saying, his accent purebred Authentiville.

"What happened?" said another.

"Open the door and alert Dr. Ronald," said the third.

"We shouldn't open the door—"

"That man needs our assistance. I'm not standing here and watching him die."

"He won't…"

"Open it!"

There was a sound like a birdsong, a little chirrup of electronics as the lock's configuration was altered. Then came the abrupt sound of rushing air as the transparent wall was parted, creating a sliver of vacuum that filled in the blink of an eye.

Footsteps. The guards were in the cell, one leading the charge, the others tentative, following a few steps removed.

"Hey, Wertham? Wertham. Wake up."

A hand touched Wertham's shoulder then, pushing at him gently, then more firmly as the words came again.

"Wertham?"

He felt himself being rolled over and laid out on his back on the cot. Hands touched his body, fingers brushing his face.

"I don't think…" the guard just above him said. "I think he's stopped breathing."

"Are you sure? Let me see."

Another guard came forward. Wertham heard the boot heels clip-clopping on the floor as he approached, felt a strong grip on his forearm, something press lightly but firmly against his chest.

"You're right," the second guard agreed. "He doesn't appear to be breathing."

He wasn't. That was a part of the mechanism he had employed. It shut down everything but continued to feed oxygen to his brain, a bubbling super-jet of oxygen that not only prevented any deterioration in brain operation but actually enhanced the functionality of the organ. It would burn fully an hour, if necessary, though with each passing minute the danger of such an input increased tenfold. The body of man was not designed to take such enhancements; Wertham had trained for this moment for fifty years.

"Did you get hold of the doc?" one of the guards asked, the one who had first come to Wertham's aid.

"Ronald's coming back now," the guard farthest from Wertham confirmed. "He'll be here in two minutes."

Of course he will, Wertham thought. It's all a part of the plan.

"Good. Seal the room."

"What? You think Wertham could…?"

"Doc Ronald's got a warp key," the guard assured them. "He'll unlock the shield wall when he arrives. Better not to take the chance until then."

As they spoke, Wertham felt something being pressed against his face, a bulging muzzle of a mask clinched over mouth and nose. The hissing sound of escaping gas came to his ears, distant now as he crouched in his hidden pocket of time, behind the geometric shapes that no other man could ever perceive. They were trying to revive him. Chest compressions. More oxygen. But the body was dead, and it would remain so until he was ready to strike.

AFTER THE MEAL, the Cerberus companions were invited to join King Jack and Queen Rosalind at what they called "the Happening." With Jack carrying the energy rod lightly in one hand like a walking cane, they strode through the magnificent corridors of the royal residence until they reached one of the upper stories.

"The palace is the hub of our operation here," Jack explained. "Our citizens would be much impoverished without the work that goes on within these walls."

The corridors were wide as highways, and though not busy there seemed to be a steady stream of people going back and forth, hurrying about their palace business. Many of these people looked identical to the hairless servants who had waited on the royal party at the meal, Kane noticed, and he wondered if they were some kind of clones or similarly artificial humans.

Other people seen in the corridors were wearing grand clothes, cloaks, capes and towering headdresses that loaned their figures sweeping lines as they moved. It gave the whole place the feeling of being inside a painting, each line a graceful sweep of the painter's brush.

King Jack stopped before the open doorway to a room, inviting his guests to peek inside. The Cerberus warriors stepped closer. Within was a dark room illuminated only by what appeared to be glowing round portholes set within the walls, and it stretched back close to two hundred feet.

A figure sat at each of the portholes, peering into it, and all wore dark visors over their eyes. There were a hundred such figures in the room, and above their circular portholes loomed larger oval screens, like eggs resting on their sides. Each figure was dressed in the same black leather tunic and conical helmet, as well as the tinted visors. Kane noticed something else about the figures, too—they had heads and torsos, but no legs. Instead, their bodies seemed to be cut at the waist where they connected to fixed chairs bolted to the floor.

"What are they doing?" Brigid asked, pitching her voice just above a whisper.

"This is the tabulation room," Queen Rosalind said. "The information they receive here comes from the operators of the Happening. It's here that the data is pulled together and fed through our maps to find specific markers we've identified."

"Like triangulating a site?" Grant suggested, at which the queen looked confused. "Um…figuring out where a location is based on other known locations," Grant elaborated.

The queen nodded. "That's a fair summary," she said. "We work through the basic four dimensions, plus the quantum factor that can alter or distil time if we need to pluck an item from a particular period."

Kane's eyebrows rose. "Time travel? You're capable of that?"

King Jack fielded the question with a chuckle. "Not time travel, as such," he said. "The Vooers in this room are capable of manipulating very small sections so that we might slip an hour or two either way to capture what we need. It allows us to backtrack a little when we need to."

Kane, Grant, Domi and Brigid watched as two golden spacecraft launched on the large oval screen. They were pebblelike, resembling the ones that had grabbed Grant's Manta.

"More scout ships," King Jack explained. "I guess we're having a busy few days right now."

Then, with a gesture of his golden energy rod, the king led the group farther down the corridor. As they walked, Brigid raised another question.

"You called those people—*Vooers?*" she asked.

"Visual Observation Operatives," King Jack explained. "It's a meticulous and exhausting task. The Vooers are bred specifically for the job."

Brigid nodded as though accepting this at face value. However, it added strength to her suspicion that this society had perfected the art of genetic manipulation, growing a workforce designed for specialized functions.

A few yards farther along the corridor they came to another doorway, inside which stood a long room filled with equipment and manned by four women. The room was barely illuminated by a faint glow of blue radiating from the walls. Huge machines covered the ceiling and floor, and as the Cerberus crew looked more closely they saw that it was all interconnected, feeding to six strange-looking constructions posed at intervals around the vast room.

Within the room, each of the women was sitting before a bulky unit that was vaguely reminiscent of an old cathode ray television set, with a flat, oblong screen behind which was a thick block of machinery. The machinery was mostly hidden behind metal sheeting, but there were vents through which a throbbing white glow could be seen, as well as snaking pipes and chimneylike constructions that chuffed exhaust into the air of the room. The exhaust by-product was invisible, but it created a heat haze above the chimneylike towers. Despite this, the room itself was ice-cold—so cold that the coolness seemed to seep from the doorway as they neared.

The units themselves included a chair and visual screen, a little like a flight simulator.

Women were working three of the units, while another woman sat making notes as one of the users dictated, her face close to the illuminated screen. There were three further units, but they showed darkened screens.

The women at the units looked young and slim, and Kane guessed that none of them was over twenty-five. They were dressed in white minidresses that came down just past their hips, thigh-high boots and hair bands that held back their long tresses.

"Of course, you don't stumble on alien material by chance," Jack explained as they entered the room.

It was notably cooler in here and there was icy condensation on the walls.

"This here's the Happening," Jack explained. "It clues us in on what's out there before it happens."

"Before—?" Brigid queried.

"The Hyper Advanced Prediction Prophesying Engineered Nodule with Integrated Nano Gate—that's its full name," Jack explained. "It sorts the quantum pathways and detects the most likely outcome of any given event."

"A fortune-telling device," Grant translated. He had seen similar items before, and they rarely amounted to anything more than a way to trick the minds of the people watching, usually to scam them for money or possessions.

"Let me show you," Jack said.

As he spoke, Queen Rosalind stepped over to the nearest functioning unit and spoke a few words to the female operator. The young woman dipped her head courteously to the queen before stepping out of the chair and helping the blue-haired queen into the seat. As the Cerberus team watched, Rosalind adjusted a headpiece that enshrouded her whole head until only her mouth could be seen.

"We have six of these units in all," King Jack said as his wife calibrated the settings. "Three of them will be functioning at any one time, checking the quantum pathways in the search of useful tech that might otherwise have been left abandoned and unnoticed."

"Three?" Brigid queried.

"We need three because it's all about probabilities here, not absolutes," Jack told them.

The operator who had been using the machine stepped in to help the queen, guiding Roz's hands to the control panel where she took hold of twin grips with her slender fingers. "It sticks a little, Your Majesty," the operator said with obvious embarrassment. "Be careful when looking fourteen weeks hence, it can get stuck and we have to reignite the system."

"Thank you, Betassa," the queen said. "I'll keep that in mind. Take a break and find yourself something to eat. I won't hog this unit for very long."

"As you will, Your Majesty," the operator said.

Betassa departed with a timpani drum of receding heels.

"I don't trust this," Kane muttered, pulling Brigid to one side. "A cache of alien technology—it's too good to be true."

"But it makes sense, Kane," insisted Brigid. "We've been investigating the fallout of alien interference ever since we left Cobaltville—in fact, it was that same alien interference that set us on the path of exiles cast to the Outlands."

"Even so…" Kane began uncertainly.

"Think about it," Brigid stressed. "All that alien tech had to end up somewhere, right? We're looking at it. A whole city of it. Every invention here owes its existence to alien technology."

"Which puts us where, exactly?" Kane wondered.

"If we could trade with these people," Brigid mused, "acquire their technology—it could literally change the world."

Kane nodded. "Lakesh would have a field day," he said. "That's for sure."

Brigid turned back to the king and queen, indicating to Kane to do likewise. It seemed that Queen Rosalind was ready to show them the full extent of the Happening's powers.

The cold lights flickered and dimmed as the machine whirred to life.

Chapter 12

The Happening hummed in the darkened room, a low growl at first that grew higher in pitch as its engine fed more power to its software. In the control chair, Queen Rosalind was barely moving, the golden helmet covering her features almost entirely so that only her mouth showed. Her mouth twitched in the slightest of smiles as her hands worked the ball-like controls on the machine's surface.

As his wife worked, King Jack outlined the procedure. "We've been scouring the planet for alien artifacts for a long time," he said. "In fact, it's alien technology that formed the foundation of this whole city."

"How long ago was that?" Brigid asked.

Smiling, Jack shook his head. "A long time," he said wistfully. "We've been here a lot longer than you've been alive, Brigid."

"This whole place is founded on alien tech?" Kane probed.

Jack nodded. "I don't expect I need to tell you folks that there's a lot of alien material all over the globe, with more of it appearing periodically. There was an alien craft docked in orbit until not much more than a year back, for example. When the thing went kaboom, we had people in place to pick up the debris.

"And that's where the Happening comes in. See, it's drawn to alien technology—stuff that doesn't belong, you might say. The machinery is sensitive to the appearance and use of that technology, which is to say if someone fires up a Tuatha de Danaan music gate, the Happening will get a bead on it and start working out where that technology will most likely end up."

"So you steal it?" Kane asked.

"No," King Jack assured him. "We're not interested in getting into squabbles of who owns what. We tried that for a while, back in the early days of Authentiville. Lot of bloodshed on both sides—you can probably imagine. Wasn't worth it. There's plenty of stuff that's been left out there unguarded and forgotten about. Most people don't even notice it, though from what your friend Domi told us, I'm guessing you folks are the exception."

Grant nodded. "We've met with our fair share of alien problems over the years," he lamented.

Around them, the other operators were continuing with the monitoring of their units, oblivious now to the presence of the monarchs and their guests. The room had a curious stillness to it with a kind of tension to the atmosphere, like a packed theater moments before the performance begins.

"What the Happening does is put together the pieces of the puzzle," King Jack continued. "An alien spaceship appears in orbit, the Happening is on it, figuring its vector and probing the future to figure where it'll wind up—could be two, three months from now. As that moment gets closer, the Happening sorts through the possible options and the information becomes more definite."

"Then it's Schrodinger's Cat technology," Brigid said with sudden understanding. "You work out what's there and then factor in all the likely outcomes until one emerges that's right."

Jack looked at her with his open, kindly face. "I can't say I know about this dingy cat you mention, but your summary sounds about right. The Happening draws together echoes of the future and forms a likely outcome for any given event.

Once we've got that, we can set our scouts out there to pluck the artifacts we need at the optimum moment.

"Of course, that's only half the process," the king continued. "Once we have it in hand, we still have to comprehend and refine that material to find its best use."

Brigid's eyebrows raised with surprise. "You're improving on alien tech?"

Jack shrugged. "Nothing to say we can't, is there?"

As the Cerberus warriors pondered that, Queen Rosalind spoke from behind the metallic veil of the Happening headgear. "Something's coming through now," she told the others, and the screen on the front of the machine flickered to life.

A mist appeared on-screen, and then an overhead view of the ocean formed from the mist. The view was very high up, for even once the mist had parted there were still clouds obscuring the blue-green water, wisping through the foreground like trailing steam.

"Ocean," Rosalind said, her mouth carefully forming the word. "I see the ocean."

"We all see the ocean," Domi agreed, and Brigid shot her a look to quiet her.

"Something beneath the waves," Rosalind continued, either ignoring Domi's comment or unaware of it. "A shape, like a pyramid."

The view rotated and closed in on the ocean surface, and the Cerberus companions became aware that something odd was happening. While the eighteen-by-twelve-inch screen appeared normal enough, flat like a picture or a television monitor, an added dimension seemed to be taking form behind the image, granting an incredible sense of depth to the picture as it shifted on-screen. Both Brigid and Kane had seen its like before, recognizing the effect.

"Is that…Annunaki technology?" Kane whispered uncertainly.

Brigid nodded.

Although the setup was different, it was recognizably derived from the astronavigation chairs that were in use on the Annunaki mother ship, *Tiamat*. At least two of those chairs had made it to Earth after the destruction of the great dragon ship itself. One had cropped up in the Louisiana bayou, where it had been mistakenly called a "Voodoo Chair" and been used in conjunction with opiates to generate startling visions in the user's mind. Brigid Baptiste had very nearly been consumed by such a chair as it attempted to synergize with her, hooks anchoring themselves into her flesh until Kane had pulled her free.

Kane had encountered another astronavigation chair under less fraught circumstances and had utilized the chair's mapping functionality to locate Brigid during the period when she had been in the thrall of the Annunaki god-prince, Ullikummis. That chair had been stored among the many incredible artifacts inside a museum in the hidden city of Agartha, whose guardian, Balam, had allowed Kane access to the chair during the God War.

Neither Kane nor Brigid truly understood the functionality of the astronavigation chairs beyond their observation that they operated concurrently on both the physical plane and the mental one. The way in which they cooperated with a user's thoughts made the chairs seem almost alive.

Standing protectively behind his wife, King Jack nodded at Kane's query. "We learn to mix and match here," he told his guests. "A bit of Annunaki know-how in the right hands can work wonders."

"Is it safe?" Brigid asked, recalling her experience with the Voodoo Chair.

"We've been using this stuff a long time, Red," Jack assured her with a smile. "I wouldn't put my wife in something I'd not had checked over with a fine-tooth comb."

Turning her attention back to the screen, Brigid saw that the view of the ocean had become an overlay to the pyramid shape. The pyramid was dark, as if it was a shadow projected against a wall by a bright light, its silhouette visible but its details uncertain.

"I can't tune in on the details yet," the queen admitted with a note of strain in her voice. "Let me try…"

On screen, the image shifted, rotating 180 degrees as the Happening software tried to generate a clearer view. Around the image, dark spots had appeared, like ink bubbles in the blue of the ocean.

"What's she doing?" Grant asked.

"Tapping the quantum pathways," King Jack explained. "The Happening doesn't just show pictures of the future—it works the odds. The path of least resistance is usually the most likely outcome of a given event, is what they tell me. But sometimes finding that path can take a little patience."

Brigid nodded in comprehension while her companions still looked mystified.

"Sounds like a load o' mumbo jumbo to me," Grant muttered.

"No, it's not," Brigid told him. "The Cerberus computers use a similar system, running analysis software to predict everything from earthquakes to system overloads. What this Happening unit does is fundamentally the same—it applies a complex logarithm to discern the most likely result of a given set of circumstances."

Overhearing this, King Jack strode across to where Grant and Brigid stood and looked the ex-Magistrate in the eye. "You don't believe in this stuff, do you, son?"

"I have trouble with it," Grant admitted. "Some of the time."

"And yet, you and your friend came here piloting Annunaki TAVs. You're obviously familiar with stuff like this chair," Jack said with a kind of kindly sincerity, as though trying to pierce the veil of Grant's distrust.

"I've seen a lot of bad come out of that technology," Grant said before gesturing to his colleagues. "We all have."

"The Annunaki," Jack stated, "the Tuatha de Danaan, the Rakshashas—they're all gone now. Only their hardware survives. The old gods are dead and we're what took their place—the people of Authentiville."

"Then you're the new gods?" Kane asked. "Is that it?"

Jack patted Kane on the arm and smiled. "Gods crave to be worshipped. All I crave is a hot bath and the company of good friends from time to time," he assured them all. "Let the deities worry about the things we don't care for. I'm just an ordinary man living an ordinary life."

Looking around the room, Kane bit back his response. Now was not the time to tell Jack that his life was anything but normal.

"Tell you what," Jack said. "Looks like Roz is going to be a little time tapping into that pathway there. Why don't you and I go take a look around the city? Bring your friends, too, those who want to join us. I'll show you how things work around here, give you a better handle on how it all fits together. Figure I can maybe open your eyes to what the *ills*—" he winked as he said the word "—of all that alien technology have actually brought us."

"I'd like that," Kane admitted, and Grant nodded, too. The two of them had been nearly inseparable since their days as Magistrates—whether Grant cared for the royal tour or not, he would stick with Kane and provide backup if it proved necessary.

Brigid continued to watch the screen where the shadow pyramid was taking shape. "I'll stay here," she informed Kane without looking up. "I'd like to get a clearer idea of how the scouting procedure works."

Domi shrugged as Kane turned to her. "Seen the place already," she said in her clipped way. "You go. Want to talk to Brigid, anyway."

Kane and Grant followed King Jack out of the darkened room, leaving Brigid and Domi to monitor the predictive machinery with the queen. Jack's staff lit the way in a glow of fearsome energy.

WERTHAM WAS IN the fight trance now, his whole body coiled and ready to attack while his mind swam in tranquillity, watching the clock.

All three sentries had been poised close to Wertham's apparently dead body when it had moved. The movement had been sharp and sudden, the way a dead frog's legs will scissor at the introduction of an electric current.

Wertham himself was still a half step outside of his body, waltzing in the alien geometry that hid itself from human eyes. His body followed his commands now, but not in the way a man might command his arms to rise or his legs to walk. No, this was more akin to the manner in which a farmer will instruct a sheepdog, sending it this way and that through a sequence of yips and whistles, commanding each turn of the body remotely in a synergy of master and devotee.

Wertham saw the guards only as luminous hard planes, their beating hearts held strong in their cores like traffic lights.

The first guard reacted to Wertham's flinch. "What th—?" he began.

But already he was too late.

Wertham's arm thrust out, the straight edge of his hand striking the guard beneath his jaw, obliterating his windpipe with a single blow. The guard sagged back from the cot, his hands grasping up at the armored collar of his uni-

form, the awful, animal sounds of choking spewing from
his open mouth.

"Ben, what happened?" his colleague asked. His attention was distracted in that instant and he watched Ben limp
back and down, tumbling to the deck as if he were a tower
of clothes piled too high on laundry day.

Wertham's body was all sharp angles now, hard lines and
furious energy that was barely restrained by its flesh. He
moved from the cot in a whirlwind, a spinning, twirling dance
from bed to floor, left leg snapping out in a blurring kick, the
angle impossible. The foot connected with the second guard's
chest, slamming against the hard armor there with the clang of
a bell being struck. The second guard was driven across the
room with the impact, whirling through the air before striking
the back wall—the translucent one that could be parted only
by a guard's key—in a drumbeat of soft flesh against solid
barricade. He sank to the floor, eyes swimming out of focus.

The third guard reacted swiftly, whipping himself out of
reach as Wertham's other foot cut the air toward him in a
swishing arc. The foot missed by a fraction of an inch, and the
guard drew his baton from its holster at the top of his thigh.
The baton emerged seven inches in length and the thickness
of a wineglass, but Wertham watched as the guard flicked his
wrist and the length quadrupled, turning the short stick into
a powerful club. He had never given his jailors cause to employ their defences before—objectively, he found this whole
experience fascinating.

Wertham's flesh was following the pattern of the fight
trace, slipping into a charge, body dropping low as he powered toward his remaining foe. The guard beside the wall
was recovering, which meant he ought to curtail this before
reinforcements could be called.

The sentry with the baton stepped back, securing a two-
handed grip on the weapon and holding it upright before him

like a cell bar. Wertham had no time to acknowledge the irony; already his body was switching from the charge into an upward leap, effortlessly springing from the floor. His left foot connected with the extended baton, slapping against it with a clap of noise and using it to climb higher into the air even as the guard fell back with the sudden shift in weight and balance.

The guard tried to change his attack, but he was too slow. To Wertham, deep in the fight trance, the guards moved with all the speed and purpose of a still photograph, each shift in the fight seen not as a motion but rather as a new pose to be accounted for and conquered at his leisure. Fight mathematics—simple for a mathematician of Wertham's ability.

Still balanced on the outstretched baton, the prisoner's right leg whipped forward, pointed foot meeting the guard's faceplate and shattering the visor he wore there. Toughened crystal composite spread across the room as the visor broke, sharp shards driving into the guard's face in gashing red lines.

The guard tumbled back, his grip loosening on the baton as he rolled to the floor. Wertham sprang as the guard fell, moving through the air almost as if afloat before landing on the far side of the room.

Calculation: the baton-wielding guard would take 2.3 seconds to recover. In that time, Wertham turned his attention back to the guard slumped against the wall, reaching for him with both hands and yanking him from the floor by his collar. Like the rest of the guard's suit, the collar was made of composite crystal, forming a shell-like armor over his whole body, which left only his mouth and a tiny section of his throat exposed. A helmet hid the rest of his face and head, the tinted visor disguising the vacuous expression on the vat-grown man's face.

Wertham hefted the guard up, using his powerful leg muscles to drive the startled guard toward the ceiling.

Wertham had always been thin—dangerously so, some would observe—but he was wiry. Furthermore, he could access hidden reserves of strength that few men would ever stumble upon by using the alien drugs he had discovered and developed in his most productive years. The guard slammed against the ceiling with a crack and his neck caved in, spine crumbling in on itself—not through the power of Wertham's attack but through the perfect angle at which the blow had struck. It was all mathematics.

At the same instant, the guard who had tried to use the baton on Wertham was staggering to his feet. He heard the noise as his colleague's neck snapped, felt it like a shock wave. Instinct kicked in and the guard ran, leaping the outstretched edge of the bed and darting through the open doorway that led to what had served as Wertham's living quarters for the past seven centuries.

"Attempted breakout in progress at the moral foundry," the guard said as he dashed past one of the L-shaped seats in the room. A transference mic embedded in his helmet picked up the command automatically, relaying it to the sentry station two floors below. Wertham was the only prisoner Authenti-ville had ever known, yet by convention the guards had been trained to refer to the area rather than the prisoner—to keep things impersonal.

Still deep in the fight trance, Wertham followed.

Chapter 13

Once again, they took to the skies. This time, they traveled on an open-sided disk over the rooftops of Authentiville, with King Jack standing at the control console, working the metallic bubble with a simple series of squeezes and turns.

Kane recognized the configuration of the disk despite the surface differences. In their tussles with the Annunaki, the Cerberus rebels had seen sky disks in operation. Incredibly fast-moving while in the atmosphere, sky disks were saucer-shaped vehicles equipped with low-observable camouflage screens that made them appear as little more than a shimmer in the air. When that camouflage was powered down, the surface of the sky disks looked like mercury, a beautiful liquid silver. Each vehicle housed a cabin inside, where the pilot and passengers would sit. This one, however, was something different. While it ran on the same basic principles, this disk was smaller and open to the elements, more like a platform than what man had once called a "flying saucer."

"Feels sturdy enough. You make this baby yourself, Your Majesty?" Kane asked.

"Not me," Jack told him. "My pit crew came up with the modifications, but they're tinkerers and the modifications are never ending. Always they see ways to improve on what we have. I think Ronald was a part of the original design team, in fact."

Grant warily eyed the bubble that Jack used to pilot the craft. "Looks kind of simplistic," he observed.

King Jack smiled. "The greatest technology is deceptively simple, don't you find?"

Grant nodded appreciatively as the disk soared over the golden rooftops.

"Where are you taking us?" Kane asked as he watched the bright buildings idle past below.

"Just for a look around," King Jack replied in a booming voice.

Kane estimated that they were three hundred feet above ground level—whatever that meant for a floating ville—but the disk felt steady enough. It was as if they stood on a travelator that imparted a slight sense of shuddering as it moved but nothing more.

The floating vehicle's passage was quiet enough, but the sound of rushing wind made it difficult to be heard at a normal speaking volume. The king was used to raising his voice.

The platform cut a graceful line across the ever-changing sky, weaving between the taller buildings as it crossed the magnificent city. Other vehicles whipped past, one-person and two-person transports, along with larger vehicles like the steed, and even the single sets of wings that Ronald and Domi had called pegasuits. Grant spotted a woman followed by three children, the oldest maybe six years old, whipping through the sky wearing pegasuit wings. They hopped out from the corner of a high-rise like birds learning to fly before doing a circuit of the building's upper levels and returning to the spot where they had started.

"Learning to fly," Grant said with a chuckle. It was truly another world.

"I think that was Raka' technology originally," King Jack offered. "Made a heck of a difference when we stumbled upon it and figured out what it could do."

It was the second time Jack had mentioned the Raka' or

Rakashashas, Kane realized. Kane made a mental note to ask Brigid who or what these Rakashashas were.

Beneath them, they saw people going about their business in streets paved with slabs of copper. The people wore elaborate costumes, supple armor often in garish colors, capes, cloaks and magnificent helmets on both the men and the women. Everyone looked in the peak of physical fitness, and while there was some differentiation between them, almost everyone was tall and slender with the muscular physiques of athletes. There did not seem to be any old people in the streets or the buildings that they passed.

Far below, Kane spied a silver stadium with clear flags fluttering from its arches. The flags were made of some translucent material, capturing the colors of the rainbow sky as they whipped in the breeze.

"What's going on down there?" he asked.

Obligingly, King Jack dipped the sky disk down for a closer look.

The stadium was filled with several hundred spectators, their eyes glued to the action on the track. The track was sandy-yellow and featured several dozen land vehicles vying for position in a frenetic race. The vehicles were of several types built around a large single wheel to which the rider had been strapped. The vehicles looked both very fast and very dangerous, but King Jack gave a reassuring laugh at Kane's surprised look.

"Don't worry," Jack said. "The riders are mostly pilots from the scout division. They enjoy the speeds the wheel-rigs can reach, and they hardly ever crash out. There are trained apothecs on hand to handle things if anyone does, with a regen pool on-site."

Kane and Grant barely followed the man's explanation. They recognized most of the words but it was almost as if he was speaking another language.

"How many people live here?" Kane asked, raising his voice over the rushing wind.

"At last count, Authentiville housed somewhere in the region of four thousand people, including children, plus the Gene-agers, of course," King Jack told him as they pulled away from the stadium and its wheel-rigs. "But that was a few years ago now, I'm afraid. Record keeping never was my strong point."

"What are the Gene-agers?" Grant followed up. "You make it sound as if you don't count 'em."

"Every society needs certain conditions to prosper," Jack replied easily. "Workers, drones. The Gene-agers aren't real men, just functions brought to life. They keep the ville operational."

Grant nodded. It sounded a lot like slavery to him.

They continued hurtling across the sky, passing other flying vehicles and individuals wearing the pegasuit wings. Passing close to a tower shaped like a pepper grinder, Kane and Grant saw what appeared to be some kind of literary event through the windows. There were people dressed in gaudy clothes, unlike the supple armor the Authentiville citizens seemed to favor, and as they sped past, a figure wearing a giant puppet suit emerged from behind a curtain, using gestures to make the monstrous arms and legs move.

King Jack directed the flyer low over a green field of grass that topped a golden rectangular building. Cows were chewing their cud and a herdsman—dressed in blue armor with a sweeping cape—stood watching them from close to the building's edge. As they neared they saw the herdsman was holding something to his mouth—a long, narrow pipe like a wind instrument—into which he blew. The cows turned in unison and lowed at the king as he passed, while the herdsman waved a salute, his cape billowing out on the wind in the wake of their passage.

"Some Tuatha genetics in those beasts," Jack told them casually. "The herdsmen use harmonics to make the bovines responsive."

"You hear that?" the first guardsman asked his colleague. "A breakout?"

A light flashed to life on their console, and a map of the cubelike apartment in which Wertham the Strange was incarcerated spun continuously on the fifteen-foot-high screen behind them.

"Impossible!" his colleague insisted, though his hands were already in motion over the master control panel. "Lock down everything to ensure that nothing can come in or out of that cell until we give the all clear."

"That would, of course, mean damning your colleagues to death," another voice said.

The two guards looked up and saw Dr. Ronald gliding into the reception area from his parked transport outside.

The guards looked at him hopefully. "What can we do, then?" the Gene-ager operating the control board pleaded.

Hidden from their view, Ronald's hand brushed against a switch located in the left arm of his motion chair. Twin darts launched from the chair, flitting across the room like insects before finding their targets in the throats of the two men. "I suggest dying," Ronald told them as he guided his chair behind the desk until he was at the control panel.

Both guards slumped in their chairs, making hacking noises as they struggled with the fast-acting Annunaki poison that was now coursing through their veins. The poison was a derivative of a very successful anesthetic that the good doctor utilized in his operating theatre. The mixture had been tweaked ever so slightly, on Wertham's instruction, to induce an immediate allergic reaction that, coupled with the anesthetizing properties of the mixture, left the guards unable to move their chest muscles and breathe.

Gently, almost lovingly, Ronald pushed the closest of the guards from the operating panel so that he could reach its controls.

WHILE THE QUEEN worked the unfathomable Happening device, Domi drew Brigid aside and spoke to her in a low but giddy voice.

"Brigid, it's so good to see you again," said Domi. "I'm so glad you guys made it here."

"We wouldn't leave you for the world," Brigid reminded her. "Plus, Lakesh would have killed us ten times over if we hadn't willingly volunteered to find you the very second you went missing."

Domi looked pensive. "Missing? Yes, I suppose I am. Oh, but it's so wonderful. You've seen this place. These people—they live among the stars."

Brigid nodded warily, sensing her colleague's enthusiasm.

"And Brigid, they take me for who I am," Domi continued. "They've shown me more acceptance here than I've ever felt out there—on Earth."

"You're—*we're* still on Earth," Brigid reminded her. "At least, technically."

"But it's different here," Domi continued, a broad smile lighting up her face. "Brigid—I want to stay."

Brigid was taken aback and, wrong-footed, she struggled to respond. "Domi, I…" she began. "We have the means to get home now."

"No, I'm not a prisoner here," Domi said a little more forcefully than Brigid expected. "I hadn't thought about Cerberus since I got here, not until I was told you guys had arrived. I want to stay. I *fit* here."

Brigid didn't know what to say to that. Domi was, without

doubt, an outcast at the Cerberus headquarters. Her strange appearance, coupled with her often primitive outlook, made her an anachronism among the scientists and technologically adept warriors of the Cerberus operation. More than once Domi had felt rejected, pushed out by the very people who should be her friends there, and while Brigid herself had never turned Domi away, she knew that others—including Grant—had.

"You mustn't make any hasty decisions," was all Brigid could think to say. Yet even as the words left her mouth she knew it was a ridiculous thing to say to a free spirit like Domi: every decision that the albino girl had ever made had been hasty and barely considered. She lived by instinct and wit, not by planning the way the other supposedly sophisticated members of Cerberus did.

Brigid wanted to say something else, something about Lakesh and how much he would miss her, but at that moment she struggled to frame it into a sentence without its sounding like emotional blackmail. "Domi, I think that maybe you need to think…" she began. Then her eye was caught by the queen. "What is it?" Brigid asked, leaning closer.

"Trouble," Queen Rosalind bit out. "Trouble's coming. Soon."

"How soon?"

"Soon enough. It's so catastrophic that it blocks out everything else," said the queen. "I can't see past it. That's why I couldn't peer into events in the water."

The two Cerberus warriors watched as the screen showed the golden city in the cosmic rift, just as they had seen when they approached it on their landing vectors. But this time there was smoke pouring from the buildings, darkening the rainbow sky.

Chapter 14

King Jack's sky disk hurried on, cutting its silent path above the city, past the anvil-shaped building whose walls were dominated by the waterfall. The water glistened with rainbow highlights as it caught the swirling colors of the impossible sky.

"How long have you been here?" Kane asked King Jack.

"Out here in the warp or the city itself?" King Jack asked. A question for a question.

"Either. Both," Kane clarified.

The armored king looked wistful for a moment, rubbing his chin with his free hand before answering. "Time tends to lose its meaning after a while, don't you find?" he said.

"What about you?" Kane asked. "You mind my asking how long you've been on the throne, Your Majesty?"

Jack laughed, easing the disk down to a section of the city characterized by lower buildings. "As long as I can recall," he said, "they've always called me 'the king.' The more things change here, the more they stay the same."

"How old are you?" Grant pressed.

Jack laughed at the man's directness. "Younger than the Annunaki, that's for sure."

Kane was beginning to understand, or at least he thought he was. Authentiville was caught in a fractal node between realities; it was a city riding the tides of a cosmic rift. Who knew how his traditional concept of time related to these people? He eyed King Jack again, figuring the man for maybe sixty years old. His wife was perhaps five years younger, but both of them were in such good physical health it was hard to say. Heck, they could be a hundred and sixty—even five hundred and sixty!—and Kane wouldn't be able to tell.

Below, the city was awash with miraculous devices. Whole walls glowed to illuminate the alleyways, moving walkways ran between the high storys of the buildings, and people navigated the city by all sorts of means, from wheeled boards on which they could barely get both feet, to wild pods arranged in long strings, one after another, like the segments of a worm.

King Jack's sky disk swooped down towards the industrial sector of the ville.

"Hang on," Jack advised as he guided the vehicle down among the belching chimneys, their hot vapor clouding in mists.

As Ronald dealt with the sentries on duty in the reception area of the prison block two floors above, Wertham the Strange was chasing through the rooms of his apartment of incarceration after the rogue guard who had eluded him. The lights that glowed across the walls flickered as the control board downstairs was manipulated, giving the incarceration area the feel of being in the center of a fireworks display. Ronald's doing—to disorient the sentries.

The guard, whose designation was one-nine-seven-one, had dropped his baton. He couldn't quite process what had happened. It had taken just minutes for the whole situation to spiral out of control. Wertham was a model prisoner, at least in so much as he was the only one to ever exist in the history of Authentiville, and he had never shown any desire to escape. Perhaps he didn't want to escape now, one-nine-seven-one realized. Perhaps he just wanted to hunt men for sport, just as the royal hunting parties would track deer out in the rooftop plains on the first of the month.

One-nine-seven-one had no weapons now, and was merely endeavoring to create as much space as possible between himself and the deranged chemist. The flickering lights were not helping; his Gene-ager eyes did not respond quickly to changes in illumination, the need had not been foreseen, so that ability had not been factored into his genetics. It was hard to see where he was going, and he ran into a low table in the living area and tripped over a chair as he passed out of the room.

Wertham moved noiselessly behind him, his body flowing like water from room to room as he chased the footsteps of the retreating guard. The sentries had locked the cell complex upon entry, which left the guard in question trapped with Wertham on the prowl. Hundreds of years before, King Jack had forbade any kind of ballistic weaponry, which left the guards relying on sprays and batons—neither of which the guard had about his person now. Naively the three Gene-agers who had come to check on the apparently hurt figure of Wertham the Strange had believed that they could overpower him should the need arise. He was, after all, just one man, and a physically weak one at that. But Wertham had been experimenting with the alien drugs for centuries; he had discovered the fight trance around the time that surface man had invented eyeglasses.

Ducking left, one-nine-seven-one found himself in the bathroom facilities of the locked complex. His breathing was coming fast now as, despite being in prime physical condition, he felt fear for the first time in his artificial life. His partner had had his windpipe crushed, a spewed trail of red running down his face. The other had struck the ceiling with such force it had either cracked his skull or snapped his neck—the guard couldn't be sure which.

His fervent gaze raced around the bathroom, searching, searching. Maybe there was something here that he could use as a weapon. The hygiene unit was a broad, square structure that immersed the bottom half of the human body. Beside it, the bathtub was shaped like a shell, a jet of water coming from above on vocal command. Nothing there, only cleansing products. The guard couldn't know that Wertham had used those very products to create his fight trance drug, siphoning and testing them in different combinations, utilizing flecks of the paint that daubed the bathtub to add to the mix as he put his fearsome mind to work for this very day.

The bathroom featured two doorways—the one through which the guard had entered, leading into the living space, and a second one at its far end that led around to a sparse clothing storage area, which in turn led around and into the bedroom once more. There were no closable doors within the prisoner's apartment; everything was open and everything could be seen.

Nowhere to hide.

He stood with his back to the wall by the second doorway, concentrated to calm his breathing. The guard activated his helmet comm again. "Come in, control—what's going on down there?" he demanded. His voice sounded harsh and breathless with its edge of panic.

As he did so, a voice echoed through the chambers. It was Wertham. "They call me strange," he said, "because they fear what they can never understand. Do you fear me?"

The guard clenched, trying to locate the prisoner by the sound of his shrill voice. It was all hard surfaces in the bathroom, causing the sound to bounce with a cruel echo, masking its source. He looked around him, left and right, searching for any sign of the prisoner in the flickering light. Then he saw the shadow, peeping through the doorway like a grim specter.

The guard moved, hurrying toward the shadow, cinching his body against the wall closest to the doorway so that he might ambush Wertham. Both of them were unarmed;

he at his physical prime, Wertham a weakling. It should be easy. But he knew it wouldn't be—he had seen how Wertham moved while possessed by the fight trance, had witnessed the incredible feats he seemed to perform with ease.

The guard's heart beat against his chest.

Buh-boom, buh-boom, buh-boom, buh-boom.

Chapter 15

Wertham the Strange stepped through the gap an instant later, head down, arms outstretched, hunkered into himself to present a smaller target and to keep his center of balance low. The Gene-ager guard whipped around, bringing his knee up toward Wertham's crotch.

The knee struck, missing Wertham's groin in the flickering illumination but driving against the side of his leg with such force that it would have knocked another man off his feet. As it was, Wertham danced backward, taunting with a brash "Hah-har!" Truly the appellation of "Strange" had been well attributed, one-nine-seven-one thought as he followed up his blow.

Wertham blocked a punch to his face with his forearm, sweeping it away and throwing off his attacker's balance. His open left hand rushed toward the guard's disguised face, slapping against his exposed chin with a clap of applause. The guard staggered back, taking two steps away from the wall before catching his heel against the edge of the shell-shaped bathtub. He struggled to remain upright, feeling the sting of that blow to his chin.

Wertham stepped closer, a cruel smile on his thin lips. "You held me here without question," he said in a voice like a snake's hiss. "Ignored my pleas. Now you will plead to me, and—trust me—I shall ignore *your* pleas."

The guard brought his fists up to strike Wertham again,

but Wertham moved faster, brushing them away before driving a vicious kick to the man's gut.

The guard doubled over with the blow, toppling into the bathtub. Wertham was over him in an instant, clapping his hands against either side of the man's helmeted head.

"Breathe deep, brother," Wertham instructed cruelly. And then he gave the command—"bathe"—and the water began to pour from the ceiling-mounted spigot. It came in a torrent, as if the two figures were poised under a waterfall. Wertham bowed his head as the water lashed against his shoulders, pulling the guard's head up until it was directly in the path of the powerful jet of water. The guard spluttered, struggling to breathe as the water drilled against his face with ferocity. Every time his head tipped back Wertham pulled him forward, forcing him to remain in the direct line of the powerful jet of water.

Fifty seconds later, the guard designated one-nine-seven-one was drowning, water filling his lungs. His struggles stopped forty seconds after that, and then his spluttering ceased shortly afterward.

When Wertham let him go, the guard sank beneath the now-filled bath, his body no longer moving, no longer alive.

"THERE ARE SOME bad people on the rise," Queen Rosalind intoned softly as she sat on a comfy chair to the side of the Prophecy Room. She was clearly shaken, even though it had been almost ten minutes since she had seen the strange patterns on the receiver screen. Brigid theorized that the user must connect with the machine on a psychic level, similar to the astronavigation chairs she and Kane had sampled. Rosalind's skin had turned pale, her ruby lips taking on the lighter pink of a blush.

"Can I get you something, Your Majesty?" Brigid asked. "Another glass of water?"

Rosalind looked at her, her neon-blue hair brightening and dimming as if alive. "You're very kind, Brigid," she said, pressing her hand against Brigid's. "Don't lose that."

Brigid looked at the woman askance, absorbing what she had just said. "Why…do you say that?" she finally managed.

Queen Roz's face took on a solemn aspect, and for the first time Brigid truly saw the weight of years in that face. There was wisdom there, and eyes that had seen more than the queen could ever recount. "The life you live, the war you fight—these things can change a person," Roz said. "But only if they let it."

Brigid felt the blush of embarrassment rise to her cheeks. Not very long ago, she had been turned by "the war," as the queen had called it, and had momentarily become a darker aspect of herself, a vile creature called Haight. It had been a combination of brainwashing and regret that had brought upon the Haight persona, but deep in her heart Brigid feared that it might one day return. As Haight, she had shot Kane. He had forgiven her, but if the personality re-emerged, Brigid could only guess at what it would be capable of.

As Brigid's thoughts wandered, Domi returned with a second glass of water for the queen.

"Your Highness," said Domi, handing the glass to the neon-haired woman with a respectful dip of her head. She did not seem to have noticed how pale Brigid had gone in the meantime.

Brigid watched as Domi waited on the queen. This was not like Domi—the albino woman was a free spirit. True, she had sold herself into sexual slavery once, years before, in an attempt to become a part of Cobaltville's protective environment, but that had only given her even more reason to despise any form of servitude. Brigid saw the change then, even as she thought it. Domi was not serving the queen out of obligation or respect. She was doing it because she wanted to be here, to ingratiate herself, to stay. Domi's words came back to Brigid from just a few minutes before—how she had found her place here in the cosmic rift, how she felt at home among these people with their future technology and strange society. Brigid couldn't help but wonder if Cerberus had already lost one of their brightest and best warriors.

"You ever heard of an ageless pool?" King Jack asked as he stepped from the sky disk with Kane and Grant.

He had landed the graceful vehicle in an open area before one of the towering factories. The building's exterior walls were a burnished golden and they caught highlights from the shimmering sky that surrounded the floating city. High above them, three towering chimneys bent upward into the air, not straight but curved like bows, pouring a steady stream of water vapor up into the air. The vapor was clear, misting just a little to create a miragelike heat haze in the air immediately above the industrial district. It struck Kane as a good metaphor for Authentiville in general—the whole golden metropolis had the appearance of a mirage.

Down on the ground, the streets were a rich, reddish-copper color. Up close, Kane and Grant saw that the streets were paved in a mosaic fashion, tiny tiles interlocking to form the surface like pebbles on a beach. It made the streets seem less garish up close.

Besides the royal sky disk, there were other vehicles parked outside the factory, though not as many as Kane would have expected for such a huge facility. In fact, there were barely a dozen other craft parked there, and they included two sky platforms like Jack's and something that resembled a snail made of metal probing outward in front with a spiraled passenger compartment in the rear that stood eighteen feet high. The snail-thing had wheels with thick tire treads, each wheel coming up as high as the ex-Magistrate's shoulder.

Despite his suspicions, Kane played dumb as Jack led them across the courtyard and into the factory building. "Ageless pool? I don't think so." It was better to let the old man show him than to try to second guess, and maybe reveal something he would have rather kept to himself.

Jack smiled as he strode into a vast, two-story anteroom dominated by towering pillars. Inside the anteroom, the building had a familiar scent. Both Kane and Grant recognized it immediately. It was the smell of a Chalice of Rebirth. The Chalice, or Cauldron, of Rebirth was an Annunaki-Tuatha hybrid design that consisted of a bathing pool into which warriors could dip to repair their wounds. The units had turned up in a few places in mythology, most notably the Irish myth of the Cauldron of Bran. Cerberus field teams had stumbled upon a few of the pools during their travels, and had even employed one to repair one of their colleagues.

The walls here were lit, like those of the palace, by hidden illumination. It created a translucent sheen to the walls, not so bright that it was hard to look at yet radiating enough light to make the place feel welcoming. One peculiar effect of this lighting was that it threw almost no shadows—because light was coming from everywhere, it meant that the shadows it cast were very short, a little like standing out in the midday sun. The effect was momentarily disorienting to Kane and Grant.

There was a single desk in the anteroom, taking up about a quarter of its length along the left-hand wall, like the bar in an old drinking establishment. The desk was manned by two figures—stylized women rendered in a silver metal that seemed almost liquid in nature. As Kane strode past he noted that neither figure had legs. They were propelled along the desk via a swiveling arm-type arrangement just below its surface.

The silver women spoke in near unison. "Good afternoon, Your Highness."

Still talking with Kane and Grant, King Jack acknowledged the greeting with a vague wave of his gold-gloved hand. "When I came across my first pool I didn't have clue one what to do with it. Figured out later it could heal wounds. Took us a while to work out how to get one here and get it operational."

The trio of men walked toward a doorway at the far end of the anteroom. The doorway was nothing more than a gap in the wall reaching all the way from floor to the ceiling sixty feet above. Perspective made it look narrow, but as they neared, the Cerberus men saw that the doorway was almost wide enough to fly a Manta through. As they got closer, they could hear the thrumming sounds of machinery along with the steady drone of voices.

"Through here," Jack said.

Past the towering doorway was a vast chamber with a sunken center, around which ran a walkway wide enough to drive an automobile or a Sandcat. The sunken area was a quarter mile across and half that again in width, taking up a rectangular space that encompassed most of the high room. It was surrounded by a continuous narrow metal band covered in glyphs and symbols.

Amber liquid bubbled like liquid sunlight in the pit, which was so vast it moved with its own tides. Great cauldrons fed the pool, pouring hundreds of gallons of liquid into the colossal reservoir. There were several dozen people in the pool, stripped for swimming or bathing, along with several boat-like vessels floating across the golden lake.

"Phew," Grant whistled. "That's one mighty big pond."

King Jack laughed. "It is at that, son, but you've probably noticed by now that I never do things by half in my kingdom."

"You built this?" Kane questioned.

"A lot of people think I did," Jack told them both with a wink. "That's why they call me the king. Hey—who am I to say otherwise and shatter people's illusions? People need heroes, Kane."

"Then you're a hero?" Grant asked him.

"We can all be heroes," Jack told the Cerberus men earnestly. "It just depends on how people choose to tell our stories."

Together, the group strode across the walkway toward the edge of the ageless pool.

WERTHAM'S FACE TOOK on the look of sweet serenity as the trance passed. His true mind reengaged with his body, swimming out of the fugue state and back to the real world. He was still standing in the shell-shaped bathtub, the stream of water flowing over his back and shoulders, covering the corpse in the tub at his feet.

"Cease," he said, pushing back his wet hair from his eyes. Above him the jet of water came to an abrupt stop, no longer filling the exquisitely designed tub.

"Void," Wertham said.

Openings appeared around the bathtub at the command, like mouths amid the water. The bathtub began to empty, the level of warm water sinking as Wertham stepped over the lip of the tub and down onto the floor.

He left wet footprints as he walked through his apartment prison, making his way back to the bedroom where the guards had first discovered him.

When he reached the bedchamber, Wertham saw the figure waiting on the other side of the barricade. Dr. Ronald was still dressed in his immaculate high-collared uniform, resting in the sleek conveyance he required to transport his body in light of his ruined legs.

"They should have fixed those for you," Wertham said as he stepped over the dead figure of a guard. The guard's visor was shattered and his head was dipped into the shoulders where his neck had been crushed. "Then we might not have been here."

Ronald was obviously shocked by the dead bodies of the two guards, but he covered it well.

"Surely you've seen corpses before, Doctor?" Wertham teased.

Uncomfortable, Ronald ignored the comment. "Are you ready to go?" he asked.

"A moment," Wertham said.

Wertham kicked one of the dead guards from the foot of the bed and sank down on his haunches. The sallow eyed man reached for the bed and lifted it a few inches off the floor, pushing back the mattress and working at a rudimentary catch there. A moment later, Wertham pulled loose the bottom strut of the bed, a fourteen-inch length of metal, circular at its cross section. He twirled the batonlike strut in his hand so that it caught the flickering lights of the cell. Satisfied, he stepped through the security wall to join his accomplice in the outside world.

"Do you know I have not stepped out of that cell in seven hundred years?" Wertham remarked as he made his way with Ronald to the elevator. "I don't know…" he mused. "I expected it to feel more…earthshaking, somehow."

"Five sentries are dead," Ronald reminded him.

"Sentries and centuries," Wertham trilled. "Ever in the way of man's goals. Ignite the Doom Furnace, brother—to work!"

With that, the two men stepped into the air-powered chute that would take them down to the entry level, and from there to the palace to take control of Authentiville.

BESIDES THE SEEMINGLY perfect figures in the water itself, there were a number of people wandering about the edges of the ageless pool. Kane and Grant recognized these as Geneagers, of the same servant class who had served their meal in the palace. Up close, the Gene-agers had pallid skin with dark circles around their eyes, and though dressed in bright, utilitarian outfits, they all wore the same blank expression. Each one appeared to be male, with his head shaved, but up close Kane noticed there was more to it than that—none of the Gene-agers had eyebrows or any sign of facial hair. Furthermore, while they were all equally well built, at least two of the servants were female, the swell of their breasts disguised by the taut garments they wore.

"How many of these guys do you have?" Kane asked as King Jack removed his crimson cloak.

Jack thought about this for a moment as one of the Gene-agers took the cloak. "We keep fifteen hundred to cover the basic operations of the ville, from day care duties for the children to running the machinery underpinning this very facility," he explained. "They're very adaptive, although they burn out after about twelve years."

"'Burn out'?" Grant repeated, alarmed at the implication. "These are people…aren't they?"

Jack smiled that winning smile of his once again as he drew the golden rod he had brought from the throne room. It never seemed to leave him. He waggled it before the nearest Gene-ager—a male wearing an emerald one-piece suit. At the wave of the stick, the Gene-ager's eyes went black and he bowed his head infinitesimally.

"What—?" Grant began, but the king was not finished.

The two Cerberus warriors watched as Jack motioned with the golden stick, stepping closer to another of the servants. This figure did the same, as did a third standing a few feet away.

Kane was eyeing the rod warily as he asked the question on both men's minds. "How did you do that?"

"They live and breathe," Jack explained. "But they're significantly less than human."

Chapter 16

Serra do Norte, Brazil

Twin cones of multihued light materialized from the ether, one above ground and the other, counterintuitively, beneath, forming an hourglass shape amid the greenery of the dense forest. Streaks of lightning hurtled within those eerie cones like witch fire, creating an impossible sense of depth within those swirling lights.

It was the interphaser, Cerberus's teleportation device, appearing out of nowhere. Birds squawked at the strange intrusion, while rodents scampered back to their burrows or hid themselves amid the low-hanging ferns, turning startled eyes away from the sudden burst of light.

A moment later, the multicolored cones coalesced into four silhouettes as the Cerberus recovery team appeared from the quantum ether. There were four of them in all—Falk and Cataman for the investigative side, Edwards and Sinclair for security.

Edwards was a tall man with broad shoulders and a body language that spoke of aggression. He didn't walk so much as prowl, and he didn't speak to people, he talked at them. Or shouted.

His hair was shaved to a faint shadow on his head, and his right ear was mangled where a bullet had clipped it. Edwards wore a camouflage jacket with loose pants, the legs of which were marked with a half-dozen pockets, each one bulging with supplies. He was checking a Beretta 93-R pistol in his hands, assuring himself that it was loaded. He also wore a rifle on a strap across his back—an M-16 derivative manufactured in the late twentieth century by Colt.

Sinclair was the other part of the security detail, a dark-skinned woman whose short hair was cropped close to her scalp. She wore a flak jacket and camo pants, and like Edwards she had armed herself with a lightweight pistol—in her case a Smith & Wesson 0.45 Third Generation with a magazine clip in its butt. Like Edwards, she had trained in the deadly arts of combat—in her case, as a Navy SEAL back in the late twentieth century before being held in suspended animation for two hundred years inside the Manitius Moon Base. She had been with the Cerberus unit ever since, acting in a security role.

The third member of the group was an ageing man with a slightly stooped bearing. He was a pale man with salt-and-pepper hair brushed back from the sides of his head in two extravagant wings. It gave him the air of an addled professor, an impression his singed lab coat only served to enhance. This was Roy Cataman, one of the more recent additions to the Cerberus scientific community. Most recently, Cataman had been pivotal in an investigation into an ancient super-soldier program.

Mariah Falk rounded out the team, exhausted from worry but determined to see things through to the bitter end.

Edwards was striding out of the mystical light show almost before the quantum gate had sealed and he called to Mariah as he marched.

"Whereabouts is the spot where you found the spaceship?" Edwards barked.

Mariah trotted after him, still trying to get her bearings after the teleportational jump through quantum space. "About three miles distant," she said, recognizing their location—

it was the same spot where she and Domi had arrived just a day before. Was she really so tired she'd forgotten how fixed parallax jump points were?

"About three miles—or three miles?" Edwards snapped impatiently, intruding on Mariah's thoughts.

"Two and three-quarter miles," Mariah replied, holding her irritation in check. "Bear west-southwest."

Edwards nodded indifferently, consulting an electronic compass clutched in the palm of his hand. "Have arrived at location," Edwards confirmed, engaging his Commtact without bothering to alert Mariah or the others. "Everything quiet. Am checking it out." With that, Edwards scurried off into the underbrush, the Beretta pistol in his hand.

At the jump point, Sinclair was carefully packing away the interphaser unit while Professor Cataman was merely endeavoring to catch his breath.

"You okay, Doc?" Sinclair asked as she placed the pyramid shape of the interphaser inside the foam-lined case the team had brought with them for that purpose.

Standing bent over with his hands resting on the tops of his legs, Cataman brushed Sinclair's concerns away with a wave of his hand. "I'll…be…fine in a…moment or two," he said weakly.

Interphaser packed, Sinclair strolled over to join the scientist, a smile of concern on her lips. "Takes it out of you the first time, doesn't it?"

"What does?" Cataman asked.

"The interphaser jump," Sinclair said.

Cataman glanced up at Sinclair to agree, but as he did so he swayed on the spot and Sinclair had to grab his arm to steady him. "It rather does," Cataman agreed after taking a deep breath. "Thank you, Sinclair."

As the two of them spoke, Edwards reappeared from his brief jaunt to scope out the area. "All clear here," he told

Sinclair. "There's evidence of some building, but it's just ruins now. Let's move this party out and get ourselves posted at the last known location of Kane's team."

Sinclair nodded. "Agreed. Roy? Will you be okay?"

Cataman straightened up gently. "Yes, I'm sure the walk will do me some good. Clear my head."

Edwards looked at Cataman and shrugged. Civilians! May the barons save us from them.

Though Edwards could not guess it, the ruins that he had found were from an ancient temple that had once dominated the riverbank close to their set-down point. Like many of the so-called parallax points that the interphaser tapped into to ferry its passengers about, this area had once been revered as a sacred site by primitive peoples. A few paces ahead, Mariah Falk was eyeing the afternoon sky as the others sorted themselves out. It was a crystal-clear blue with only a few delicate, featherlike wisps of white cloud floating high in its glorious depths.

"We're moving out, Mariah," Sinclair told her as Edwards marched on ahead. "You okay?"

"Yep," Mariah assured the ex-Navy officer. "Just thinking about the blue sky and how, back where we started, they used to have that phrase—*blue-sky thinking*. You remember that?"

"Yeah," Sinclair told her. "Positive thinking with no road-blocks to your ideas, or something like that."

"Something like that," Mariah agreed. "I guess whoever thought of it never lost a friend to an alien kidnapping, huh?"

Sinclair looked gravely at the geologist. "We'll find Domi," she said. "We'll find all of them."

"We'd better," Mariah said. "Otherwise, I'm not sure I'm going to be going out in the field ever again."

Chapter 17

Location unknown

"They're significantly less than human," King Jack had said just a few seconds before. The statement hung there in the bathing house like a lead weight.

Kane and Grant were aghast at the king's words, but the golden-armored monarch did not seem to notice. He continued to wave the golden shaft that he carried in a broad, sweeping arc. As he did so, every one of the Gene-agers that manned the washrooms seemed to fall asleep, bowing their heads so that their chins struck their chests.

"They're designed to respond to the Glorious Omni-Device—or God Rod," Jack said proudly.

The Gene-agers bowed their heads for a five count until Jack raised the rod and with a smile brought them all back to life. The Gene-agers continued about their business as if nothing had happened.

"You see?"

"Seems like you have the ultimate control here," Grant said, watching as the slaves continued about their tasks.

"A monarch rules," Jack reminded him, "and he takes the can, sometimes, too. But without that man to look up to, things soon devolve into anarchy."

"Now, that I can vouch for," Kane agreed. He was thinking of the mess that North America had been left in when the barons disappeared several years ago, a mess it was still working through.

"So long as I've got this," Jack continued, showing Kane and Grant the golden rod, "there's nothing in the warp that's going to worry anyone."

Kane eyed the God Rod, trying to make sense of what it was and what it did. "Yeah, I noticed that back in your palace," he said. "What is that thing? Magic wand?"

Kane and Grant watched as energies coruscated across the rod's surface like waves crashing on the shore. "It attracts and holds energy," Jack told them, "and it's bonded to my genetic code. That means no one but the king gets to play the shut-down trick with the Gene-agers here."

Grant shot the king a dark look. "Still looks a lot like slavery to me," he said. "And in my experience, that isn't something that ever ends well…Your Highness," he added after a moment.

"They're not man enough to be slaves," King Jack assured him. "They're just automatons made of flesh. Human robots."

"And you never fear they might rise up against you?" Grant asked, uncomfortable with the situation.

Jack shook his head. "This system has been in place since before your granddaddy was a twinkle in *his* granddaddy's eye," he boasted. "We pulled away from the surface a long time ago, and we did it because some of us could see the way things were down there and figured that it wasn't ever likely to change.

"Look around you—look at what you're experiencing," Jack told them both. "The king is showing you around his city. I have nothing to fear from my subjects. We have no crime. We want for nothing. This isn't an Earth state where people will try to take what they don't yet have. We're beyond that—*centuries* beyond that. It's possible to achieve when people work together. When there's trust."

"What about weapons?" Kane asked. It was a grim question, but one that had been on the minds of both Cerberus men from the moment they had landed here.

"Weapons," the figure in the gold armor repeated, pronouncing the word with gravitas, almost as though it was a weapon itself. "We once had weapons, centuries ago, back when we were naive and still finding our way. This city existed even then, constructed on the technology that we'd found out on the coast of Ireland. But we weren't so fast back then, hadn't tapped the right mix of junk to make that possible, so we had to rely on weaponry to keep us alive when we jaunted over the surface.

"Some people figured that was fun, a kind of vacation from the luxury here," Jack said darkly. "Weapons were found and adapted and, yes, they got used. I used them, too, I'm not ashamed to say."

"But now?" Kane encouraged.

"One day my son made a life on the surface and he didn't come back," Jack told him, and Kane saw the look of pain in the king's eyes. In that moment, King Jack looked older. "It wasn't long after that that I decreed all weapons be stored away forever, and that any new technology we found was defanged the way a snake charmer defangs his snake. I don't like weapons, and Neal's disappearance made that decision much easier for me to make."

"Your son was called Neal," Kane stated, piecing the story together.

"Yes." Jack nodded, his expression dour. Then he looked up at Kane and Grant and the old smile reappeared as if in some magic act—now you see it, now you don't. "I believe I promised you fellas a chance to go swimming," he said cheerily.

A moment later, Kane and Grant were stripping out of their

clothes and shadow suits and joining the king as he paddled out into the shallow end of the amber pool.

ONE OF THE rooms of the royal palace was given over to a display of ornate fountains that utilized a combination of water and colored light. The fountains had been designed by the most proficient artists in the kingdom, and they covered such diverse subjects as scenes from Greek mythology—here a hydra with thrashing necks made of water, there an arrow striking Achilles's heel in a jet of crimson light—to undersea fancies of dancing fish and mermaids, all of them lit in the greens and blues of the ocean depths.

Queen Rosalind had retired to her chambers after thanking Brigid and Domi for their kind help during her momentary aberration at the prophetic machinery. Domi had led Brigid here, explaining it was an area of tranquillity and meditation, and that she had already settled on it as one of her favorite areas of the magical palace.

Brigid's eyes widened as she took in the enclosed area of fountains. It stretched the length of several football fields, with a majestic fountain every ten yards, placed one next to the other like exhibits in an art gallery. A dozen or so people milled about the vast room, taking up positions on benches and playing some derivative of chess or drafts in the illumination cast by a fountain.

The walls were lit from within, a soft shine that did not hurt the eyes, and many of the fountains radiated an internal glow. High above, at the top of the huge room, a line of skylights looked up into the rainbow whirl of the cosmic rift.

"Well?" Domi prompted, reveling in her friend's surprise. "What do you think?"

"It's beautiful," Brigid said, struggling to take everything in. "Bending light and water like this—simply breathtaking."

"There's a few places just like this in the ville," Domi explained, sitting on a bench seat, "as well as others that do similar things with three-dimensional paintings and colored wood. The whole ville is geared toward artistic expression."

"So I've noticed," Brigid said, joining Domi on the seat. "The whole palace is a marvel of statuary and ornate carvings. I guess that's what happens when a society no longer has to struggle to achieve its goals. It turns to art."

"Or to finding other places to rule," Domi said dourly.

"Yes, territory can be a big driving factor for any society," Brigid agreed. "I wonder why King Jack's people never expanded onto the surface. With the tech they have up here they could have conquered most of Earth's peoples in a matter of a few days."

"I think they feel safe here," Domi said, running her alabaster hand through the trickling waters of a fountain. The fountain sculpture showed a fishing boat called by sirens and veering onto the rocks. "They've almost unlimited space to expand, and existing in a quantum warp they have no predators, no threats."

"Not even from within?" Brigid asked. Then she shook her head. "I keep forgetting that you've only been here for a day, Domi, hardly any longer than we have. You seem so... at home."

"I am at home, Brigid," Domi told her. "What possible reason could make me leave?"

Brigid's gaze left Domi and turned to the falling water of a fountain designed to look like a charging centaur. The centaur's feet were lost in the mist of water where it struck the fountain's base, while light reflected across its flanks to suggest movement.

"Brigid?" Domi prompted. "Why don't you stay with me? The people here have made me so welcome. I'm sure they'd be only too happy to have a mind like yours here, contributing to their bank of knowledge."

Brigid smiled at Domi's words. What she said was probably true—King Jack and his people seemed very welcoming to newcomers. They hadn't once asked for Brigid and her colleagues to justify their reasons for being here. However, what had most struck Brigid was not the words, but the fact that they were being uttered by Domi of all people, the most taciturn and withdrawn member of the whole Cerberus operation.

Her plea was not just heartfelt; it was eloquent—more eloquent than she had ever known Domi to be. Brigid looked around the vast room, scanning for something she could not put her finger on. Could it be that there was something here, in this room or in the palace or perhaps even in the whole of the floating city that was boosting Domi's intellect? And was it affecting all of them?

AT THE EXACT moment that Brigid Baptiste was marveling at the tranquillity of Authentiville, Wertham the Strange stepped onto the landing pad of the prison complex with Ronald floating beside him in his automated motion chair. Ronald's private air mule was waiting at the end of the landing platform, a hundred feet above street level. Square in shape with windows all around, the compact vehicle was reminiscent of an alpine cable car.

As Ronald made his way to the air mule, Wertham halted a few steps beyond the open doors of his prison, taking in the view of the golden city, breathing in fresh air for the first time in seven hundred years.

Ronald turned back. "You like what you see?" he asked.

Wertham nodded. "The question is, do *you* like it, Doctor? Is it what you want?"

"You know me, Wertham," Ronald said, opening the door of the mule with a wave of his hand. "I'm a simple man with simple tastes. A kingdom of this size will be more than adequate for my needs."

"Which leaves me with the surface world," Wertham mused.

"If you are able to tame it," Ronald reminded him.

Wertham laughed as he stepped into the mule with Ronald. "Oh, I'll tame it all right. When I'm done, Earth will bear my face on its largest continent, and every living person will know only one word, and that word shall be my name."

At the vehicle controls, Ronald toggled a switch and set the mule to rise from the landing platform. In a few seconds, the private vehicle was passing through the sky above Authentiville. It cut an effortless path between other vehicles as Ronald guided it to one of the vast parks that dominated the ground level.

"The city looks smaller than I remembered," Wertham observed as he stood before one of the mule's panoramic windows. "Funny how things become bigger in one's mind over time."

A moment later, the mule touched down at the edge of Pacifist Park, which covered almost three acres of land. Surrounded by a golden barred fence, the park featured softly undulating hillocks and just a few trees; perfectly trimmed grass carpeted the whole thing in a swathe of green.

As the mule powered down, Wertham was pleased to see people were out enjoying the park, sunbathing in the rainbow glow of the vortex, children running around playing children's games.

"A lot has changed," Wertham exclaimed as he surveyed the park and the towering skyline looming behind it.

Ronald looked up at his associate from his chair. "You don't recognize it, then?"

Wertham showed him that terrible smile, the one that spoke of inhuman genius, of insights that man was never meant to know. "They could only disguise so much," Wertham said, twirling his silver rod in his hands like some sinister majorette. "Shall we?"

Ronald followed as Wertham stepped from the mule's ramp and out into the green park. "They used the camouflage tech we found on the sky disks," Ronald explained.

Wertham nodded. "I see." He knew the technology that Ronald was talking about. The Annunaki sky disks had been equipped with technology that would adopt the color of their background, making them appear as just a shimmer in the air when they flew within the atmosphere. It was a way to hide them in plain sight. Though Wertham could not see it, he guessed that the same technology had been retooled to create the illusion of the beautiful park he saw before him. And yes, it was an illusion, formed of hard light.

Wertham closed his eyes for a moment, mentally consulting the circuitry within the silver-skinned rod he had secretly constructed during the years trapped in his cell. The old plans formed before him, a web of ancient catwalks that had not been trodden upon for almost a thousand years.

"Move left," Wertham instructed, and Ronald guided his motion chair until he was in line with where Wertham was indicating.

Then, with a twist of the silver baton, Wertham tapped the hidden technology beneath its skin and felt the shimmer tech that held the park in place. Something winked out in his field of vision as a great plain of grass simply vanished to be replaced by a gap sunk into the earth. The people who had been on that patch of grass—fifty square feet of it in all— screamed as they began to fall, the hard-light hologram that had been holding them up winking out of existence. They tumbled down into the body of the thing that resided below, great cavernous lines of metal sunk deep into the foundations of the floating city.

Other people in the park turned at the sudden change,

shouting and pointing at the eerie sight of the ground literally ceasing to exist. Down there, beneath the illusion of perfect grass, lay a great industrial structure, all hard lines and sheer metal. Wertham watched as another batch of people disappeared with another turn of the rod in his hands, plummeting down into the forgotten industrial complex. Behind him, the mule sat on what was now an island of grass between the ancient catwalks.

Ronald's expression was fixed as he watched more people fall to their deaths. "You could have let them go," he said.

"Why?" Wertham replied, a cruel edge to his voice. "They didn't let me go—why should I do any different for them?"

As he spoke, another great swathe of the perfect grass winked out of existence, leaving in its place a chasm down into the guts of Authentiville. Sounds of shrieking filled the air.

Chapter 18

Its name was the Doom Furnace and it had lurked beneath Authentiville for almost a thousand years, like a sleeping creature of myth waiting to be reawakened. Wertham the Strange strode across its high catwalks to the song of screaming, staring down into the seemingly bottomless chasm that was the Furnace's kiln. Around him, park-goers were still falling, dropping into its abysslike depths, unable to foresee where the narrow catwalks would materialize as the ground beneath them winked out of existence. Only Wertham saw that, thanks to the Devil Rod.

Up ahead, a child stood on the narrow walkway, staring down into the darkness, screaming for his mother.

"Your mother's dead, child," Wertham said as he approached. "But whatever's left of her body will be recycled to make something new and wondrous, a whole new complexity of human."

"Wh-wha—?" the child stuttered, unable to comprehend the man's strange words.

Wertham sneered and slapped the child across the head, knocking him so hard that he slipped from the narrow walkway and disappeared into the dark. "Children," he muttered. "They ask for everything to be laid out for them, and yet they still don't understand."

Down below him, just a few hundred years before, fires had burned as weapons of cosmic destruction were forged and perfected. Great burning pools of lava had been tamed and utilized to make the greatest weapons that man would ever know. Each of those weapons had been based upon the designs that Jack's people had found—great Annunaki warships and flyers, mobile cannons that used sonics to fell whole populations or to superheat water so that it turned to steam so swiftly that it burned the flesh from their enemies' bodies in the blink of a now-lidless eye.

Like so much of Authentiville, the Doom Furnace was hidden beneath the streets, way down in the guts of the platform upon which the city was balanced. Through a careful manipulation of quantum mechanics, those guts extended almost infinitely, creating a tesseract of near-limitless space in which to house the great industrial complex on which the city relied. The food its citizens ate, the water they drank, even the air they breathed—all of it was produced beneath the city itself, vast plantations and moisture farms and air farms located beneath the streets and manned by the Geneagers who never tired and never questioned.

But this part had been sealed off, all entryways blocked, disguised and covered by Pacifist Park and its illusory idyll. A hardlight projection of quietude paving over the glorious industry of war.

"How long has it been?" Wertham asked, taking in a deep breath of dead air. He asked the question of the skies around him, as if interrogating the cosmos itself.

"It's a thousand years since Jack shut this down," Ronald said. "He did it after his—"

"Yes, I recall why he did it," Wertham interrupted. "To think that the man would halt the Doom Furnace like that, when so much could have been built here." He looked down into the vertiginous chasm, spying the glint of smart-metal far below where the old warships waited, mothballed for a millennium.

Ronald watched as Wertham closed his eyes, consulting

and manipulating those hidden shapes he had spoken of time and again, twisting the batonlike device in his hand.

Below them, deep in the bowels of tesseract space, a flame lit, igniting the ancient forge for the first time in ten centuries.

Wertham sneered as the great industrial machine came to life around and beneath him, the nightmare shapes of warships lit in bloodred by the burning flames of the forge, weapons of delusion waiting in the shadows. The Doom Furnace was operational once more, its song of war reverberating through the streets around Pacifist Park.

Minutes later, Ronald's mule pulled up at the service entrance of the palace to disgorge its two occupants. They entered the vast kitchen of the palace like a storm rolling in from sea, brushing past the cooks and waiting staff as they hurried toward their destiny.

Identifying the head chef on duty, Ronald guided his chair over to him and addressed him with authority.

"The king?" Ronald demanded of the head chef. "Where is he?"

The chef wore a towering white headpiece within which a thermal gauge constantly informed him of fluctuations in ambient temperature that might affect his culinary masterpieces. The information was fed from the hat straight to his brain, bypassing any need for him to look away from his hot and cold creations.

"Where?" Ronald repeated, grabbing the chef by his lapels and dragging him down to his level in the chair.

"The king left," the chef stuttered. The chef always knew of the king's movements, for it was his responsibility to feed the man—and some would say that this, in itself, was the most important job in the whole kingdom. "In the company of the visitors. I don't know where."

"And the queen?" Ronald snarled.

"In the throne room," the head chef replied, wide-eyed. "She requested a small meal of nutritional exactitude, Your Honor."

"I remember where the court is," Wertham assured his accomplice. "Let us surprise her with a little dessert to go with her nutritional request. Something—semilethal."

The head chef watched bemused as Wertham the Strange exited the kitchens via the service elevator, rocketing up through the levels of the palace to the royal court.

The head chef let out the breath he had been holding as Ronald left the room. He wondered not what this augured, but rather what meal would be best to serve in its light. But then, as a Gene-ager, the head chef was given to little in the way of free thought.

At amber.

The color swirled around their bodies, running over muscles made tight by their time in the cramped cockpits of the Manta craft. It felt warm and relaxing, like the embrace of a familiar lover.

"You know, Your Highness," Kane remarked, "this is just what I needed."

"Me, too," Grant agreed.

It was remarkable, really. Both men had seen a Chalice of Rebirth before—several times, in fact—but to find one so large and so readily accessible to any inhabitant of this incredible city was beyond their wildest imaginings.

The Chalice of Rebirth utilized nano technology to re-create tissue cells, replenish blood and otherwise repair damage to the human body. Kane had been dunked in one of the pools by accident not so long ago, and the effect had been to repair a gunshot wound he had sustained, as well as accidentally mixing his DNA with that of an alien chip of rock embedded in his eye. The experience had affected his comprehension for a while, leaving him with memory echoes of another creature.

Here and now, there was no damage to repair. Neither Kane nor Grant had been wounded; neither man needed this fix. Yet they had agreed to join King Jack in the pool as a show of solidarity.

Around them, at the edges of the rippling pool, a dozen Gene-agers waited patiently, ready to fulfill the orders of any Authentiville citizen without question.

"I try to take a dip once a week," Jack explained. "Keeps the old aches at bay and helps the mind relax."

"I dunno," Grant said. "Seems to me you have a pretty relaxed setup here anyway. In the palace, I mean."

King Jack looked at him, his clear blue eyes amused. "You're still worrying about the Gene-agers aren't you, son? They won't hurt you."

"It's not me I'm worried about," Grant told him. "Any society predicated on slavery falls apart sooner or later. That's a historical fact."

"That's *your* history," Jack told him, "not ours. Things are different up here. We bred the Gene-agers to perform the tasks we require and they've done so for as long as most people here can remember. What's more, they'll keep doing so after you're long gone. Things don't change. We're a captured sliver of time out here, away from the petty squabbles of the surface people. And that's the way we like it."

"Things always change," Grant said, but he tried to make a joke of it, splashing the amber liquid over himself as he dunked his head under the surface.

THE ROYAL COURT was quiet, its functionaries going about their business in near silence. Queen Rosalind sat alone, staring into her hand mirror, tracing the age lines that marred her face. Using the Happening had taken a lot out of her, and neither she nor Jack had told the strangers how much of the user's energy the Happening drained in its functioning. There were things one didn't share with strangers.

Like much of the Annunaki technology on which it was based, the device employed an organic dimension that meant it needed to bond and engage with the user before functionality was achieved. Roz had been kept physically young by the pools of regeneration, but using the machine was truly a young person's game. In future, she reminded herself, she should leave its function to the genetically manipulated staff who were grown to use it.

"It's a terrible thing, getting old," she remarked to herself. But it was something the people of Authentiville need never fear, not with the Ageless Pools serving their needs.

It was at that moment that the figures appeared in the colossal chamber, flitting across the surface of her mirror as she brushed at her neon hair. She spun in her throne, turning to see who they were.

"Ronald—?" she began before gasping. The other figure was familiar to her, as well, and his appearance here brought with it a sense of dread.

"Well?" Wertham the Strange demanded, wielding the silver-colored rod in his hands. "Aren't you going to welcome me back to the palace, Your Majesty?"

"Get out, Wertham," Rosalind spat out, rising from her grand throne. "You shouldn't be here. You should be..."

"What? Imprisoned?" Wertham challenged her. "Imprisoned for my expansive ideas? Is that how you remember it, even after all these centuries? Or perhaps it is the centuries that have made you misremember so much, casting me in the role of villain in your simple play."

Around them, the people of the royal court were clearing the room, sentries marching to see what the fuss was. But before they could do anything, Wertham waved the silver rod he carried at them and, as one, they halted in place, their eyes losing focus.

Rosalind's dark eyes fixed on the rod that Wertham was holding in his hands, and her heart sank as she realized what it was. "What is that?" she demanded. "You don't think for a moment that you can…"

"Replace the king," Wertham finished. "I've had seven hundred years to think on that fact, ever since your husband incarcerated me for suggesting we reach beyond the borders of this little idyll in the stars. And you know what? Yes, I think I can replace the king. But I won't. No, I've promised that role to another."

"Wertham, no," Rosalind pleaded. "You're unwell. Your mind…it's…"

Wertham held up the proxy God Rod that he had created, tooled from the bar that held his bed together, worked with circuitry that had been smuggled into his prison over the period of a decade, stripped and repatched, so that now it worked in a manner only his fertile mind could possibly have conceived. "It begins this day," he announced. "The Era of New Gods."

Wild energies exploded from the false God Rod, burning a hole in the air, fizzing with their barely restrained fury. The sentries remained unmoving, their Gene-ager minds idling as they awaited new commands.

Rosalind gasped as she finally realized the enormity of what the device meant. With it, Wertham could control all of Authentiville, including every atom of salvaged alien tech that had been put to use there.

"Today, your whole world changes," Wertham told her as he strode across the room toward the twin thrones.

Rosalind stood, blocking Wertham's path, but he shoved her aside. She hissed like a cat as she was knocked against the side of her towering throne. Then Wertham slipped the silver rod into place in the mount between the thrones, guiding it inside the circles of gold where King Jack's God Rod belonged. For a moment, Wertham's rod glowed with sinister promise.

"Today, everyone's world changes," Wertham snarled as the base of the holder linked with his false God Rod, firing the palace's power through its sleek lines. Now the throne was Wertham's to control.

All around Authentiville the lights began to dim.

Chapter 19

Kane and Grant climbed from the pool.

"Got to admit, I feel refreshed," Kane said as he reached for his clothes.

Grant agreed. "Yeah, nothing beats a dip in the nano-soup," he said with a laugh.

As they spoke, both men noticed something almost subliminally, and Grant was the one who gave it voice first. "Did the lights just flicker?"

"I…think they did," Kane agreed hesitantly.

A few paces across from them, King Jack was being helped back into his armored garb by two of the Gene-agers while a third proffered his freshly laundered cloak.

"Your Highness," Kane began respectfully. "Do the lights often dim in this place?"

The king ran his left arm down the sleeve and into the golden glove of his armor. "They shouldn't," he said, bewildered. "Why do you…?"

Before the monarch could finish, the lights faded a second time. Only this time, it was more pronounced as the illumination slipped to darkness for fully three seconds.

"Now, that time I saw it," Jack admitted as the lights came back on with no discernible hesitation. "This is most peculiar. I have never known the illuminants to fail like that."

"How do they work?" Grant asked, securing his boots before reaching for his duster. The long coat was made of a Kevlar/Nomex weave, making it both flame retardant and able to deflect bullets. At that moment, Grant felt suddenly in need of the shield it provided.

"They're a semiliving ecosystem that runs behind the walls of most of our buildings," King Jack explained as he stomped across to the nearest wall. Beside him, the three Gene-agers kept pace, still holding his cape and God Rod, as well as one entire sleeve of his armor.

Jack stood at the wall, concern on his features as he ran the fingers of his ungloved hand along it. It was clear that he was searching for something, and in an instant he had found what he was looking for—a hidden panel. Three feet square, the wall panel opened on a hinge, revealing what appeared to be a growth of lichen beneath. The lichen glowed, providing the illumination. The Cerberus explorers had seen something similar some months back when they had found themselves exploring the Ontic Library, a grand storehouse of Annunaki knowledge located under the Pacific Ocean.

"Doesn't need feeding," the king explained, checking over the mossy growth. "Takes all it requires from the air. Place like this, with the pool—it's ideal. Plenty of moisture in the air. Even if the lights fail elsewhere in the kingdom, this, of all places, should be immune to a problem."

Kane was running over what Jack told him. "If this stuff is—what-chu-call-it?—semi-alive, then what would cause it to shut down like that?"

Still probing the moss with his bare hand, Jack shook his head. "Now that, son, is a very good question."

Jack took the God Rod from the servant before running it swiftly over the lit wall. As he did so, the Gene-ager sagged, as did the others still holding segments of King Jack's armor.

"What happened?" Kane asked.

All around, the Gene-agers were shutting down, each of them bowing head to chest the way that King Jack had demonstrated earlier.

"Are you doing that?" Grant asked warily.

"Not me," the king admitted. He sounded worried.

As he spoke, the open wall panel flickered and went dark. All around the room, other walls switched to darkness along with the ceiling panels. Worried voices came now from the pool behind them, asking what was going on. The only glow remaining was from the golden rod of energy in the king's hand.

"This is bad," King Jack muttered as he ran the glowing God Rod before the open wall.

"Your doing?" Kane asked.

"No," Jack stated. "And what's more, it can't be anyone else's. Not without access to the God Rod. And there's only one of those."

DOMI VISIBLY FLINCHED as the lights dimmed in the water arboretum of the palace. There was still light in the vast room—a line of skylights set in the roof let through the multicolored glow of the warp—but it felt suddenly gloomy and dangerous.

"What's going on?" Brigid asked, getting to her feet.

Domi shook her head. "I've not been here long, but I've never seen anything like this," she said. "The lights don't even dim with nightfall."

Does a place like this even have nightfall? Brigid wondered. An experienced fighter, she had adopted a combat stance, keeping her center of gravity low, wary of an attack. Her emerald eyes scanned the darkness within the arboretum, the awe-inspiring fountains standing in thick shadow at points around the chamber.

Domi was on her feet, too, sniffing at the air, her ruby eyes shifting right and left as she searched for the source of the sudden loss of light. "Something's happening," she said. "Something bad. Just like the queen said."

"There's bad and there's bad," Brigid replied as she led the way through the room at a trot.

Domi kept pace with her and in a moment the two women were back at the tall, open doorway through which they had entered this wing of the palace. Through the door they saw that the whole palace had been thrown into darkness. The walls and ornate light fixtures had lost their glow, leaving the interior of the palace in thick shadow.

"It's you, right?" Domi whispered, adopting a position just behind Brigid.

"What?" Brigid whispered back.

"Wherever you go, trouble follows," Domi teased.

Even in the diffuse light coming from the skylights, Brigid could see the glint of Domi's teeth as the feral girl smiled. Brigid smiled back.

"We better check things out," Brigid said. "Find out where the queen is in this…power blackout. I have a feeling we may not like the answer."

Domi agreed, nodding her head resignedly. The two Cerberus teammates had infiltrated too many places and seen too many things to believe that this was simple happenstance.

Seeing her chance, Queen Rosalind began to run, scampering away from the twin thrones as the lights of the palace flickered and died. The only light in the throne room now came from the imitation God Rod, a sparking upright line between the thrones as energy coruscated across its metal surface.

With alarming speed, Wertham reached out and grabbed her, snagging her flowing blue tresses and bringing her down to her knees with a whiplike gesture. Her capes spread around her as she crashed to the hard floor.

Queen Rosalind shrieked as Wertham dragged her up the few steps and back to the towering thrones. She could hardly keep up with him as he tugged her hair, kept slipping on the polished floor and dropping down to her knees. But he would not slow down.

"Let go of me, Wertham," the queen yelled. "What you're doing is insanity!" The queen's words echoed across the throne room.

Without slowing his pace, Wertham glared at her, revealing his teeth in a fearsome grin. "Isn't that what you said about me at the trial, Roz? Didn't you call me insane then?"

Wertham slung the queen back onto her throne as though discarding trash. He paced along the steps of the dais, eyes growing wider as he examined the empty throne of the king. It had changed since he had last seen it: the filigree was more delicate while the thrones themselves were more sturdy, larger and more imposing. Ceremony again.

"Wertham…" Roz pleaded again, but Wertham shot her a cruel look and she sank into silence, but only for a moment.

Ronald glided closer, bringing himself to a halt at the foot of the tiny flight of steps that led to the thrones.

Queen Rosalind lay sprawled in her seat, clutching at her scalp where Wertham had pulled her hair. She warily eyed the false God Rod that Wertham had put into the space vacated by King Jack's own device. The rod was glowing brightly, fluctuating with powerful energy. But to Rosalind's eyes, the energy spewing from the rod looked wrong. It was a darker color than King Jack's, full of purples, indigos and sickly yellows, like the changing colors of a bruise.

"What have you done?" Roz choked, barely able to say the words.

"*My* God Rod," Wertham said, settling into the king's throne. He looked uncomfortable, squirming there like a child. "I made it with all the little forgotten pieces that were left behind. Ronald helped me acquire them."

Roz shot a look at Ronald as he glided over in his hover chair. "Ronald? Is this true?"

"Nothing will change very much," Ronald told her. "Not for you. You'll still be queen, but the kingdom you oversee will be bigger—much, much bigger."

"What are you talking about?" the queen demanded, pulling herself up in her throne.

"Wertham had the idea," Ronald explained. He maneuvered his chair up the steps until he was in line with the thrones, sitting beside the queen. "We've spent our lives hidden in this rift, peeking out only to scavenge before we go running back to our little bolt-hole in the ether. That's Jack's fault, Your Highness."

"He's still your king," Rosalind reminded him.

"Not for much longer," Wertham said in a singsong voice as his hand played across the hilt of the silver God Rod. He closed his eyes, feeling the energies in flux and guiding them with his mind. He could see the hidden shapes, and he still remembered the four extra senses he had discovered that had granted him a fuller appreciation of the world.

"What are you planning to do?" Rosalind demanded.

"Two kingdoms, working in tandem," Ronald said as Wertham sank into a trance, communing with his God Rod. "One here, functioning as it always has, generating new uses for the old technology..."

"And one down there," Wertham interjected, pointing to the room's polished floor, "on the surface of the planet." Open, his eyes glowed with a sickly green luminescence, the force of the palace energies now running through him.

Rosalind gasped when she saw Wertham's eyes. "And what?" she spat out. "You'd rule them, you lunatic?"

"Not me," Wertham confirmed. "Not both, anyway. Ronald here will be taking Authentiville to new and greater heights. He's been doing the king's development work for the past three centuries anyway. And yet, Jack never repaired his ruined limbs."

"He couldn't," Roz began. "He tried but the neural pathways proved…"

Wertham hushed her with a look. "And me—I'll be down there among the old race, putting things together the way your precious, short-sighted husband should have done a thousand years ago when he had the chance. Instead of falling asleep at the tiller and squandering all our marvelous advances." Before Rosalind could say a word, Wertham held up a hand and corrected his statement. "All *my* marvelous advances," he growled.

Rosalind looked shocked. "You mean—to kill the surface people?"

Wertham shrugged. "We'll sort the wheat from the chaff," he said calmly, "and bring the old and short-lived human race up to scratch. They'll wear my face and live only to chant my name. Perhaps I'll train them to sing my name so loud that even you will hear it, out here in the cosmic rift."

Roz looked from one man to the other, unable to believe what she was hearing. It was a coup. "And which of you will be the king?" she asked, her voice taking on a taunting tone. "The madman or the cripple?"

Ronald lashed out, striking the queen across the face so hard that she sank down in her seat, horrified at what Ronald—trusted aide and advisor to the throne—had just done.

Wertham took her goading more calmly. "A kingdom for each of us," he said.

Roz wiped at her mouth, tasting blood there. "The people will never accept it. They love Jack."

"Jack will be dead inside of an hour," Wertham assured her. "The Gene-agers will see to that."

"No, you can't!" the queen shrieked.

Wertham looked at her, his eyes afire with that terrible green flame. "I control them now," he trilled. "They perform my will. I designed this system, remember? Ultimately, it answers to me."

"You can't," Rosalind repeated, sobbing.

Wertham ignored her. "And as for the people of Authentiville," he said, "they will accept it because we shall have a continuity of ruler. *You,* my dear Queen Rosalind, shall be at Ronald's side once we put things in motion."

Chapter 20

In the darkened regeneration baths, Kane detected movement to his side. He turned, bringing his empty fist up as a figure approached the king from out of the darkness.

It was one of the Gene-agers, back to life once more, with arms held out, hands open. Behind him, the two who had been holding the king's armor had also emerged from their mental coma, and they began to stride toward the king where he worked at the wall panel.

"It's all right, Kane," King Jack assured him. "These guys won't hurt you."

He was wrong. In the darkness, Kane and Grant saw the Gene-ager reach for and grab King Jack, pressing hands to his throat and squeezing. King Jack gagged, sinking to his knees as much in surprise as with the force of the sudden attack.

"Wh-what are y-you doing?" Jack choked. "Let…go of me. I am your…king."

The blank-eyed Gene-ager wasn't listening, or if he was, he didn't have any respect left for the aging monarch's authority. King Jack waved the God Rod uselessly, but it didn't affect the Gene-ager's stranglehold. His hands tightened around Jack's throat, squeezing tighter and tighter. They were hands grown in a vat, designed for the most arduous of manual labor. Each one could crush a walnut without straining. Jack felt the raw pain in his throat as his windpipe began to mangle, saw bright spots rush across his vision in the darkened room. "Hk…"

"Step away from the king," Kane ordered.

At the same moment, he heard Grant rumble a warning. "Kane."

Kane glanced back, saw more figures moving in the darkness. They were also Gene-agers and they were moving quickly, swarming across the walkways and dropping down from the overhead catwalks, converging on the point where Kane and Grant stood with the king by the wall. They ignored the other patrons of the baths, instead cutting a path to just one target—their king.

Without a second's hesitation, Kane locked his arm around the one who had grabbed King Jack and pulled from behind, using leverage to drag the man back. Surprised, the Gene-ager let go of the monarch and slid backward across the slick decking. Kane thrust his knee into place as he loosened his grip, tripping the Gene-ager so that he crashed down on the deck.

"It's impossible," King Jack muttered incredulously as he rubbed at his neck. "The God Rod's not working on the Gene-agers. Impossible."

While Kane was dealing with the first attacker, Grant had slipped on the electrochemical polymer lenses he carried in his duster, placing them like a pair of sunglasses over his eyes. The lenses drew on all available light and enhanced it, granting the wearer a form of night vision even in pitch darkness.

A blank-eyed figure—one of the two who had been assisting the king with his armor just minutes before—swept the empty armored glove at the king's face like a club. Still kneeling, Jack tried to duck back as it sailed at his head. The bulk of this strange makeshift weapon missed, but the metal fingers sheared across Jack's cheek, scoring three parallel lines where they struck. Moving fast, Grant grabbed the Gene-ager by the arm and yanked hard, dragging him back and down with all his prodigious strength.

Caught unaware, and solely focused on his assignment to assassinate the king, the Gene-ager staggered in place. Grant played the advantage, driving a fist into the creature's face like a hammer blow. The Gene-ager's nose caved in with an audible snap, and the dead-eyed man swayed in place.

To his credit, the Gene-ager tried to fight back. He drew the metal glove up again, raising it like a baseball bat and swinging it at Grant's head.

Grant sidestepped, turning his head as the golden glove swished past. Then he took a step closer to his foe and grabbed the front of the man's tunic with both hands, pulling him down and to the side. Wrong-footed, the servant-turned-killer caromed over Grant's shoulder and slammed to the floor with a crunch of bones.

Grant turned back, assessing his foe through the enhanced vision of the lenses. The Gene-ager wasn't moving and Grant figured him to be unconscious. There wasn't time to check—not with figures converging on them from all sides.

The other servant fared little better as Kane dropped low and pitched a sweeping kick in his direction, yanking his surprised foe off his feet as he reached for King Jack from behind.

"What's going on?" the king sputtered, struggling back to his feet. "The Gene-agers…?"

Kane pushed him back against the wall, reaching for his own polymer lenses and slipping them over the bridge of his nose. "Stay here," he said. In an instant, the once-dark room took on an eerie green glow, and moving figures came to life amid the long shadows. He could see, too, the bathers where they waited in the water or had pulled themselves up to the side. They looked confused but not yet frightened. They had no idea that their ruler had just been attacked.

"What do we have?" Kane asked Grant.

"Company," Grant said, eyeing the figures shambling through the darkness. "A lot of it. I count fifteen hostiles, heading this way and moving fast."

"They're converging," Kane confirmed as he saw the scene fully for the first time through the night lenses. As he spoke, he flinched the tendons of his right wrist, sending his hidden Sin Eater out of its holster and into the palm of his hand.

"Gentlemen?" King Jack pleaded. He stood by the wall, rubbing at his throat where the rogue Gene-ager had tried to choke him. "I can't see a darned thing!"

"We can. Your faithful servants just turned on you," Kane outlined briefly.

"What?" King Jack spit. "But that's impossible. The Gene-agers…"

"Not now, Your Highness," Kane instructed in a hiss.

Choosing his first target, Grant powered his own blaster into his hand, though he held off shooting as he watched the Gene-agers amass on the same level of the pool, approaching determinedly from all directions.

"Keep back," Grant commanded in an authoritative tone.

The figures kept coming. In a second, one materialized off to Jack's left. The figure was running at full tilt, brandishing a hunk of metal pipe as a kind of club. Probably an engineer or handyman, Kane guessed, skewering him in his sights.

The dull-eyed man swung his makeshift weapon at King Jack, who had the sense to duck as he saw the movement in the flickering light of his staff. The pipe slammed against the wall with a clang, but the Gene-ager was drawing it back immediately to attack again.

Kane snapped at his trigger, sending a short burst of 9 mm bullets at the servant's torso. The figure with the pipe staggered in place with the violent impacts before dancing into the wall a few inches from King Jack's head, much to the monarch's surprise.

"What's going on?" Jack asked, bewildered. "I ain't never seen the test tubers go nuts like this."

"My guess is something's controlling them," Kane told the

old man. "Based on the way they all turned on you together like this. They received some kind of command."

"That's impossible," Jack insisted. "Only the God Rod has the wherewithal to—"

"You have another of those things anywhere?" Kane demanded, cutting the man off. "A spare? In the palace maybe?"

"No," King Jack insisted. "One king—one rod. Why would I need another?"

"Then I don't think the other one was made with you in mind, Your Highness," Kane told him grimly.

Grant surveyed the open area of the pool, watching as more Gene-agers appeared from various doors and walkways, moving swiftly toward the Cerberus warriors.

"Kane…?" Grant said warningly.

"I see 'em," Kane said before turning back to the golden-armored figure of the king. "Your Highness, do you have a bodyguard?" Kane asked. "Maybe someone who might have been following us at a discreet distance to make sure you were safe?"

Jack shook his head heavily. "No, nothing like that. There's never been the need."

"That's a shame," Kane told him. "Because we could use someone like that right now who knows the lay of the land."

"We need to get out of here," Grant added. "It's too open. We can't protect you."

"Protect me?" King Jack sputtered.

"You're going to have to trust us, Your Highness," Kane said. "I think you're in real danger here."

As Kane spoke, another of the Gene-agers bolted for the king. Grant squeezed the trigger of the Sin Eater and sent a single round into the figure's leg, the sound of the recoil loud in the open space. The Gene-ager doubled over and sank to the floor, hands pressed to his ruined thigh.

Grant turned to Kane as the figure fell in the darkness. "So what now?"

Gun raised, Kane used his free hand to gently shove the king in the direction of the entry doors. "Apologies for the rough treatment, Your Highness," he said, "but we're a little rushed."

King Jack nodded. "Understood," he said, picking up his pace as they made their way to the doors of the colossal bathing room, hordes of deranged Gene-agers chasing silently after them.

Chapter 21

Domi and Brigid found themselves in a corridor of colossal proportions that, like the fountain area, had been plunged into darkness. The palace felt still and frightening in the darkness, unidentifiable sounds echoing from the distance, the low susurration of scared voices buzzing like nightmare insects.

Further along the enormous corridor, Brigid could just barely make out bewildered figures moving about or sitting on decorative benches and seats that had been placed at intervals along the walls.

"It looks as though it's affected the whole palace," Brigid said, peering down the corridor.

"Not just the palace," Domi stated as she padded over to a nearby window. "Look."

The window dwarfed Brigid and Domi, standing fully four times their height and constructed of huge panels of glass, each one big enough to pass a full-grown ox through. Brigid joined her companion at the window, peering through one of those enormous glass panels.

This section of the palace was quite high up, and it granted a clear vista of one section of Authentiville. It was hard to make out at first, with the ever-swirling lights of the "sky," but after a few seconds Brigid saw that no lights were showing in the golden spires of the city itself. "What's happened?" she asked, barely breathing the words.

Domi turned away from the window, her head whipping around as she sensed something behind them. "Brigid..."

Brigid turned at the warning, watching as the dark silhouette of the albino girl marched off into the shadows. A moment later, Domi was lost to sight—or she would have been had Brigid not plucked a pair of night lenses from her jacket pocket and secured them on the bridge of her nose. The lenses were of the same type used by Kane and Grant.

Through the night-vision lenses, Brigid saw Domi hurrying away down the darkened corridor, sticking close to the walls. Up ahead, four hulking figures were stalking toward them both. They looked humanoid, but their proportions were larger, like those of a gorilla. Each figure had the hairless head and blank features of a Gene-ager, but these were larger than the ones Brigid had seen in the dining room, as if primitively stretched. One of the hulking figures was carrying a woman over its shoulder; patently unconscious, the woman did not struggle.

Behind the hulking Gene-agers, more figures became visible within the darkness, but these were better dressed, clearly members of King Jack's royal court. They had their heads bowed and shuffled along, one after the other. Brigid recognized Betassa, the blond-haired woman who had been operating the Happening machine when the queen took her place among them. Betassa's white minidress looked rumpled, and her hair hung limply about her face as she bowed her head in supplication.

What's going on? Brigid wondered. Why aren't they fighting back?

But the answer struck her, even as she said it. No one did anything because they had rarely known violence in this city, and not for perhaps a thousand years. What guards existed here were for show, part of the pomp and ceremony that ancient kings were expected to have. If there was a response to violence of this sort, the court had forgotten it.

Behind the masking shades of her night lenses Brigid

was rolling her eyes. "A society with the survival instinct drummed out of it," she muttered. "Will wonders never cease?"

Brigid counted twenty courtiers in total and, straining to see, she noticed there was something glowing faintly around their necks.

"Join the line," the Gene-agers instructed in one voice. "Follow the group."

Domi, meanwhile, had slipped into the shadows between two chairs that had been backed against a wall, hunkering into herself as if to become a smaller target. Her keen eyes made out the figures, too, and she could smell the fear in the air.

It took Domi just a moment to guess what had happened. The palace had been somehow overrun by these Neanderthal brutes and they were placing everyone in custody for whatever cause they served. She watched as a figure farther down the corridor was added to the line of prisoners, a halolike band of energy placed around his neck by one of the bald-headed humanoids before being pushed to join the rear of the trudging line. The ring around his neck throbbed with light for a moment and Domi saw what seemed to be a spear of needle-thin energy spike into the back of the next prisoner in line, linking the two collars as effectively as a chain.

Brigid joined Domi, her movements silent in the darkness.

"I don't know what we've stumbled upon," Domi whispered, "but it doesn't look good."

"Agreed," Brigid said.

"But why aren't they fighting back?" Domi asked.

"The people here don't know how to fight," Brigid whispered. "It's unknown to them."

The Cerberus warriors watched the towering Gene-agers grab another courtier—this one a woman in emerald-green finery—and add her to the strange line of cowed prisoners.

Domi brushed her arm against Brigid to get her attention. "We have to do something," she said in a low voice.

Brigid wasn't so sure. "Domi, this isn't our world. It's not our fight. We don't know what the sides are, or the stakes."

Domi was busily removing her boots as Brigid spoke. "But we know wrong when we see it, Brigid," she insisted.

The albino woman had never been comfortable in any clothing that restrained her, and seeing her remove her boots like this felt to Brigid as if it was an obscure victory of "her" Domi over the one who desired to remain here.

Brigid reached down to the holster at her hip and pulled her blaster free. The TP-9 slipped from its holster with a faint swish of leather and then it was in Brigid's hand once more, a familiar weight in her grasp. Her left hand moved to check the safety without looking, while her eyes remained fixed on the strange line of prisoners and their guards who were marching down the corridor.

"You brought a blaster," Domi whispered. "Good move."

"Let's hope I live to appreciate it," Brigid said before standing up and striding to the center of the corridor, placing herself midway between the walls. She raised the blaster in a two-handed grip, pointing the muzzle at the line of prisoners and their captors. "Nobody move!"

IN THE DARKNESS of the bathing house, Kane, Grant and King Jack slipped from the magnificent pool room and out into the lobby. King Jack was bravely leading the way, the glow of his God Rod the only light by which he could see. Kane kept pace, while Grant brought up the rear, peering over his shoulder every few steps to warily eye the rogue Gene-agers tracking them.

"They're right behind us," Grant reminded the others.

As they entered the anteroom, where a sliver of rainbow sky winked through the parted doors at the far end, Kane reached forward and tugged at King Jack's cloak, pulling the man to a stop.

"What is it, Kane?" the golden monarch asked.

For a moment, Kane said nothing. Through the electrochemical polymer lenses, the lobby was as Kane remembered it, with towering columns and the single, barlike desk along one wall. But through the night-vision lenses, Kane could see two dozen Gene-agers striding back and forth, guarding the far door, inside and out. Until he had evidence to the contrary, Kane had to assume the entire slave caste had turned against the monarch—and that the God Rod was now powerless against them.

Sensing the presence of their ruler, the two artificial women at the desk spoke in near unison. "Did you enjoy your dip, Your Highness?"

Alerted by the sound, the Gene-agers peered up the length of the anteroom and began to stride menacingly along it, walking in step.

"You know any other way out?" Kane asked Jack, his voice an urgent whisper.

"What? Why?" Jack sputtered.

"Trouble, and a lot of it," Kane explained shortly. "Now— other exits? Yes or no?"

The old king thought for a moment, while behind them at the door into the bathing area, Grant pumped off a triple burst of fire.

"You want to hurry things up?" Grant hissed. "We have a lot of unpleasant company back here and they're gaining fast."

They were closing in the anteroom, too, Kane saw. He stroked the trigger of his Sin Eater, sending twin bullets at the nearest two figures as they strode closer and watched in grim satisfaction as the Gene-agers fell. But there were others to replace them—even as he watched, more of the dead-eyed servants came striding through the far doors of the anteroom from the streets beyond, blocking out that sliver of rainbow sky and the golden glow of the streets.

One of the genetically manipulated servants had reached King Jack by then, arms outstretched to grab him. The king stepped back, swinging the God Rod like a baseball bat. The blow struck his would-be attacker across the jaw, and the Gene-ager staggered back, rolling over the surface of the desk.

"The God Rod may not control them any longer," Jack said breathlessly, "but it's still good at keeping them in line."

"We have a lot of them to keep in line, Your Highness," Kane replied.

King Jack waved his glowing energy rod in the direction of the reception desk where his attacker had toppled. "This way," he instructed.

Kane snapped off a shot, downing another of the threatening figures in the darkness. Then he and Grant were following the monarch as he strode behind the desk. The twin silver figures at the desk turned to face their king, asking again about his dip, but the king ignored them, playing the God Rod over a panel directly behind them.

Through the polymer lenses, Kane watched as the panel slid back, revealing an access into the heart of the building. More Gene-agers were closing in on all sides—Kane estimated at least thirty swarming on this spot and another dozen approaching from the pool area. He placed himself back to back with Grant.

"Let's clear the field," Kane instructed.

Together, the Cerberus warriors blasted a stream of bullets at King Jack's approaching foes, turning together in a practiced clockwise rotation so as to send bullets in every direction. The brutal sound of 9 mm slugs ripping through vat-grown flesh and masonry thundered in the air, and the Cerberus men observed emotionlessly as swarming figures dropped all around them. It was not pleasant work but it was necessary—whoever had possessed the previously docile slave caste had murder in mind, and right now Kane and Grant were caught like rabbits in the headlights.

Close by, King Jack slipped into the access way and watched in horror as his makeshift protectors cleared the first wave of would-be assassins.

Kane raised his voice over the staccato sound of gunfire. "Let's get moving," he told Grant.

"On three," Grant agreed, using their age-old system.

A moment later, the two men were weaving through a flurry of attackers, their Sin Eaters still spitting bullets as figures leaped at them from all directions.

Jumping onto the reception desk, Grant kicked out and behind him, knocking back two Gene-ager servants as he dived for cover. Beside him, Kane bounded past the desk, slapping it with his palm as he swung the Sin Eater around to send another hail of bullets at their attackers.

With the shriek of bullets still echoing in the air, Kane and Grant disappeared through the access hatch and into the guts of the building. Jack passed his glowing God Rod over the access panel once more, and the metal plate slid back into place, hiding them from view. As the three of them disappeared, the high voices of the twin receptionists could be heard. "We hope to see you again soon, Your Highness."

THE THUGGISH GENE-AGERS stood perplexed as they stared down the barrel of Brigid's gun in the shadows. Light filtered through the windows from the rainbow swirl outside, but this whole section of the vast, highway-wide corridor was obscured by shadow. Behind them, the prisoners looked similarly bemused by Brigid's command that they not move.

Here was a hidden nation that had not seen a handgun, she realized, that had no frame of reference for the thing she was holding as a threat.

For a few seconds the confused Gene-agers looked from Brigid to one another, trying to work out what authority she had and how she thought the strange black item she held would help her. Then, as if they had independently settled on the same conclusion at the same time, the four brutish figures turned back to Brigid and shouted a single command.

"Join the line," they commanded. "Follow the group." Each colleague shouted the very same command a split second out of sync, creating a singing-in-the-round effect.

Being genetic constructs, it was plausible that they really had come to the same conclusion at approximately the same moment. That was the only way that Brigid could think to explain it.

Great, she chastised herself. You really thought this through!

Then the four brutish figures began to march down the corridor toward Brigid, their large strides eating up the forty feet of distance between them.

For a fraction of a second, Brigid wondered what to do. Should she shoot to wound? Fire a warning shot? Take one of these monsters out?

Caution won out. Brigid shifted her aim until it was above the heads of the approaching figures before squeezing the trigger and firing a single 9 mm bullet. The discharge sounded loud in the corridor, and the Gene-agers slowed momentarily as the blast went over their heads, ripping into the wall to their left in a burst of splintering wood. Then they started moving again, faster this time, charging what was left of the distance between themselves and their prey like a football scrimmage.

"Join the line," they said in imperfect unison. "Follow the group."

Brigid lowered her aim, centering herself as she targeted one of the two figures in the middle. Better to pick one of those off where the others could see and have it act as a warning.

Aiming for the central figure's legs, Brigid squeezed the TP-9's trigger and sent another bullet hurtling through the air. It struck the Gene-ager in the fleshy portion of his right hip, but Brigid felt little satisfaction as the false man flipped over himself and dropped to the floor.

Again, his colleagues slowed, but only for an instant. In that moment, Brigid saw the fallen Gene-ager roll back up to a standing position and begin charging at her as though nothing had happened. Her bullet had struck him—but whatever they were made of it was a lot stronger than human flesh.

Brigid stood in the path of the charging brutes, her finger steady on the trigger. Shooting them was not the answer—or at least, it offered no guarantees. Then what?

"Stay back!" Brigid cried.

Out of options, she blasted again. Her bullets sounded loud in her ears, and she heard several strike flesh with a familiar dull, wet sound.

And then the first of the monstrous figures was upon her, and Brigid felt the hard impact as he slammed against her. Her breath blurted out of her lungs in something between a cough and a growl, and Brigid skipped backward while the figure kept running, forcing her back.

Faster and faster Brigid scrambled as the Gene-ager drove her onward, unable to get her feet under her. The TP-9 blasted another shot into the air without her aiming, its thunderclap echo loud in Brigid's ears. Suddenly she struck something, slammed against it so hard that it gave, breaking with the impact of the two bodies.

The next thing Brigid knew, both she and her assailant were toppling out of a shattered high window of the palace, with the street a distant golden streak somewhere far below them.

Chapter 22

Kane and Grant followed King Jack as he led the way down a tight tunnel within the depths of the bathing house. The floor was pitched at an angle, sending the three of them deep below the surface. Kane wondered how deep they could go, knowing that the city resided atop a floating disc. The tunnel itself smelled of damp and metal polish, and there were pipes running along its ceiling and walls, with couplers and valves located at roughly every fifth step.

The tunnel was narrow, too, just four feet wide and barely seven feet in height. It seemed somehow more cramped after the endless wide expanses of corridors and rooms that defined the palace and the bathing house.

"You come down here often?" Kane quipped.

"Not for a few years," King Jack answered without turning to address at Kane. "Probably not since this place was built, now that I think about it."

"And when was that?" Grant asked. He was reloading his Sin Eater as the group jogged down the tunnel, slipping the dead clip into a pocket of his duster.

"Before you were born," Jack told him.

Having experienced the Ageless Pool, Kane and Grant realized how difficult it was to guess the king's age or that of the rest of the population of this incredible hidden realm. With their constant access to a Chalice of Rebirth, it was entirely plausible that these people were as close to immortal as any human could get. The question was not how long they would live, but rather when they had been born. What moments in history had Jack and his people witnessed? Been a part of, even?

After a couple of minutes, the cramped tunnel opened up into a huge unlit room that stretched back farther than anyone could see in the darkness. The room was cluttered with what looked like the early products of the Industrial Revolution. Great brass cooling towers and storage units dominated, reflecting the glow of Jack's rod as it played on their polished surfaces. A labyrinth of pipework ran across the ceiling, linking each containment unit and pumping materials between them. Clouds of vapor hung heavy in the air, and the walls were slick with condensation.

"What is this place?" Kane asked, but he could already guess. "Pump room?"

"Precisely so," Jack confirmed, motioning with his glowing rod, unaware of how his companions could see with their special lenses. "These units power and filter the pool water, regulating the chemical compounds and ensuring the Ageless Pools remain topped up and fully functioning."

His words echoed from the pipes, reverberating around the room in whispers long after the king had finished speaking.

Grant looked around warily, the nose of his Sin Eater poised before him. "And this place is unmanned?" he asked.

"Not usually," King Jack replied, a furrow of vexation showing on his aged brow. "I guess once the—whatever it was—*signal* was sent out, the assigned Gene-agers came topside to hunt for me."

"I'll check around," Grant said, slipping deeper into the shadows, "and make sure we don't have any nasty surprises waiting."

Kane remained with Jack, reloading his Sin Eater as they spoke. "So, you finally acknowledge that they've turned against you," he said, scanning the vast room.

"I'm not a fool, Kane," Jack chastised him. "An optimist, maybe, but never a fool. I just didn't want the Gene-agers to turn rogue like that. What would make them do such a thing?"

"Beats me," Kane said. "You said your God Rod controlled them?"

"Absolutely," Jack agreed with a nod of his head. "The rod works as an omni-key, operating the main systems of the city and accessing all minor functions through them."

"Like a kind of master program," Kane mused, slowly beginning to comprehend. "But you said you have the only one. The queen doesn't have one?"

The aging monarch shook his head. "Nobody but me," he said.

"And there's no possibility that someone could copy it? Clone it?" Kane asked.

"The technology involved is unique," Jack said. "It's a combination of Danaan harmonics and Annunaki organic channeling."

"But it can't be replicated?" Kane pressed.

Jack shook his head heavily. "The only man who was able to bind those two facets together like this was Wertham, and he's…well, he's no longer in the picture."

At that moment, Grant returned from scouting, the Sin Eater poised and ready in his hand. "You said you have a big slave population, chief." He checked King Jack as he materialized in the tiny circle of light cast by the God Rod.

Jack thought for a moment. "We employ various strands of Gene-agers to run municipal facilities like the pool, act as construction detail, work the transport system and…" He sighed. "I'd say there must be close to fifteen hundred active genetic servants, Grant, if that's what you're asking me."

"Different types?" Kane asked, seeking clarification.

"We grow them for specific roles," King Jack explained. "Some are more hardy than others—the repair workers who keep Authentiville afloat are able to survive in a vacuum, for example."

Kane raised his eyebrows and let out a low whistle. "Pretty tough."

"There's a real possibility that all of them have been reprogramed to hunt you down," Grant said. "All fifteen hundred of them."

While King Jack tried to comprehend this, Kane's mind raced back to something he had said a few moments earlier.

"You said one other guy could work your God Rod," Kane recalled. "Wertham?"

The king nodded his head heavily. "Wertham the Strange," he said with a sigh. "One of the most brilliant minds that the world has ever known. The man had what one can only call an instinct, a gift. He was able to look into the alien technology we discovered and create uses for it like no one before or since. Wertham helped design the system of filtration that the Ageless Pool operates on, so that we no longer had to rely on the fixed locations of the Chalices of Rebirth. That innovation changed our society."

"What happened to him?" Kane asked.

King Jack sighed heavily once again. "Wertham saw new ways to utilize alien technology, but his experiments took him beyond that. He was a close friend of mine and we would talk at length about his dreams. He wanted to tap into the aliens' way of thinking, to see things as they saw them. So he began to experiment with Annunaki foodstuffs, nutrition systems, medicines. He distilled them, imbibing sufficient quantities to alter his way of thinking."

"You mean he drugged himself?" Kane asked.

Jack nodded. "At first it was occasional and very controlled," he continued. "Wertham would use the effects of these alien proteins to, as he put it, *make his mind run sideways*. He once told me that we all have clockwork brains, and if we could only make the mechanism run backward we would be able to see the whole world in a new fashion."

"Alien narcotics," Grant grumbled. "Now I've heard it all."

"Wertham became fascinated by the things he saw," Jack told them. "Little wonder, given the things he told me about. And I suspect that those were merely the tip of the iceberg."

"What happened to him?" Kane asked. "Overdose?"

"No," Jack said. "Wertham's insights became muddled, dangerous. He began talking of invasion, of domination of the surface people. It was nonsense—we had already renounced arms after my son was killed. I would suffer no warmongering among my staff, not even talk of such.

"Wertham built something in secret," Jack continued solemnly. "A suit powered by will, which he believed could conquer the surface without any loss of human life. *Our* human life, that is. The surface people would die."

"But they're—we're—all the same, aren't we?" Kane asked.

"Yes," Jack said. "I started my life on the surface, as did many of the people here. Chance allowed us to create the Authentiville and everything you've seen here."

"But this Wertham guy," said Kane, "wanted to start a war with the rest of humanity."

"Just so," King Jack said gravely. "And some people even thought he had the right idea. 'We can expand beyond the rainbow horizon,' they said. 'We need never hide away our miracle technology.'"

"Why did you hide it, anyway?" asked Grant.

"In my heart, I'm a pacifist," Jack said. "I've always been one. Before this, I was a peaceful man. I tried to promote that message throughout the world.

"When I found my first crashed spaceship and all that was inside, it opened my eyes to a world I hadn't even imagined. But I realized how most men would employ it. Sooner or later, someone would see the military value in such technology and they would either use it or sell it to someone who would use it on his fellow man. I didn't want that to happen so I kept it to myself. And slowly I gathered like-minded individuals around me to help guard and protect it, to hide it from prying eyes. Hence—Authentiville."

Kane nodded in admiration. The old man was right, of course—given the opportunity, it didn't take long for humans to slip into tribes and start killing anyone who didn't belong. Hot-shot technology would only create an arms race—the kind of arms race that had resulted in the nukecaust that created the Deathlands.

"What about Wertham?" Kane prompted.

"We held a trial," Jack said, "where Wertham was given the opportunity to speak and to justify his actions. He was found wanting and was sentenced to incarceration. Wertham the Strange remains the only criminal in the entire history of Authentiville."

"What happened to him?"

"He was imprisoned."

"Where is he held?" Kane asked, a familiar feeling of dread pounding at the back of his mind.

"In a humane prison in the far east of the city," King Jack said. "The prison is genetically coded to his body. There is no possibility of escape."

Kane shook his head. "Respectfully, Your Majesty, if he's the only guy who can make a God Rod and it takes one of those to turn the Gene-agers against you, I'd conclude that that prison isn't as secure as you might believe."

King Jack scratched at his chin. "Wertham has been locked in there for seven centuries," he said. "Why would he come out now? Why like this?"

"Seven hundred years is a long time to nurse a grudge," Grant said dourly.

"And a long time to come up with a plan," Kane added ominously.

Chapter 23

"Radiation levels are pronounced in this area," Roy Cataman confirmed as he consulted his computer screen.

The party of four had reached the spot where Mariah and Domi first discovered the crash-landed lifeboat and had set up a minilab to run on-the-spot analyses.

"We can also detect a vapor trail running from this point to the north," Cataman continued, flicking the view on the laptop over to a diagrammatic representation of the area.

"Meaning?" Sela Sinclair asked. She was holding a Geiger counter with which she had been gathering readings while Cataman and Falk entered the data into their portable computers. Edwards sat nearby, keeping his eyes open for danger.

"In time, we'll put the story together and trace where all our colleagues have disappeared to," Cataman explained.

"How long will that take?" Sinclair asked.

Cataman looked thoughtful, his brow furrowing beneath his wild salt-and-pepper tangle of hair. "We require precision," he said, "which will take several hours. But for the immediate, I can confirm that someone's been activating an interphaser unit in this area. Or something very much like one."

"An interphaser?" Mariah and Sinclair said in surprised unison.

Though based on alien technology, the interphaser had

been developed by Lakesh and his team at the Cerberus redoubt. Indeed, it was something of a pet project of Lakesh's, designed to replace the mat-trans, which he had helped research back in the twentieth century. To learn that someone else was using that technology was nothing short of incredible.

Sinclair voiced the thought on both women's minds. "Is that even possible?"

Roy nodded slowly. "The chances of two entirely separate entities developing the same basic technological advance independently are not as rare as one might imagine," he said. "History is full of such coincidences. For instance, the television system that became popular was Marconi's, not John Logie Baird's."

"Even so," Mariah began, but Roy held up his hand to silence her.

"As I understand it," he said, "the interphaser accesses a system of nodes called parallax points. These points existed many centuries prior to Lakesh's involvement, evidence of their importance can be found over and over in the historical documentation. Furthermore, a section of the United States military was involved in triangulating and listing these specific locations in its Parallax Points Program.

"However," the wild-haired scientist continued, "what the information I have before me suggests is that an additional parallax point, if we may call it thus, is in residence above our heads, albeit some distance to the north of our current location."

Mariah looked relieved. "That would explain how Domi's kidnappers managed to appear in a clear sky without warning," she said. "And it would also explain how Kane and Grant's Mantas were apparently plucked out of the sky while we watched on the satellite feed."

Standing beside Mariah, Sela Sinclair had put the Geiger

counter down and was busy working the locks on the inter-phaser carrying case. A moment later, she had the pyramidal unit free and was setting it up on the ground. "If there is a parallax point above us," she said, "this should be able to access it in the database."

The three of them watched as the lights on the control console at the base of the interphaser blinked to life. The tiny screen flickered for a moment, showing a map of the area over which was laid a grid. The parallax point that they had used to reach here was a fixed yellow spot on-screen. The interphaser went through its protocols, searching the database for other nearby parallax points. For half a minute, the interphaser continued to scan, finding nothing of interest. The Cerberus group felt their tension rise until suddenly a second parallax point was identified.

"There it is," Sinclair cheered. "There's our point."

Cataman peered over his glasses, leaning a little closer to view the evidence before eyeballing the sky. "Two point three miles distant," he mused. "But that's the one."

"So, what do we do now?" Mariah asked, her eyes fixed on this imaginary marker in the sky. "Jump there?"

Cataman shook his head. "If we do that, Mariah, we run a risk of materializing two thousand feet above the ground with nothing to walk on."

"And...*splat!*" Mariah said, pulling a face.

"Splat, indeed," Cataman said sagely. "Let's speak to the ops room and see if they can survey the area with our eye in the sky."

"On it," Sinclair confirmed as she engaged her Commtact.

A few seconds later, Sinclair was having what appeared to be a one-sided conversation with empty air as the Cerberus operations center acceded to her request. "They're bringing the satellite around now," she told her companions.

Bitterroot Mountains, Montana

IN THE CERBERUS ops room, Brewster scanned the satellite image on his monitor, making his report with emotionless professionalism. "Clear sky, no indication of the parallax point the survey team identified," he said. "Switching to infrared—"

The image on-screen changed to a patchwork quilt of vibrant colors as it gave a map of the heat given off by the area. It revealed nothing of note.

"—to ultraviolet—"

Again the image changed, turning into a sea of gray tones of subtle gradations, the details bleeding into one another. Again, the new scan revealed nothing of note.

"—radio emissions," Brewster Philboyd continued, increasingly crestfallen.

Again, the on-screen image changed to one of simple black and white, as if the map had been redrawn with streaks of lightning. And again, it revealed nothing of note.

Philboyd turned to Lakesh sorrowfully. "Shall I continue, Dr. Singh?" he asked.

The disappointment in Lakesh's expression was palpable. He had been hoping for some clue to Domi's disappearance, and it was all his heart could take to see that hope dashed. "Try magnification," he told his assistant wanly. "Let's not give up yet."

Philboyd's fingers scurried across his keyboard and he manipulated the satellite image further. For now, however, it was clear that Domi and her fellow Cerberus field agents were well and truly lost.

Chapter 24

The street raced up from below, faster and faster as Brigid and the Gene-ager plummeted the last dozen feet toward the ground. There were people down there, and they had suddenly become aware of the shattered window and the two falling figures hurtling earthward—or whatever-ward it was, Brigid thought. They began to shout and scream, as if they were unwilling patrons at some circus act turned horribly wrong.

Brigid was still wearing the night-vision lenses, which made things somehow less real, picking out highlights in negative as they tried to make sense of the sudden change in light.

Suddenly, Brigid saw a white streak flash across the lenses, zipping across her vision like a bolt of lightning. A millisecond later, she felt something slap against her side, and she found herself spinning in midair as her assailant's body went hurtling down toward the ground and the unwilling spectators screamed louder.

"How heavy are you?" Domi asked, her voice close to Brigid's left ear, the sentence clipped and abbreviated the way Domi only spoke when she was under stress.

It took a couple of seconds for Brigid to take it all in, process it. The Gene-ager who had attacked her slammed against the golden strip of road with a crunch of breaking bones; people screamed before he hit and when he struck the pitch became higher, more fearful. At the same instant that Brigid's fall slowed, the rushing in her ears like the ocean in a storm, a road vehicle screamed to a halt before the bloody body of the Gene-ager, and people were shouting below her.

The blood was pounding in her ears like a drumbeat. Then Brigid was lifted up, away from the street, and she saw Domi's face smiling from beneath her, the pegasuit wings extended to either side of her shoulders like enhanced shoulder blades. Fully extended, the wings had a span of six feet in total, a foot more than the petite woman's height. And they groaned with the strain of carrying two human beings, designed as they were only to lift the weight of one.

Brigid was so overcome she could feel hot tears burning down her cheeks. "Just set us down," she said. "Just set us down."

"Am trying!" Domi insisted in a frantic shout. "Not easy." She was struggling to control the pegasuit with the extra weight, and the pair of them spun dizzily in the air, whirling dangerously close to the golden wall of the palace like a sycamore seed.

Below, the driver that had almost run down the Gene-ager was out of his vehicle and checking on the man who had dropped from the palace. A crowd had formed already, and some watched in horror as the two women above them slammed against the wall of the palace in a barely controlled fall.

Still clinging to Brigid, Domi extended her legs and kicked at the palace, running at a sideways angle as she tried to keep them from slamming into the wall again. Domi left dirty footprints across a window as she scrambled down the side, and Brigid struggled to make sense of anything in her addled brain.

People on the street reacted in shock, watching their dangerous path as the pair hurtled toward the sidewalk. The two women landed in a stumble, and Domi let go of Brigid, who continued in a near-run until she batted against the wall of the palace with outstretched hands. Brigid stood there, recovering her breath as she regained her wits. Domi was crouched on the sidewalk a few feet away, visibly shaken.

"You okay?" Brigid asked, pulling herself erect with the help of the wall.

"Think so," Domi responded. Her hand tapped something at her armored flank and the wings retracted back into a blister on her back. "Didn't expect that to be quite so…quick."

"It was almost a whole lot quicker," Brigid said with the trace of a smile. "Thanks."

Domi nodded, pushing herself up from the ground. "So, what now?"

Brigid checked her blaster, assuring herself it still had ammunition. "It looked to me as if the servants were taking over the palace," she said. "Why they'd do that is anyone's guess. But coupled with the power failure across the ville, I can't help but suspect there's something bad going on. Really, really bad."

As Brigid spoke, she noticed that Domi appeared suddenly distracted. "Something wrong?" Brigid asked.

Domi had heard something. It was faint and high-pitched, almost beyond human hearing. She had to strain to detect it at all, and even then it was more like an emotion than something solid. But before she could say anything, a fanfare of music blared across the streets of the royal square around the palace, reproduced via a hidden sound system that was located on every street corner.

The people around them were excited by the noise and turned to stare at a high window of the palace. Confused, Brigid and Domi turned, too. In a few seconds they saw a figure emerge, followed by two more, posing on a high balcony overlooking the town square. Brigid and Domi recognized two of them as Queen Rosalind and Ronald, the royal aide. The third stood between the two, holding his arms aloft as he urged the crowd to quiet. This man had a sunken, skeletal face and dark hair tinged with gray, and he was wearing a simple cotton shirt and pants of matching green.

"Who is that?" Brigid asked, but Domi just shook her head.

"Loyal subjects of Authentiville," the man said, his voice enhanced somehow via the sound system. "Let me welcome you to the dawn of a new era. An era where, at last, Authentiville shall expand beyond the limits of the floating city."

The crowd around Brigid and Domi sounded surprised and confused by the stranger's statement, and there was a sense of keen excitement running through them as people stopped to listen. Domi could still hear that buzzing, too—faint but there, like the distant whine of a jet engine. It irritated her as she tried to listen to the man's speech.

"For too long," the green-clad figure continued, "this city of miracles has been under the yoke of a short-sighted ruler, one who knew only fear and never bravery. It takes a brave ruler to see the future and not to shy away from it. I am that ruler—I, Wertham the Strange."

The crowd erupted at this, muttering the name as if they could barely believe it.

Wertham waited a few moments for the crowd to quieten before continuing. "Yes, *the Strange,*" he said. "That's what *he* called me—branded me—because my ideas were too radical for him, because I wished to embrace the future. *Your* future.

"The king is no more, and we must let the old regime die with him."

Murmurs of surprise and shock rumbled through the crowd, but they quieted as Wertham continued.

"Before this day is done, we will fire our first salvo at the surface dwellers," Wertham explained brashly, "in a sustained campaign to take back what is rightfully ours—to take control of Earth, once and for all."

The crowd watched in awe as Wertham held aloft a silver baton that glowed with energy, and Brigid heard several people around her repeat the same phrase.

"The God Rod. He has the God Rod."

Then Wertham spoke with a commanding shout. "The king is dead. Long live your God Emperor! Long live Wertham the First!"

All around the royal square, the crowd took up the chant, pumping their fists in the air, while vehicle drivers honked their horns and revved their engines. When she turned, Domi was staggered to see Brigid pumping her fist, too, and repeating the chant in time with the others.

"Long live the God Emperor! Long live Wertham the First!"

"WE CAN'T STAY here indefinitely," Grant told Kane with irritation as they skulked in the shadows of the bathing-room pump house. "We need a plan of action."

They were about twenty paces away from where King Jack was sitting, ostensibly running a patrol to ensure no one snuck up on them. Oblivious to their conversation, Jack had unscrewed the bottom part of the God Rod and was fiddling with the control dials hidden within.

"You're right," Kane agreed, surreptitiously peering over at where Jack was sitting. "Whatever's going on topside, someone wants the old man—either captured or dead."

Solemnly, Grant kept his voice to a whisper. "We can't fight a war for this guy, Kane, no matter how friendly he's been. There's two of us—four including Brigid and Domi if we can contact them—against over a thousand of those Gene-ager slaves. And that may just be the tip of the iceberg."

"Yeah," Kane agreed, "and it's the rest of the iceberg that's got me worried. From what he's said, Jack there has been grand poobah of this place since it was set up, hundreds—maybe thousands—of years ago. He's benevolent, despite the wealth of technology he has, and it's that benevolence that's kept his people in check."

Grant made a sour face. "What? You think if he's deposed then whoever takes over is going to turn more aggressive?"

"Someone's trying to kill the king," Kane reminded Grant. "Short odds they're not the peace-loving type."

Grant looked uncertain. "Royal coups aren't our business, Kane."

"Quite right," Kane said. "But if that instability threatens our people, then it becomes our business. We've seen truly miraculous things since we got here. Just think what would happen if that level of tech was turned against the human race. It'd be the Annunaki invasion all over again."

"Only these people *are* the human race," Grant reminded him.

"Yeah, but I don't think *they* see it that way," Kane said. "For all its advances, Authentiville is an insular society. They've lived out here, hidden in the quantum interference between worlds, without showing any interest in human affairs. Doesn't take much for that kind of society to turn from insular to protective to warlike. I don't think we can take that risk, not from what Jack's said. Just follow my lead."

Grant nodded solemnly in agreement and paced across the pipe-filled room with Kane to where Jack waited.

"WELL, THAT ALL went rather well, I feel," Wertham said as he strode through the doors from the royal balcony. "I could perhaps use a cape, though."

Ronald followed, ushering a miserable-looking Queen Rosalind into a richly appointed parlor full of statuary constructed of now-flickering light.

"You're delusional," Queen Rosalind snarled, her eyes narrowed in fury. "They won't fall for this."

Wertham turned on her with a look of glee on his sunken features. "They already have, Roz, my dear," he snapped. "Can't you hear them chanting?" He cupped one hand theatrically to his ear, turning in the direction of the open balcony doors.

"It's a trick," Rosalind stated flatly. "My people may have fallen for it for a moment, but they'll wise up soon enough."

Wertham glared at her, the imitation God Rod glowing wildly in his hand. "*Your* people? *Your* people?" he roared. "They're mine now. The God Rod assures that."

"You're not the only one with…" Rosalind began.

"Wrong!" Wertham bellowed, silencing her. "Jack's not coming back. Like I told *my* people out there—the king is dead. I am their emperor and their god now. Me, Wertham the First!"

OUTSIDE, THE CROWD was still chanting, hyped up with excitement at Wertham's speech. They welcomed this new ruler in a way that was both immediate and fanatical. Domi could hardly make sense of it, and she equated the sense of sudden adoration with falling in love—or lust—in a fraction of a second, deep feelings emerging from nowhere.

Standing beside her, Brigid was cheering, too, applauding the speech and repeating, "Long live the God Emperor!" over and over.

"Brigid?" Domi prompted.

Her red-haired ally seemed baffled for a moment by Domi's attention, and Domi saw her blink several times in quick succession as if to clear her head.

"Where—?" Brigid muttered. "What happened?"

"You were caught up in…something," Domi explained. Then she grabbed one of Brigid's hands and pulled her through the cheering crowd. "Come on, it's too cramped here. Makes me nervy."

Brigid shook her head with confusion as they wended through the crowd, slipping the TP-9 semiautomatic back into its holster for safekeeping. All around, people were beginning to resume their lives, returning to whatever they had been doing before Wertham demanded their attention.

Brigid and Domi crossed the street between vehicles, with Domi still leading the way. The albino warrior drew Brigid into a narrow street that looked out on the palace.

"You okay now?" Domi asked.

Brigid nodded uncertainly. "It's strange," she said. "I can see the Happening, the room of fountains, the struggle in the palace corridor and how I went through the window. I can see you catching me as I fell. I can remember everything up to a few minutes ago, then it suddenly becomes…well, *weird* in my mind."

This was serious, Domi realized. She had known Brigid Baptiste from the earliest days of the Cerberus operation, and she was very much aware that the woman had an eidetic memory, which meant she forgot nothing. Or, at least, that's the way it *should* have been.

"Do you remember what that nut ball on the balcony said?" Domi asked.

"The man in green? Yes, every word," Brigid explained. "But there's something else there, too, it's as though he spoke from a gigantic light, almost like I was looking into the sun. It doesn't feel as if it's a part of my experience, more like something I saw in a drama or read in a book. Does that make sense?"

"Not really," Domi told her. But already the albino girl's mind was turning, recalling something she had noticed just before the speech started. There was a sound, Domi recalled—that strange, almost subconscious buzzing she had detected at the very upper limit of her hearing just before the royal fanfare had played through the hidden sound system. "Did you hear a kind of buzz?" Domi asked excitedly. "Before that guy started speaking?"

Brigid's brow furrowed as she tried to recall. "No, nothing."

"I heard something," Domi explained. "I don't know what it was. It was barely there, just a high-pitched note."

"Like an insect's wings?" Brigid asked. Already she was coming up with a theory.

"Kind of," Domi said. "But more—I dunno—musical, maybe? Like a note being played."

Eyeing the dispersing crowd, Brigid suddenly recognized the mania that they had all been caught up in. All except Domi, that is, with her own special set of skills. Brigid felt it, too, could still feel it, gnawing at the back of her skull. There was something in the words, then. No, not the words—but the relay system through which they had been delivered. Something that triggered a sense of euphoria in the listeners' brains.

"Subliminal conditioning," Brigid said. "Hypnosis. Something like that anyhow."

"What? You think that this Wertham guy was trying to hypnotize you?" Domi asked.

"Not just me," Brigid reasoned. "Everyone. Everyone in that crowd. Maybe even everyone in the whole of Authentiville. The sound you detected was some kind of signal aimed directly into the brain, designed to make Wertham's speech seem more palatable. Perhaps even something more than that."

Domi's face scrunched up in annoyance. "Then why were you affected but I wasn't?"

"Domi," Brigid began, "and I say this with the utmost respect and love—you are not exactly a normal or average example of the human condition."

Domi rankled at this, but Brigid continued.

"You perceive the world in a way that few of us will ever be able to define, let alone comprehend," Brigid said. "You're closer to the environment around you than anyone I've ever met. If something's out of place, you'd notice, even if you can't say quite what it is."

Mollified, Domi flicked a glance back to the street and the towering structure of the palace. "Something's out of place, all right," she said. "Did you notice Queen Rosalind up there with the speech man?"

"Yes, and the king's not come back," Brigid stated. "Wertham said he was dead."

"Yeah." Domi nodded. "And Grant and Kane are with him. Which means they may be dead, too—doesn't it?"

Chapter 25

"We can't stay here forever, Your Highness," Kane began. "Sooner or later, those folks out there are going to figure where you went and work out a way to open that door. Once that happens…"

Still studying his golden baton in the darkness of the pump room, King Jack nodded sadly. "You're right," he said. "Of course you're right."

"You said there was someone," Kane recalled. "Guy by the name of Wertham. Troublemaker, maybe."

Jack nodded. "It began when I lost my son," he said. "I became reckless. Part of me sought revenge for what had happened to him."

"What happened?" Grant asked.

Jack looked up at the two Cerberus warriors for the first time, and they could see the sadness in his eyes. "My son, Neal, was a brave lad," Jack said. "He had an explorer's heart—he was like me in that respect. He was born here, in Authentiville, but he craved experience. He wanted to see more than these walls could offer him.

"He wasn't alone in that, I should add. It's just…" The old king sighed.

Kane picked up the sentence for him. "Not all of them were your son."

"Precisely," Jack said, gravely nodding. "It's selfish, isn't it? But I suppose that's how humans are.

"Like a lot of those born here, my son went on scouting

missions as soon as he was old enough," Jack continued, "returning to the surface to search for lost artifacts from alien visitors. There was a war at that time, an ongoing and bloody conflict over territory and belief. They called it the Crusades, kings and noblemen sending armies across continents to annex lands that held cultural significance for their worldview."

Kane knew something of the Crusades. They were campaigns during the eleventh, twelfth and thirteenth centuries by Europeans, blessed by the Pope, to regain access to the so-called holy places spoken of in the Christian Bible, such as Jerusalem. Great armies of Roman Catholics were combined in this endeavor, from England, France and Germany, motivated by a fear that the Holy Land would become overrun by the enemies of Christianity. The Crusades were characterized by bloody skirmishes, and the campaigns lasted over two hundred years under various rulers with various specific aims. Perhaps the most iconic figures of the age were the armored knights who made up a small proportion of Richard the Lionheart's army during the Third Crusade in 1189.

Though limited, Kane's knowledge gave him an indication of how old Jack's story was, and how long ago it had been since he lost his son. Had Brigid been here, Kane lamented, she would no doubt have had all the facts at hand.

"This war—or wars," Jack continued, "concerned a number of so-called sacred objects. The true nature of these items was often rather different from the stories told about them—many were legacy items left over from alien incursions onto the planet Earth. The attraction for our scouts was enormous.

"Neal went to join the crusade in a place called Acre, on Haifa Bay," the king recalled.

Acre, Haifa Bay, August 1191

THE STARMAN'S ARMOR had lost none of its luster, thought James Henry as he watched him stave off another wave of the local militia. The familiar clang of meeting swords echoed through the afternoon stillness, the heat of the day mixing with the heat of battle and turning the city of Acre into a bloody mess of the wounded and the dead. The Lionheart's forces had finally gained entry into the city for the first time in many months, and here they fought with the local army while women and children cowered behind locked doors.

It had been a year and a half since James had discovered the starman on that portentous night and incorporated him into the pilgrimage. They were the Faithful of Saint Peter and they had traveled far to regain entry to the holy places, an access that had been denied them for so many years by Saladin's forces. They had come a long way from England's green fields, and the Germans and the French, too.

Where the starman came from, no one really understood but he had sworn the *votus* before the king himself and taken the cloth *crux* to show his allegiance to their righteous cause. In their quieter moments, the starman had admitted he understood little of the army's godly calling, and had joined them "to experience," whatever that meant. Whatever it did, the starman fought like a force of nature, his heavy blade whirring in the air like a streak of lightning before hacking into the enemy with deadly precision. The enemy fought like demons, dressed in pretty-colored rags, but rags all the same.

The starman struck another down with his sicklelike sword, slicing the man open from chest to groin in a brutal downward sweep of the heavy blade. Gold-tinted green, the blade, like the man's armor, showed no signs of wear, despite the battles it had fought, the corpses it had created. The starman turned as the horde of enemies surrounded him, turning his blade in a two-handed grip before driving it through the chest of the bearded figure sneaking up behind him. He struck with a measured patience, his gaze fixed on the distance, shrugging off the blows of his attackers until he could reach and repel them.

James, too, was fighting, using his own sword to meet the curved blade of a lieutenant in Saladin's army, a man with a bald head and wide streaks of gray in his ringlets of beard. Despite his gray beard, the lieutenant fought with the vigor of a man half his age, parrying every thrust James sent, driving the crusader back toward Acre's walls. They were inside the city and the sand-colored walls were spattered with red streaks where warriors clashed, turning the place into a bloody painting.

The starman's blade swung in an arc of gold, slicing two foes in one move, cutting the first clean through the torso before meeting with the hips of his companion. The first slumped to the ground screaming, his body split into two parts, blood painting the area where it fell. The second man, a kerchief over his face and a hood pulled low over his hair, shouted a curse as the sword was pulled from his hip. He buckled to the ground as the damaged leg gave way.

The starman moved on, jabbing behind with his sword's pommel and striking another foe's forehead with such force that it left an indentation in the skull.

The enemy were swarming on the starman, babbling over and over in their own tongue, "The hunter in gold! The hunter in gold!"

Nearby, other Europeans had entered the city. The army was made up of soldiers and knights, and waves of them had fallen to the enemy's arrows while others were even now being beaten back by sword and mace.

The local soldiers came at the Europeans with all manner

of weapons, holding the line as the intruders tried to move forward.

Something had been set alight close to the city gates, producing a line of flames across the street like a barricade. Knights and horses charged on, while soldiers tried to smother the flames with blankets.

James Henry pivoted on his left foot, shifting his weight and bringing himself back, causing his attacker to overreach. The Muslim lunged with his blade, driving it past Henry and almost tripping over his own feet as the weapon struck the wall.

Henry stepped into the space left by his enemy's feeble attack, stabbing his own blade forward in a horizontal thrust that split the man's torso between his ribs. The local staggered back, his body cinched to the end of the holy knight's blade, and James watched grimly as blood bubbled between the man's yellowed teeth. Then he drew his sword from the man, kicking out with one armored leg to force the enemy away. The Muslim soldier fell back, collapsing to the dusty ground, free hand gripped around his ruined chest as his blood flowed across the soil.

From behind him, Henry heard a yelp of surprise, and he turned immediately, trusting the fallen Muslim to die. What he saw chilled his heart. The starman was caught up in what appeared to be a fishing net, and when Henry scanned above him he saw men and women on the roofs of the buildings, smiling grimly at their catch. The net was weighted at its edges. Two of their own number were caught in the net, as well, one man half sticking out from the side closest to James, arms and head beyond the reach of the weave, the heavy netting having forced him to the ground.

The starman was on his knees, unable to hold himself upright beneath the weight of the net. His golden armor shone through the holes in the net, glowing like a pillar of angelic fire.

"He's down!" Henry cried, scanning for his compatriots where they fought in the city streets. "The starman's down!" He ran even as he shouted the words, scrambling across a road decorated with a half-dozen corpses, his sword trailing low to his body.

Three locals turned to face James, blocking his path with weapons at the ready. Two of the locals held curved scimitars while a third had some kind of twin-headed axe, its head better suited to cutting firewood than doing battle. All three men were dressed in dark colors, two blue and the third in robes of green and black.

Without slowing, James Henry brought his sword up in a punishing arc, hacking through the jaw of the axe-wielder. The man's face erupted in a fracture of blood, teeth flying in all directions and he stumbled back.

Henry leaped over the falling figure, bringing his broadsword around to face his next target, the scimitar man dressed in green and black. Curved blade clashed with straight as the two met, the local spitting some curse in his own tongue at the Englishman. Henry said nothing, shoving with all his might against his foe's curved scimitar and forcing him to give ground.

The other guard—the one in indigo robes—saw his chance and leaped at Henry as he clashed with his ally. The first blow struck James Henry across the left shoulder and his armor gave off a shower of brilliant sparks.

Henry grunted with annoyance, his own attack marginalized as he was forced to give ground. His sword was still locked with the first man's scimitar, so he stepped back, hooking his sword with a flourish that wrong-footed and disarmed his foe.

The weaponless figure staggered, shouting something at

the crusader and reaching into his billowing green robes to produce a short dirk whose razor-sharp blade glinted in the sunlight.

James Henry spun, whipping his sword up to meet with another man's scimitar as it hooked through the air for his head. He met the blade low on his own, deflecting the strike with a blow so powerful that both men felt it shake their bones.

The other came at him with the dirk, and Henry lashed at him with his free hand, weakening the power he could give to his sword strikes for a moment as he backhanded the man. The fool went down in a billowing flurry of green-and-black robes like the unlatching of a mainsail.

Henry's allies were appearing now, two armored knights along with several modestly dressed footmen. Several swarmed onto the fallen figure with the dirk, driving him back to the ground before he could stand, beating at him with fists, feet and blades.

"Our...star," James Henry instructed as he fenced away another low swipe from the scimitar. The words came hard, breathless. He could only hope that his meaning was clear.

Then the scimitar clanged against Henry's armor, high on the shoulder, and he felt a bite at his neck. His dark-clad foe was sneering as he stepped back, eyes fixed on the foreigner invader's throat.

In that moment, everything seemed to stop. Even the sounds of battle became distant. Henry stopped, too, feeling for his neck with his open palm. It was wet with sweat, the same way it always was in this abominable climate. But when he pulled his hand away he saw the redness on it, and when he turned he saw the same red running down his armored sleeve in a double line.

The man with the scimitar barreled at Henry again, knocking into him with his head held low to his shoulders and throwing the two of them back. Henry slammed against the ground with his attacker atop him, felt the weight slip from his hand as he let go of his sword.

Above him, the local devil held his curved blade aloft and shouted something in his own language before bringing the blade back down in a cruel arc. Henry turned away from the blade as it came down at his head, and in that moment he saw the starman had been lifted in the netting, up off the street. Still in the netting, he hung a few feet from the lip of the rooftop along with one of the enemy, his golden armor shining brightly within those crisscrossed lines, his trapped foe dead. He looked like a snared angel.

A moment later, the knife hit James Henry in the forehead and his vision fractured into a wall of red and black. He would not be going home, would not see England's green fields ever again, and that was something that, had he lived, he would always have regretted.

SALADIN'S ENEMIES HAD respect enough to consider him a military mastermind, despite their different beliefs. Whether that was true or not, Saladin could not say. But he was smart enough to appreciate that he had surrounded himself with fanatics, and fanatics tended toward narrow-mindedness.

"We have a chance to kill the hunter in gold, their false savior," one of said fanatics told Saladin as the sultan sat in his planning room with his generals, pouring over a map of Haifa Bay.

The map was scored with marks where strategies had been proposed and discarded. The foreign armies had been knocking at their door for close to two years, and Saladin was beginning to wonder if redrawing the map would be easier than losing yet more of his troops to the knights who led their charges. Frankly, it was getting hard to tell which side had the most fanatics.

Saladin's fanatic, a soldier charged with guarding Acre,

was dressed in loose brown robes wrapped in layers around his body, with a kerchief that could be pulled up over his mouth and nostrils should the wind pick up and throw sand in the air. "The one who wears armor made of purest sunlight," the fanatic said with typical wide-eyed excitement. He smelled of sweat, even from here, bringing the reek of a soldier's existence into these perfumed quarters where incense had been so carefully employed to mask the stink.

Saladin, middle-aged and feeling the weight of years and rich food, repressed a sigh and repeated what the lackey had said in a tone of disdain. "'Armor of purest sunlight'?" He stroked thoughtfully at his long, thick beard. The beard seemed to be more gray each time he looked in a mirror; so much so, he wondered if he should invest some of the wealth that being sultan of Egypt and Syria had granted him in a better class of mirror. "You make it sound as though this warrior was being bathed in the light of Allah himself."

"He fought as though he was," the lackey said, spitting on the floor to emphasize his point. "Killed fourteen of my men, two of my own brothers."

Saladin didn't bother to repress his sigh that time. He appreciated that these fanatics could get so very worked up, but it was beyond the pale when they started to be unhygienic merely to add emphasis to a statement. Where had all that started, anyway?

"We stopped him," the fanatic continued without noticing his commander's disgust. "Netted him like a fish. He struggles but he cannot get free."

"And does this glorious sun-clad warrior have a name?" Saladin asked.

"Better than that," the fanatic said, his smile revealing crooked front teeth, one of which was missing entirely. "He has a grave waiting. By your command, of course."

Saladin rolled his eyes, repressing a sigh. "Of course."

SALADIN TOOK NO pleasure in overseeing the execution of the man in the golden armor. The captive looked young, and he was handsome in his way, with sun-bronzed skin and a chestnut beard. But his skin and his beard and his armor were all marred with blood, and there was a black stain across the fantastic armor where it had been burned.

However, it was his eyes that drew Saladin's attention. They were like an animal's eyes now, the wild look of someone who was losing more blood than a man could endure. He was tied by the wrists to a post in the courtyard, and he had been forced—or perhaps had chosen—to stand as the sun set over the walls of the fort.

Saladin stood close and pitched his voice at a low level. "What did they do to you?" he asked with genuine concern.

"Everything," the prisoner replied. He spoke with an accent, though he had mastered their tongue. "They're afraid of me."

"Yes," Saladin agreed. "Already you have become a figure of mythology—the hunter in gold."

The enemy looked at Saladin with fierce defiance in his eyes. "You're making a huge miscalculation," he said. "If you kill me—if you are able—more will come, and they will wipe you from the face of the earth."

Feet together, Saladin bowed respectfully to the hunter in gold, little more than the slightest nod of his turbaned head. "I have heard such threats before," he said, "and have no doubt I shall hear them again. If I do not—if you are right—then perhaps we shall meet again on another battlefield and laugh at how foolish I must have seemed at this moment to you."

The hunter in gold looked defiant. "Perhaps."

"You have suffered enough," Saladin told him. "Death is never kind, but it can be quick. I will insist upon that."

"You will try," the starman said. "But your men will fail.

They cannot remove my armor. It's genetically tuned to my skin, there's no way for you to release me from it."

Wearily, Saladin shook his head. "Then you make it hard on yourself," he said regretfully. "Tell me, hunter in gold—what do your people call you?"

"Some call me starman," the prisoner replied. "My father named me Neal."

Saying nothing, Saladin bowed respectfully before turning away from the prisoner. What he told his lieutenants and what they chose to do, with the eyes of the fanatics watching, were two different things. But war makes monsters of the most humble of men sometimes.

Authentiville, Cosmic Rift

"WHEN NEAL'S REPORTS ceased entirely, I took a scouting party planet-side. When we found him, my son was in pieces," King Jack finished sorrowfully. "Unable to remove his armor, those animals had starved him and let him die under the heat of the sun. They had pulled apart his dried body using horses, one tied to each limb while his body was nailed to the spot."

Grant swallowed hard while Kane let out an audible gasp.

"I can only hope he was dead by then," the old king said. "To think otherwise… Well, who can contemplate such a thing about their own child?"

Jack took a deep breath before continuing, and it was clear he was visibly shaken. "I wanted to bury him, but parts of his body were missing," he said. "*They* had taken them—perhaps as trophies. Damned surface men. When I realized, I admit I lost my perspective."

Kane nodded. "Understandable. We're both sorry for your bereavement."

Jack thanked the man. "Wertham had been my trusted engineer for almost as long as the Authentiville concept had existed," he explained. "In Neal's death, he saw justification to push his exploration of the uses of the materiel we had discovered. And I didn't stop him. He believed—perhaps correctly—that the surface people we had left behind were jealous of what we had, and that they would one day come to take it from us. I should have stopped him sooner, but a part of me wanted vengeance on those who had murdered my son."

"What did Wertham do?" Kane asked gently.

"His experiments had taken him in so many different directions," the monarch in gold replied. "Where my son explored the world, Wertham chose to explore the plane of thought. He used combinations of alien nutrients to force his mind wide-open. When he came back from that vision quest, he had ideas for a thousand devices, each one almost beyond description. But there was one such device that he called the World Armor—a Target Invasion, Total Annihilation and Negation suit."

"What did it do?" asked Kane.

"Exactly what it says," King Jack said grimly. "The suit is worked by a remote operator and dropped in hostile territory. It sets a target to invade and proceeds to annihilate everything in its path."

"Sounds like a nuclear bomb," Grant muttered, and Kane nodded.

"You said this thing was built?" Kane confirmed.

"Built, yes, but never launched," King Jack replied. "At least, not to date."

"Yeah," Kane said. "That's what I was afraid of."

Chapter 26

"I still want to obey him," Brigid said, rubbing at her temples. She and Domi were prowling the street close to the palace. The citizens of Authentiville paid them no attention, going almost trancelike about their business, as if nothing had changed.

"Think past it," Domi said, snarling like a wolf. "We need to stop this…pretend-king man."

"Yes, we do," Brigid agreed, eyeing the palace entrance. It was dark there, like the alleyway where they had hidden, all power shut down. Brigid's brow furrowed. "Why would he do that?" she asked, speaking to herself.

"What?" Domi queried.

"The power," Brigid said. "The first thing Wertham did was shut down the power. Why would he do that?"

Domi shrugged. "Put people in the dark? Unsettle them?"

"Maybe," Brigid said. "Or maybe he didn't shut down the power. Maybe he diverted it for something."

"Like what?" Domi asked.

"The only way to find out the answer to that is to speak to Wertham himself," Brigid proposed. "Which means we need to get back in the palace."

"No problem, right?"

"Right."

Together, the two women slipped inside the towering doorway of the enormous building.

It was unguarded. Within, everything was dark. Echoes

drifted to them from the distance, filtering through the vast palace corridors and creating a sense of tension.

They were in the reception room where Brigid, Kane and Grant had admired the magnificent statues. Like the rest of the palace, it had been plunged into shadow, turning its towering guardians into ominous giants, not quite alive but still too close for comfort, as if they might come to life at any moment. Domi eyed them warily while Brigid replaced the night lenses on the bridge of her nose. For Brigid, the lobby came into stark contrast once more, as if someone had switched on the lights.

"It's clear," Brigid said, stepping into the room. "We're all alone."

Domi nodded, and Brigid watched as she reached around and opened a pouch along the armor's seam at the small of her back, pulling out a familiar item. It was the Detonics Combat Master that had become Domi's signature weapon. The albino girl checked the clip before flipping off the safety.

"Where now?" she asked.

"The royal court, I guess…" Brigid proposed uncertainly.

Together, the two women strode through the reception room, alert to any danger. Before they had gotten halfway, the distinct sound of raised voices filtered through the air toward them. Someone was shouting.

"WHY DID THEY listen to you?" Rosalind demanded.

Wertham pounded through the golden palace like a hurricane, with Ronald and Queen Rosalind following in his wake.

"Why would Jack's people do that?" the queen pressed.

Wertham turned on her, and she saw that his face was drawn in a cruel mask of concentration. "He who controls the God Rod controls the world," he snapped. "Did you never realize that, Rosalind dear? That that was the source of your husband's popularity?"

"No!" the queen insisted. "Jack's a good man. His people would not turn like this. You did something…"

"Yes!" Wertham screamed. "I fixed everything, repaired the stagnant mess this city has been left in. We should have been kings of Earth, not cowering here in this quantum cupboard, afraid to show our faces to the very people we left behind."

"No good comes of war," Roz said, struggling to keep up with Wertham's furious pace.

"*All* good comes of war," Wertham bellowed. "Everything you see here, everything in this whole wonderful city, is the by-product of war, Roz. Don't you realize that? Does it take my Devil Rod to make you see how much Jack has been holding us all back?"

"Devil Rod…?" Roz repeated fearfully.

Wertham waved his silver-shelled replacement God Rod before her face. "This!" he yelled. "The Domination Executive, Vanquish and Immobilisation Link—a God Rod to override everything Jack's can do.

"I designed his. Improving upon it was no trouble, although finding parts while trapped in that prison wasn't easy. Still, I wasn't going anywhere, was I? I could take my time getting it right."

They had reached the end of the corridor. Wertham turned back to Ronald, handing him the Devil Rod. "Take care of this," he said. "You'll need it…Your Majesty."

Ronald took the baton, and for a moment he was staring into its depths, transfixed by the coruscating energies that endlessly played across its surface in the colors of a bruise. "Wertham," he said, thanking the man with a nod.

"We all have our roles to play," Wertham told him. "Remember that."

Then, Wertham strode away, hurrying down a side corridor.

"Where is he going now?" Rosalind asked as she watched Wertham retreat from view.

"Where do you think?" Ronald taunted, slipping the Devil Rod into a recess of his motion chair. "He promised the people a war."

Rosalind gasped as realization began to dawn. "He wouldn't…"

Ronald gestured to one of the nearby windows. "Look," he said.

The high window gave an enviable view of the city, plunged now into darkness by the power drain. The blue-haired queen scanned the view, searching for the thing she dreaded, but she hardly needed to strain. In the darkness, the glow of the Doom Furnace was even more pronounced. It sat at the center of Authentiville like an underground stream of lava, its brilliance lighting the buildings around it in a warm glow.

"He's relit the Doom Furnace," Rosalind said. "But how…?"

"The war machine trundles on," Ronald told her, "consuming everything in its path. But don't worry—we'll have power back soon enough."

Queen Rosalind realized then what it was that Wertham had done. When he had taken command of the palace, setting his false God Rod—or Devil Rod—in place, he had channeled all the power of the city to the Doom Furnace. No wonder the streets were dark and the palace lights flickered.

Roz turned from the window. "You don't need to do this, Ronald," she said. "We would forgive you."

"I don't want your forgiveness," Ronald retorted. "I want your love. Did you never realize that?"

Roz shook her head. "That's impossible," she said. "Don't you see?"

Ronald grabbed her by the wrist and sent power to the

motion chair's mechanisms, hurrying back down the corridor toward the throne room, dragging the queen behind him. "Tunes change," he told her, "in time."

BRIGID AND DOMI watched the scene play out from a doorway recess, hidden by the long shadows that now dominated the palace. They had been drawn by the sound of the raised voices, and Domi had found a quick route here, utilizing the pegasuit's wings to glide the two of them through vast stretches of now-abandoned corridors.

"I'll stay on Wertham," Brigid whispered as the man in green stormed off. "You see if you can get that Devil Rod away from Ronald."

In response, Domi flashed a smile at her partner. There was no warmth in that smile.

The corridors of the palace were of colossal proportions, stretching through its depths like train tunnels. The darkness played to the advantage of the Cerberus women now, allowing them to move quite freely and to, by and large, hide in plain sight.

Brigid had no idea where she was. Having an eidetic memory could not magically conjure up the floor plans to the palace or give her the foresight to guess where it was Wertham was leading her. All she could do was follow and hope that Wertham didn't lead her into a dead end. At least he was easy to spot with the night lenses, the green-grass color of his prison uniform vibrant in the tans and browns of the capacious corridors. That advantage allowed Brigid to hang back, keeping the distance between them.

Brigid followed for fully two minutes as Wertham continued his erratic path through the darkened palace. There appeared to be almost no one about, just a few of the Gene-agers who appeared to be acting in some guard role now, making their own rounds through the palace. The Gene-agers showed no capacity for innovative thought, trudging their assigned routes without deviation, walking in perfectly straight lines and making right-angle turns. Brigid found that hanging back at impromptu moments allowed her to bypass these sentries, and she traveled through the corridors unmolested.

Wertham slipped down a side corridor, striding swiftly. Brigid waited at the end of the corridor, watching as his narrow-shouldered figure hurried past two more of the waiting servants, who remained statue-still by the walls. The Gene-agers acknowledged him with the slightest inclines of their heads, but Wertham paid them no attention, disappearing through an open door that was as wide as two Mantas placed end to end.

Brigid stood at the far end of that corridor, eyeing the Gene-agers through her night lenses. Avoiding the patrolling sentries was one thing; sneaking past posted guards was a different matter entirely. Brigid's hand played nervously across the gun holstered at her thigh as she wondered what to do.

DOMI WATCHED RONALD drag Queen Rosalind in the opposite direction to the one Brigid had taken. The queen was complaining and Domi could see she was struggling to free herself from the wheelchair-bound man's grip, but it was no use.

"Please Ronald," Roz cried, her words echoing back down the corridor. "Stop this madness before anyone else gets hurt."

Domi watched them from her hiding place, seeing them silhouetted against the windows as they disappeared down the huge corridor. They were heading in the same direction that she and Brigid had come from, back toward the royal court and its magnificent golden thrones.

Domi had spent a little time in the palace since her arrival a day ago, and she already knew enough to make her way around. Instinctively, Domi turned back, retreating farther into the shadows and making her own way to the royal court.

If that's where the showdown was to be, then so be it. Domi figured she could take one crippled man; heck, she might not even need her gun, after all.

THE SOUND OF Wertham's boot heels echoed through the vast vehicle store. The huge room dominated the whole south wing of the incredible palace. Within, it housed almost three dozen different vehicles, from the small two-man mules to their larger buslike brethren, the steeds. There were also several variations of sky disk, like the one Jack had taken to show Kane and Grant the city, alongside snail-like road shells, single-wheeled unicarts, levisticks, skycles, lightracers and blissiles.

Twin roads led from the hangarlike room, disappearing into huge, arched tunnels that sat against one of the walls. A farther wall was entirely open to the outside so that those craft with aerial capacity could launch in an instant, rocketing into the skies above Authentiville. This was where King Jack had taken Kane and Grant when they had left the others, and it was from this room that the group had launched in the sky disk.

Wertham surveyed the selection of vehicles that were docked here. He recognized some, while others seemed to be modified versions of craft he had been familiar with before his extended period of incarceration. Some vehicles were entirely new to him, and he eyed them curiously, his mission momentarily forgotten. The two-man mule was reliable and fast, he concluded, making his way to a bay toward the rear of the room.

IN THE CORRIDOR leading to the palace garage, Brigid was striding purposefully toward the open doorway. She could see the garage itself, and as she got closer she recognized the basic shapes of aircraft and starcraft, similar to designs she had encountered in her adventures with the Cerberus team.

It's a hangar of some kind, she realized. Which likely means Wertham's about to rabbit. Damn.

She needed a plan, and real quick, if she was not to lose track of Wertham. She hurried faster down the corridor, hand on the butt of the holstered TP-9 semiautomatic.

The two Gene-ager guards at the doorway of the garage looked up, alerted to Brigid's presence. They looked monstrous in the harsh glare of the night lenses, their faces not quite human, Frankenstein children plucked from a vat. The Gene-agers that Brigid had met so far had shown little in the way of innovation or independent thought, and she was banking on that lack of insight now to allow her to bluff her way past these two.

"Halt," the left guard pronounced.

Brigid halted.

"State your purpose," the guard demanded.

"Just passing through," Brigid replied.

The dull-faced Gene-ager looked her up and down for a moment while he processed her statement. "No one may pass but Wertham and Dr. Ronald."

"I'm on an assignment for them," Brigid replied instantly.

The dull-faced Gene-ager looked at her again, weighing her answer against his orders. "For whom?" he questioned.

"Wertham the First," Brigid said. "May he rule us through eternity."

"State your assignment parameters," the second guard said, coming alert. He had moved closer to his companion, effectively blocking the corridor and the room that lay behind.

This was not going well, Brigid realized.

"I'm to bring him something," Brigid said. "It's urgent."

The two dead-eyed guards looked at her querulously, processing her responses. "What are you delivering?" the one to the left asked. "What is urgent?"

A grim smile tugged at the corners of Brigid's mouth as she reached to her hip and unholstered her pistol. "This," she stated, bringing the weapon up. These closeted slaves had no comprehension of blasters, Brigid knew—she had discovered that accidentally when she had gotten into the altercation upstairs that had led to her being tossed through a window.

The Gene-ager to the right reached for the gun in Brigid's hand, but she pulled it out of his reach.

"Uh-uh, no touchy feely," Brigid instructed. "What I have here is for the God Emperor alone."

Brigid's eye was drawn by something behind the guards, a flash of color blending into white as the motor of a mule came to life inside the palace garage. Come on, she thought, let me through already, you brain-dead mooks.

The guards looked at Brigid, considering her proposition.

"I shall ask Wertham," the guard to the left decided. "You shall wait."

"Sorry," Brigid replied, "but patience isn't my strong point today." With that, she pulled the trigger, blasting a continuous burst of fire into the stomach of the left guard before directing the discharge at his companion.

Both guards stumbled back, the one to the left collapsing to the floor while the one on the right crashed against the corridor wall.

Brigid scampered past the falling bodies and into the garage just in time to see Wertham's mule rocket through the open wall at the far side.

"Well," she told herself. "No turning back now."

Chapter 27

"We need to keep moving," Kane said. He crouched with Grant and King Jack in the pump room beneath the baths.

"And go where?" Jack asked. He sounded tired, defeated.

"You tell us," Kane said. "Your ville, your rules. But I suggest we get out of here before the vat boys realize we're down here."

Jack nodded, consternation on his face. "There's another way to the ground level," he said, gesturing with the glowing shaft of the God Rod. "This way."

With that, the old king got back on his feet and led them past one of the mighty pumps, treading a narrow path between the pipes. Kane and Grant followed, watching the shadows through the light-enhancing lenses they wore over their eyes.

A few dozen paces later, Jack stopped at a closed hatchway before running the God Rod across a plate in its center. The hatchway looked as if it had not been opened in a hundred years, rust and dark streaks marring its once shiny surface, but it swung open soundlessly at the God Rod's touch.

Jack stepped inside, dipping his head a little to get beneath the low frame of the hatchway. Beyond, a tunnel-like shaft led upward at a steep angle, barely wide enough to accommodate a man. It featured a smooth floor almost like a ramp, and scarred walls that showed evidence of what appeared to be quite brutal impacts. The whole thing was caked in dirt and it smelled of damp.

"Where's this take us, Your Majesty?" Kane asked.

"It's an old delivery shaft that we stopped using back in the Era of the Hawk," Jack told him. "If my memory's worth a damn, then it should lead us to a storage area over to the north of the building."

Kane and Grant followed the older man as he clambered up the shaft, pressing against the sides to hoist himself forward along the steep slope. It wasn't quite mountaineering, but it wasn't an easy walk, either.

"What's in this storeroom?" Grant asked, bringing up the rear.

"It was abandoned a long time ago," Jack told him, "so, hopefully nothing much."

"So long as it ain't where you keep more slave bodies you were waiting to bring to life," Grant muttered.

BRIGID RAN THROUGH the palace garage, watching Wertham's engine lights as he shot away from the building.

"Come on," Brigid urged, taking in the contents of the room properly for the first time. "Got to be something here I can pilot."

Her eyes lit upon the familiar shape of the steed. It was the same vehicle in which Ronald had brought her and her companions to the palace when they had arrived in Authentiville. Its bricklike design looked decidedly blocky compared to its sleek stable mates, but Brigid felt confident she could fly it if she could just recall what Ronald had done.

The steed's door opened as Brigid approached, gliding back on a hidden mechanism so that it disappeared among the bank of windows.

Brigid took a deep breath. "Okay," she said. "Let's see if I took everything in."

Brigid stepped into the steed and stopped, spying the figure there with a start.

"Who th—?" Brigid began, and she stopped. Her TP-9

pistol was up automatically, poised to blast the stranger, the muzzle focused perfectly between her ribs. But Brigid stopped shy of pulling that trigger, realizing instinctively that the stranger would not hurt her.

It was the woman in the headband, one of the two who had accompanied Ronald on the airstrip to perform what Brigid suspected was a mental scan before she and her companions had been allowed to exit the grounded Mantas.

Now, the woman stood statue still, eyes wide and unfocused, the headband reflecting the lights of the sky from the distant opening that led from the garage.

Brigid stepped closer, eyeing the woman warily. "What happened to you?" she asked, bringing her blaster down but still holding it ready in her hand. "Brain seizure?" She looked at the woman's face more closely. "No, it's more than that, isn't it?" Brigid realized. "You've been…switched off."

Well, that opened up a whole different can of worms. Brigid already suspected that the Gene-agers were artificial creatures, but she hadn't much thought about the other people she and her companions had interacted with since they had arrived. It made sense, she realized. Like the Gene-agers who had served them dinner, this mind-scanning woman and her companion were in a role of servitude, as were the Vooers and the women operating the Happening. They were tools, labor-saving machines.

No time to think about that now, Brigid realized, turning her attention back to the hangar doors. Wertham's mule was still visible, cutting a path through the sky traffic.

"Right," Brigid said, passing her hand over the door mechanism to close it. "Let's see if I can remember how Ronald did this."

She took up the same position as Ronald had on their journey over. As she did so, a clear plate seemed to drop down before her eyes. It hung in the air in front of Brigid, framing

the hangar opening where she could see Wertham's flyer.
Glowing grid lines appeared across the image. Brigid realized
absently that the image must have been there when Ronald
brought them to the palace, but the projection was so specifically mapped to the pilot's retina that it could only be seen
from a single angle, directed precisely for the pilot's sole use.

Brigid's eyes flicked to Wertham's retreating vehicle. The
design was intuitive—the grid overlay showed various pathways that could be taken, the pilot need only select one and
the engine would do the rest.

Brigid felt the steed begin to move, rising from the floor
and swinging around toward the opening. In a moment she
was out of the garage and floating high above the city streets,
a rail of light forming before the strange sky craft as it cut a
path through the air.

She was on her way.

DOMI HAD BEEN keeping pace with Ronald and the captive
queen for almost five minutes now, her keen senses guiding her through the dark maze of the unlit palace, ducking
from view when she crossed the path of one of the patrolling
sentries who had been left to clear up the last of the royal
court's stragglers. She took a parallel path to Ronald, sometimes utilizing the same corridors, but often following an
alternative route, confident that he was escorting the queen
back to the throne room.

Ronald's chair glided almost silently through the corridors,
but he was still easy to follow, for the queen's reluctant foot-
falls were heavy as she was dragged by his relentless grasp.
He would not slow, nor would he allow her to, and Domi
caught snatches of their conversation as the queen tried to
reason with her once-loyal aide.

"You must stop this, Ronald," the queen instructed. "It can
only end in pain—for everyone."

"The people will accept me in time," Ronald insisted. "As will you."

"Never," the queen shot back.

Domi halted at the end of a corridor, ducking behind a purple-leafed plant that stood taller than she was, awaiting Ronald's approach. They were a few doors away from the back entry to the throne room, Domi knew. There were no guards in this area, and it provided an ideal opportunity for an ambush. Domi hunkered down as Ronald's motion chair whispered closer.

"You see only my disability," Ronald told the queen. "You fail to envisage what I am capable of."

"No, it is you who only see your disability," Rosalind told him, the regal tone back in her voice. "Wertham has poisoned your mind, infecting you with his strange ideas, turning you against…"

"Against what?" Ronald sneered. "You, Rosalind? King Jack? And what are you? My betters, is that how you think?"

"Wertham's spell has turned you against the people," Rosalind finished lamely. "You need to consider what a war with the surface will cost them."

As the chair glided past, Domi leaped from cover with the Detonics pistol thrust before her.

"What is this?" Ronald snarled as he spied the lithe figure barreling toward him in the semidarkness.

Then Domi's leg came up in a swift kick, and her boot connected with Ronald's jaw, knocking him back in his seat. He slammed the headrest with a grunt of dispelled breath, and the motion chair edged backward several feet with the impact while he let go of Roz's hand. Wrong-footed, the queen collapsed to the floor, tripping over the retreating motion chair.

Domi moved fast then, rolling forward and reaching with her free hand for the replica God Rod where Ronald had placed it in a sheath at the side of his noiseless conveyance.

"Game's over, traitor boy," she snarled as her hand closed on the Devil Rod. Holding it, Domi felt its pulse as though it was subtly changing size with each erg of energy that channeled from its core, almost alive.

Ronald's eyes narrowed as the albino woman danced away, Devil Rod in hand.

"Now, I guess you have a way to talk to your buddy so you're going to tell him to stand down," Domi ordered. "And after that we'll see about getting the pair of you a nice cosy prison cell together or whatever it is that the people do here."

Without warning, an electrical lance discharged from Ronald's chair in a single, dartlike bolt, cutting the space between them before striking Domi's chest. She glowed for a moment as electricity played across her whole body, before sagging to the floor with a crash.

"Stupid immigrant," Ronald muttered, bringing the motion chair around and snatching the Devil Rod from the floor where it had fallen from Domi's grasp.

"Domi—no!" Rosalind gasped.

Ronald looked back at her. "Come, my queen," he instructed. "We have a kingdom to rule."

KING JACK REACHED for the hatch at the end of the shaft and ran his God Rod over its sensor. The hatch was square with rounded-off corners and it squealed as if alive when it swung open. Ideally, either Kane or Grant would have gone first to ensure that they were not walking straight into an ambush, but with the tight proportions of the shaft, such a move was nothing short of impossible.

"This way," Jack said, stepping out into the room beyond.

Kane followed while Grant struggled out of the narrow hatchway last of all.

"What did you use that for?" Grant asked as he clambered uncomfortably through the tight gap.

"Supplies," the monarch said vaguely. He was scanning the room, using the light cast by his God Rod to see. It was a vast room, two stories in height, rectangular in shape so that it felt long and narrow. The walls featured some struts on which large, sealed boxes had been hung using thick leather straps. Each box looked large enough to house a modest-sized family along with their pets.

There was no internal illumination in the room other than what poured from Jack's baton, but a small line of windows ran high up along one of the long walls, displaying the golden towers of Authentiville and the rainbow mosaic of sky above them.

Kane and Grant scanned the room, too, splitting up to make a more difficult target, and swooping around the king. Their lenses brought the whole room into stark relief and they spotted the Gene-agers waiting there.

Four Gene-agers were poised statue still, until they saw the light of the God Rod. It seemed to act as a beacon, and immediately they began moving menacingly toward the king's position.

"Get back, Your Highness," Kane shouted, commanding his Sin Eater back into his hand from its hidden sheath with a flinch of wrist tendons.

Almost before the Sin Eater was in his palm, Kane felt the arm of the nearest Gene-ager slap against his chest, shoving him aside.

"Not so fast, bozo," Kane growled, bringing the Sin Eater up against the mindless creature's gut and stroking the trigger. The Gene-ager seemed to collapse into itself, its clothes smoldering with propellant.

Behind Kane, Grant put his hand out before the king and guided him back, searching for cover. "These guys move pretty fast," he observed.

"Yeah, they're…" King Jack began, but suddenly a fifth

figure was on him, having dropped from his hiding place atop one of the hanging crates.

Grant moved without conscious thought, bringing his right hand out in a ram's-head punch as the attacker reached for the king. The blow connected with the back of the thing's shoulders, much farther back than Grant had planned, and again the thought occurred to him that these people were moving faster than he expected.

Grant's punch did just enough to knock the Gene-ager off balance, and the man stumbled as he reached for the king, snagging only a handful of his red cloak.

Then Grant was on him, driving a second punch into the slave's emotionless face, following up with a third strike low to the body that knocked the wind out of the Gene-ager.

The Gene-ager reeled in place, struggling under the force of Grant's controlled attack. He brought up one arm to stave off Grant's next blow, but Grant surprised him by commanding his Sin Eater into his hand and snapping off a single burst of fire in place of the punch he had telegraphed. The Gene-ager staggered back, collapsing to the floor with a hiss of pain.

"Come on, Your Highness," Grant instructed, pushing King Jack toward one of the walls where he could better protect him.

Kane, meanwhile, was hurrying across the room toward the next of the dronelike servants, his Sin Eater held in line with the rapidly approaching figure's face. "Who commands you?" Kane snapped. "Who do you obey?"

The Gene-ager ignored him, moving with a burst of uncanny speed and swiping at the pistol.

"Kane, look out!" King Jack called from his hiding place. "They're mover drones, they can move twice human speed if they need to."

"No kidding," Kane growled as he was knocked back by

the blow to his gun. He spun wildly toward one of the swinging crates, his feet leaving the ground entirely.

Across the room, Grant had ushered the king behind the cover of a jutting pipe that stood almost three times his height. "Fast movers," he muttered, shaking his head. "Time to break out the heavy artillery." Then, Grant was reaching into the hidden pocket in the lining of his coat to retrieve the Copperhead subgun, keeping the pipe between himself and the approaching servants. In a moment, the weapon's two-foot barrel was thrust before him like an accusation and he squeezed the trigger. Two more Gene-agers went down in a fury of sparks, bullets cutting through them in a storm of 4.85 mm pain.

The remaining Gene-ager had followed Kane where he had dropped. Kane had hit the floor hard, and for a moment the whole room seemed to be spinning. The shadow was the only alert he had that the Gene-ager had followed him, but he whipped his gun up, instinct-swift, and pulled the trigger. The Gene-ager swung back in a blur, and Kane's bullets shot past him with a cacophony of noise.

"Kane?" he heard Grant calling to him from his hiding place. "Kane? You okay?"

"Get the chief out of here," Kane shouted back, regretting once more how their Commtacts had failed once they had passed into the cosmic rift. Still, the old man was important, and if he didn't survive, then Kane figured it was even money that none of them would.

Kane watched from the corner of his eye as Grant seized the opportunity to run, ushering King Jack toward a door set within the wall beneath the windows. Kane's attacker turned, hearing the sound as King Jack ran the God Rod across the door's sensor plate, commanding it to open for the first time in years.

Without targeting, Kane sent a cluster of bullets at the

Gene-ager, rattling the floor at his feet. The Gene-ager turned back to face him.

"Uh-uh," Kane said. "You're not done with me yet, pretty boy."

As Grant and King Jack disappeared through the unsealed door, the fast-moving Gene-ager came at Kane again, stomping toward him as the ex-Mag struggled back to his feet. Through the miraculous lenses, Kane saw a second figure moving amid the forgotten storeroom—one of the Gene-agers he had thought he had already dropped. Damn, these guys weren't just fast, they could also take a good pounding before they went down.

Kane darted aside as the nearest Gene-ager threw a punch at his face. The movement was eye-blink fast, and the balled fist cut through the air with an audible whistle.

Then the other one blurred across the room, some kind of metal bar in his hands. Grim-faced, the Gene-ager swung the bar at Kane. The ex-Magistrate ducked, and the bar whipped just inches above his head. Kane didn't know what the weapon was. It looked something like a crowbar or maybe a long-handled wrench, but he was pretty sure that with enough force it could still bash his brains in or maybe even take his head clean off his shoulders. Time to end this, then.

Kane ducked as the armed attacker took another swing, but he realized he was backing into a corner as the first Gene-ager rounded on him. All of a sudden Kane had run out of options and his backup was nowhere to be seen.

Chapter 28

Brigid had lost Wertham.

But the sensor-ware of the steed hadn't. Under her mental instruction, it shot across the sky, weaving between the tallest buildings of Authentiville as it sought its prey.

Wertham's vehicle was faster, and he had had a head start, but the steed tracked his path unerringly, displaying his route on the heads-up grid that flashed across Brigid's retinas.

"Just incredible," Brigid muttered as the steed hooked around another golden tower a hundred stories above the street.

As they passed the tower, Brigid saw their destination for the first time. It looked like the inside of an automobile engine had been enlarged and sunk into the ground, existing now in a great hole drilled beneath the city. The pit glowed with a soft orange radiance, the color of smelting metal.

Brigid had passed here before, she recalled, her eidetic memory filling in the details as the steed swooped lower, angling toward the ground. But it hadn't been a pit then; it had been a park or field, a great swath of grass imprinted on her memory.

"What did he do?" Brigid wondered as the steed dropped toward a landing platform. There was one other vehicle there—Wertham's two-seater mule. It was time to finish this.

KING JACK STEPPED from the storeroom and stopped so suddenly that Grant almost crashed into him.

"Your Highness?" Grant asked.

They were outside, a little above street level on a balcony wide enough to be used as a turning circle for a Sandcat. The city was dark, the sky reflected from the shiny towers but their internal illumination dimmed. The phenomenon encompassed the whole city, Grant saw as he took in the view. But out there, somewhere between those now-dark towers, there came a glow like a volcano.

"It…can't be," Jack said, shaking his head.

Grant peered behind him, checking that nothing was following them through the door. He just hoped Kane was okay in there. When he turned back to Jack, he saw the look of consternation on the old man's face.

"That glow," Jack explained. "Someone's lit the Doom Furnace."

"Which means what, exactly?" Grant asked.

Jack's eyes widened in horror. "The Doom Furnace is a maternity ward for weapons, Grant. If it's active again, then it means someone plans to take us into war."

"With whom?" Grant asked. "I got the impression you were safe here in this…rift."

"The only war would be with the surface people," Jack told him. "Your people. Earth."

KANE WAS TRAPPED in a corner between two walls of the storeroom, the massive crates hanging overhead on their leather thongs. The Sin Eater bucked in his hand, unleashing a stream of 9 mm bullets. The bullets whined in the air, but the Geneagers merely swept them aside, arms moving in a blur as they sped up. They had got the speed of Kane's shots now.

These people are human tractors, Kane realized. Grant's Copperhead had enough punch to knock these maniacs down but not the Sin Eater—all its 9 mm discharge could hope to do was slow them for a moment. Worse still, these particular vat-grown men were so durable that they could recover from a few shots—maybe not indefinitely, but that was little comfort when one of them was swinging a steel bar at your head, Kane thought.

Kane rolled, ducking under the metal bar as the Gene-ager on his right swung for his head like a baseball pitcher. He had nowhere to run now, trapped in a corner like this. It was all he could do to avoid that swinging hunk of metal.

But before Kane could recover, the other Gene-ager—this one unarmed—came at him, delivering a powerful knee to the side of his leg. The blow seemed to reverberate though Kane's leg bone, and he toppled to the deck, his right flank slamming against the wall as he sank. Kane gritted his teeth against the sharp pain in his leg. It would pass—he just had to stay alive long enough for that to happen.

When he looked up, they were headed toward him, two of them, dull expressions like the simpleminded. They were feet away, coming at him with murder in mind. They could move faster, they were stronger and they were utterly fearless in their mission. If he didn't stop them now...

Kane's mind raced, the experience of a thousand altercations running through his brain, a hundred different combat scenarios, a dozen different moves he might employ pared down in an instant to one option. Kane took careful aim with his Sin Eater and squeezed the trigger. A burst of 9 mm titanium-shelled bullets blasted from the muzzle, whipping past Kane's attackers, up toward the roof above them, and drilling through one of the leather thongs that held the crate above them in place.

The crate was the size of a two-car garage, and it was held aloft by the application of perfect balance, two thongs keeping it high above the floor. Kane's bullets clipped one of those tethers, fraying it as they passed through the material. Kane drove himself backward, pressing his back against the wall and drawing his legs toward him as the tether gave with a sound like a tree trunk splitting. The crate swung like a pendulum, sweeping in a swift parabola and knocking Kane's attackers off their feet like bowling pins.

The crate came to an abrupt stop as its leading edge met the floor, ripping into the decking there with a screech of metal on wood.

Kane stood, breathing heavily. The crate had missed him by six inches. Maybe. Two figures lay mangled beneath it, slapped to the ground by the swinging box before getting their legs caught under it as it met the immovable floor. There was blood there, and flesh and bone, all of it mashed into a streak that spread across the floor where the crate had struck. Kane looked away, disgusted.

MOMENTS LATER, KANE joined Grant and Jack on the balcony outside the storeroom.

"Everything okay?" Grant asked as Kane appeared.

"Dandy," Kane said, brushing a finger to his nose.

Grant smiled. Kane's gesture was known as the one-percent salute, a kind of ironic code between them. It highlighted that no matter how well things may be going, there was always that one percent margin where just about anything could and would go wrong. Kane and Grant generally employed the old code when things seemed at their most dire. And nine times out of ten, the situation got worse before it got better.

"We have our own problem out here," Grant explained, and he indicated the glow on the horizon. "See that? The king tells me it's some kind of munitions plant that's been called back into action."

Kane listened as Grant and King Jack explained what it meant. When they had finished, he turned to Jack and asked what they could do to stop the projected war with Earth.

"I need to get back to the palace," Jack said. "Powering up the Doom Furnace would have required the God Rod, and it can only be engaged from the throne hub. If we can get there, maybe I can turn things back somehow."

Kane nodded. "Archimedes once said, 'Give me a place to stand and a lever long enough and I shall move the world.' And you've got the big lever."

King Jack searched the street, getting his bearings. "But my sky disk is right across the other side of the building," he explained. "Do you think you boys are up to facing off against more of the rogue Gene-agers?"

Thoughtfully, Kane peered back at the building and then out across the street. There were vehicles there, some moving and some parked. As he watched them a plan started to form. "Your Highness, have you ever boosted a car?"

WARILY, BRIGID STEPPED from the steed and stalked across the towering walkways of the Doom Furnace. Beyond them, a sheer drop fell away to the burning pits of the forge, churning out space hardware for the first time in almost a thousand years.

From up here, the whole system looked automated, great arms moving caldrons of boiling metal into ingot molds, vast banks of cooling jets hardening the results as each armored plate was produced. A mighty tower of water fed a miniature lake that was used for cooling, hanging high above the forge in a gigantic bowl.

To one edge of the pit, a sunken platform ran almost the whole length of the underground factory. The platform contained finished items—gigantic gun emplacements, huge beam weapons like radar dishes, each one made mobile by a single, ball-like device locked to its base, and each as tall as ten men. There were vehicles there, too, two vast land tanks as long as battleships, gigantic caterpillar treads running the length of their bodies. And there were other, smaller vehicles that still dwarfed a baronial Sandcat. Figures were marching in file around the platform, priming the weapons and manning the hulking vehicles as they prepared for the first wave of Wertham's assault.

Brigid ducked as something came rushing upward from the depths of the forge pit. It was a one-man flyer, designed like a sled with a swept-back screen on the front, behind which a Gene-ager worked the controls. Brigid recognized a cannon-type nose poking from the front, and she wondered what ammunition it required. As she watched, a second flyer zoomed up out of the darkness, followed by a whole squadron, at least a dozen moving in formation up into the sky above Authentiville.

Brigid moved across the walkway, feeling decidedly under-armed for whatever was coming next. "Where the heck is Wertham?" she wondered, eyeing the network of walkways that led down into the belly of the forge. A few figures moved around there, many of them carrying materials destined for the production plant.

Then she spotted Wertham, his bright-green jumpsuit marking him out amid the sea of grays and blues of the Gene-ager workers. He was below her, striding purposefully along a wide walkway toward a boxlike unit that jutted from one wall, its proportions as large as a house. Brigid watched as he reached the box and slipped inside.

"Okay, God Emperor," she muttered, fingering her holster. "Time to meet someone who doesn't take so kindly to your mind manipulation."

THE WALL LIGHTS blinked on as Wertham entered the forgotten room on the edge of the Doom Furnace. His face broke into a giddy smile as he stepped into his old laboratory.

Even in the strip lighting, it was clear that the room was

vast, big enough to house a sporting event. Every wall was carved with handwritten notes etched into the walls themselves. There was a lot of empty space here that had once held items of alien salvage, and Wertham could see the cage that had once been the focal point of the nexus area where he would test the destructive limits of a new discovery.

The lab had been located here, back when the Doom Furnace was active, to provide a place from which to test and oversee new prototypes as they were forged and put through their paces.

Now it was a shambles. Things were broken, desks overturned, paperwork singed or burned away entirely, leaving only the covers of once-bound volumes remaining. His bed, as comfortable as it was practical, had been broken apart and only the legs remained, its base torn away for scrap.

"I guess no one expected me to return," Wertham stated archly when he saw the state of the bed.

He kicked through the dusting of debris that littered the room. "Jack should have burned this place the moment he had the chance," he said. But he hadn't because he was scared of what he might burn, of what might explode or be set off to do untold damage. So he had ordered the place trashed, instead, believing that locking it away like this would somehow last forever.

Wertham moved over to one of the upturned desks, searching a line of cupboards secured directly to the wall above it. The cupboards were missing their doors now, and their contents were strewn halfway across the floor, ransacked and destroyed. Wertham brushed the remaining debris aside and reached deeper into the center cupboard.

"A warp in a warp," Wertham muttered cryptically. "A rift in a rift. There."

As he said it, Wertham's arm stretched beyond the back of the cupboard and disappeared into and through the wall.

Many years ago, Jack had constructed this city inside a quantum field beyond the reach of normal man. Authentiville existed in a cosmic rift, ever in flux with the real world. For Wertham, it had not taken much to switch the frequency to create his rift within the rift, a place where he could hide his most ambitious designs should anything ever happen to him. Within that quantum pocket, Wertham grasped something metallic that looked like a bunch of tangled wires.

Wertham carefully unfolded the wires until a circlet was revealed. The circlet was topped with three strips of wire, each no thicker than a man's pinkie finger. Wertham took the strange item and placed it over his head like a crown. It felt just like he remembered from all those years ago, and already the impossible shapes were playing before his eyes.

Sitting on the fire-scarred desk, Wertham scowled in thought. "The world's a big place," he recalled. "I'll have to personalize it."

"BEEN A WHILE since I did this," King Jack admitted as he fed power to the lightracer's control console.

Barely wider than a man, the lightracer was shaped like a spear and stretched back to a length of fourteen feet. More than one half of that length was taken up with engine, a solar drive that fed a nuclear reaction through the vehicle's synapses to power it. One single back wheel dominated the design, cutting through the vehicle and standing to the height of a man, two feet above the low-slung body of the lightracer itself.

The king accelerated from a standing start to 90 miles per hour in less than two seconds, cutting a path through the street outside the regeneration baths, trusting the avoidance software to keep him safe as the vehicle wove through traffic. Despite the gravity of the situation, King Jack was grinning.

Behind Jack, Kane and Grant were kneeling on the low floor, wedged into a space no larger than the pilot's seat of the Manta. Kane peered over the king's shoulder as the dark city whizzed past at incalculable speed, wincing and ducking as they darted around slower vehicles on their passage back to the palace. Despite their velocity, the lightracer made a sound no louder than a gnat's wing.

"Are you sure you know how to drive this thing?" Kane asked, his heart racing.

Jack laughed. "Ah, you can't teach a new god old tricks, son," he said, working the controls.

Through the windshield, Kane saw what looked like a service truck pulling across two lanes as it made a turn. The lightracer clipped past it with inches to spare, nothing but a blur on the road.

Pushed right up against Kane, his knees up against his chin, Grant closed his eyes in a slow, meditative blink. "You know," he said, "if we make it back to the palace I'm telling his wife."

BRIGID CLAMBERED DOWN the crisscrossed walkways of the Doom Furnace, moving as swiftly as she could toward the door through which she had seen Wertham pass. Somewhere in the back of her mind she could still feel the tickle of that bogus instruction to obey, and each time she became aware of it she would clench her hands tight, pushing her fingernails into the fleshy part of her palm until it hurt.

"Keep with it, Baptiste," she told herself, trying to think what advice Kane would give her.

She slipped down a winding metal staircase to bring her level with the doorway she sought. As she reached the bottom step, she spotted five dull-faced servants trudging toward her. They carried boxes of tools and equipment, each one filled to the brim, each one heavy enough to require a wheelbarrow for a normal man to move.

The Gene-agers stopped when they saw Brigid there, eyeing her suspiciously. "You don't belong here," the lead slave said, dropping his box of parts.

Oh, boy, thought Brigid, here we go again.

Chapter 29

Wertham was alone in his all-but-forgotten laboratory. He had spent seven hundred years alone in the single prison cell of Authentiville. Solitude held no fear for him now.

He reached for his hidden cache of mind drugs, a specially adapted mixture of Raka' and Annunaki proteins and solvent compounds that he had stumbled upon and refined centuries before. Like the crown, the cache was where he had left it, hidden in a rift pocket disguised by one of the shapes that were impossible for a normal man to see with the naked eye.

The drug looked like a tiny capsule, smaller and rounder than Wertham's little fingernail. He slipped it onto his tongue, reveling in the unpleasant taste, familiar even after all these centuries without it. The pill melted with a fizzing sensation, much as a meringue will disintegrate on the tongue, and Wertham felt things begin to slip inside his skull and his body, the way a contact lens will slip over the eye.

Hearing, sight, smell, touch, taste. Five senses.

Become six. He could *gloud* the air now.

Become seven. And now he could *frieb* the trace heat coming from the wall lights.

Become eight. He could *ize* the trace he had *friebed*.

Become nine. And to *tomp* the very room with all its angles and planes.

They were senses impossible to describe without experiencing them firsthand, new senses that expanded Wertham the Strange into a whole other scale of being. An existence kaleidoscoped with glory.

He felt the buzz of his new set of senses, four new abilities acting in conjunction with the old familiars. They would all be necessary for the Titan work he was to do next.

The sensor rig was perched atop his head, its metal pads making contact with his cool skin. Wertham took up a position on the lip of an overturned desk, perching there like some hungry bird of prey, and gazed about the room. He could still see the shapes that hid themselves from human eyes, the shapes that only the alien races were supposed to see. They rotated in the shadows, glistening like diamonds, twinkling like stars seen between the clouds.

Nine senses fed information to him as he slipped his consciousness into the new form, seeking it out with the headset, discovering it right where he had placed it all those hundreds of years before. The Titan.

BRIGID HAD FACED Gene-agers before, so she didn't hesitate this time. Instead, she charged at the nearest, the one who had dropped the box he was carrying as he formed his accusation, pulling her TP-9 from its hip holster.

The TP-9 sang its song of menace, a stream of 9 mm bullets launching from the sleek black muzzle and drilling into the chest of the artificial man. The Gene-ager stumbled back with the impact, surprised and wounded at the same time, dark ooze spreading across his overalls where his skin had been pierced.

Brigid used the man's surprise to her advantage, flipping herself in midrun so that her body dropped low, taking all of her weight on her right leg as her left kicked up. The toe of her upthrust boot connected with the Gene-ager's jaw, and his teeth closed with a loud clack. The artificial man was knocked back with the blow, staggering to keep upright.

Brigid continued to move, slipping from high kick into a crouch and sweeping the TP-9 in a low arc before her. As the first Gene-ager tumbled to the stone catwalk, Brigid's bullets cut the legs out from under the next two, sending one of them staggering over the edge of the walkway while the other crashed to the floor. Brigid ignored the cry of surprise as the Gene-ager disappeared over the side of the catwalk, her heart pounding faster now, the pulse of adrenaline throbbing behind her ears.

The last two Gene-agers were only now beginning to react to this mystery attacker with hair the color of the furnace below. They dropped the crates they were carrying and ran at Brigid, hefting long-handled tools over their heads as makeshift weapons.

Brigid sprang back up to her feet, targeting the two figures as they charged her. The first reeled back at the hail of bullets, but the second reached near enough to throw his weapon, launching it across the space between them like a spear.

Brigid saw the metal shaft glint with the red radiance of the furnace as it sailed toward her, and she sidestepped just in time to avoid its impact. Then she was moving again, sprinting toward the remaining Gene-ager, ejecting the empty clip of the TP-9 as she ran.

A moment later she was on top of the false man, and she brought her knee up in a swift jab at his groin. The Gene-ager took the strike without reacting, reaching for Brigid as she tried to pull away. His arm snagged her right shoulder, pulling down to prevent her using the semiautomatic pistol. Brigid didn't care—the weapon was empty right now, which meant it was little more than deadweight until she could reload it. Instead, she brought her left arm around, flattening the palm like a knife and using its side to strike a blow to the slave's throat. The Gene-ager's eyes bugged as he felt the blow, and his grip on Brigid slackened for a fraction of a second.

That fraction was enough. Brigid pulled her right arm free from her assailant's grip and spun away in a graceful pirouette.

The Gene-ager recovered from the blow to his neck, rubbing at his throat with annoyance. Then Brigid dropped low, snagging her left leg behind his and flipping him onto his back. The Gene-ager toppled back, kicking out as he slipped over the side of the catwalk. In a second, he was tumbling down into the artificial lake of water that waited beneath the door in the wall, colliding with it in a great splash. Brigid watched for a moment as the replica man flailed in the water, struggling to keep himself afloat. There was no time to wait to finish him off. She had to keep moving.

Brigid was not a killing machine, but she could kill if she needed to. More importantly, these semi-men were some kind of clones; she was sure of that much, and while she didn't have the full story yet, she trusted her instincts enough to dispatch them without it weighing on her conscience. Whatever Wertham was doing, she had a nasty feeling that bumping off a few artificially grown men would pale into insignificance by comparison.

THE ROYAL PALACE came into view through the lightracer's windshield like a behemoth rising from the sea. The structure took up a whole city block, and with the lights of the city out it looked all the more ominous as if it waited for them to enter and challenge it.

Kane muttered a curse as King Jack pulled the lightracer to a stop, the braking mechanism just as noiseless as the engine had been at full speed. "You've really got to warn us when you're going to do that," he told the king as he swallowed the bile that had appeared in his throat.

"Sorry, fellas," King Jack said amiably. "I clean forgot the two of you didn't have a velocity belt between you."

Kane didn't know what a velocity belt was, but he guessed it was some kind of gravity dampener, similar to the one used in the Mantas to prevent a pilot blacking out while traveling at very high speed.

The front of the lightracer peeled away like a waterfall, and Jack clambered from his seat and out onto the street. Kane followed with Grant pulling himself free of the space he had been wedged in during their rapid trek across town. Grant stood for a moment, bent over with his hands on his hips, trying to catch his breath.

"You boys up to this?" Jack asked, looking from Grant to Kane.

Kane nodded as he reloaded his Sin Eater, tossing the dead clip into the driver's seat of the spear-shaped vehicle. "Yeah, let's get you seated back on the throne."

Behind Kane, Grant reloaded his own Sin Eater, as well as his Copperhead, and together the three men hurried up the grand steps that led into the palace.

THE TITAN CAME awake at Wertham's command, the designer's mental faculties charging his masterpiece.

The Titan waited deep in the cavernous recesses of the Doom Furnace, where it had clung for seven centuries in the timeless void of the quantum rift, poised like a nesting bat. It looked like a man, or a mockery of a man, dressed in armor plate that shone despite all its years of neglect. Nothing rusted in the nonspace of the quantum rift, nothing aged, not really. Only people became older, and the residents of Authentiville had even found a way to get beyond that.

The Titan wore armor the color of the sunset and a helmet that towered high over its head like a hood. As Wertham sent the command to engage, lights came to life across its towering crown, and its eyes glowed a deep, fiendish red that lit the cave around the furnace as brightly as the furnace itself.

Each arm on the mighty battle suit was ninety feet in length, each leg a hundred feet. Its fingers were large enough that a man could stand on just one of them, and a single clenched fish was enough to crush a modest-sized building.

The expression on the face was fixed in a grimace, with down-turned mouth and scowling eyes.

Wertham could feel through the suit, sense the world coming alive around him as the Titan—or more properly, the Target Invasion, Total Annihilation and Negation suit—powered up after seven centuries of waiting. The Titan itself knew nothing of this stretch of time—it could have been built just a week ago or a million years ago, it didn't matter. All it knew was the mind that sat within its shell, and that was all it would ever know.

At a single command, the Titan began to move, mighty limbs shuddering as it rose from its seven-hundred-year nest in the shadows. The eyes surveyed the cavern by the furnace, watching emotionlessly as Gene-ager slaves scrambled out of its path. High above, the fleet was amassing, ready to go to war.

Through the eyes of the colossus, Wertham saw the rainbow swirl of the quantum pocket where lightning played, ever at a distance from the golden city that had hid there for a millennium. The Titan suit could feel; every inch of its armor body, every ounce of its armored flesh felt in a way that defied description. Wertham needed the drugs just to enter this trance, to give himself enough senses—nine in all—to function within the artificial body. Only he could do this, only he could control it.

With a single command, the Titan disengaged from the floor and began to rise, levitating on the field of birth energy that had waited all these centuries to be engaged.

BRIGID WAS AT the outside door of the laboratory when she heard the rumbling beneath her. She stepped away from the door and walked to the lip of the rocklike walkway, peering over the edge. What she saw made her heart race.

There, rising on a tide of energies, was a gigantic man dressed in red armor. She ducked back as he came crashing through the walkway, shattering it. Brigid cried out as the walkway snapped in two, the floor dropping away from her as she ran back to the doorway of the hanging laboratory. She reached out, grabbing the door handle with her free hand, hanging on for dear life as the walkway crumbled away beneath her feet.

Within moments, all that was left of it was a semicircle around the door, jutting out just nine inches from the wall. Using the door handle for support, Brigid stood there on tiptoe as the armored figure hurtled past like a launching rocket, a fantastic cushion of energy trailing and propelling it from deep inside the structures of the Doom Furnace.

Brigid watched, hanging from the door, as the figure ascended. Its proportions were almost more than she could contemplate. It towered at least two hundred feet in length, head to toe, perhaps more. It was hard to tell because it was moving so fast. Brigid watched as the Titan rushed up into the sky, joining the rest of the fleet that had gathered there.

"What the heck have we gotten ourselves into?" she muttered as she dragged the door open and pulled herself from view.

A moment later, Brigid was inside the corridor leading to Wertham's laboratory, the reloaded TP-9 held ready in her hand.

WERTHAM EXPERIENCED THE sense of being born as the Titan suit ascended into the sky above the Doom Furnace. Through the eyes of the armor, he looked left and right, admiring the invasion fleet he would lead to planet Earth.

With a single mental command, he began to drift, floating

on the cosmic tides, fluttering away from the golden city of Authentiville like a feather on the breeze. A million tons of smart metal—the same substance that had been discovered on the skin of the Annunaki sky disks, which could expand and contract as required—dropped from the impossible city into the rainbow swirl of the quantum night, plummeting into the opening maw of a parallax point.

Target: Earth.

Chapter 30

Serra do Norte, Brazil

"What the hell is that?" Edwards barked, drawing every-one's attention.

The investigation team had moved from the area where the alien lifeboat had been buried, trekking closer to the spot that Roy Cataman had identified with the parallax point in the sky. It was unspoiled forest here, green and lush with the call-and-response birdsong playing through the air from the middle distance. Cataman, Mariah and Sinclair turned at Edwards's surprised shout.

"Up there," Edwards told them. "Where the prof says our parallax point is."

Something glistened in the sky like the morning star.

Edwards was already delving into his backpack for his binocs, a confused scowl darkening his sun-reddened face.

"I see it," Cataman said. "Shining. What is it?"

Edwards had his binoculars to his eyes now, their strap dangling beneath his chin. Sinclair drew her own pair from her field kit and whipped them up to her eyes.

Through the magnifying lenses, Edwards and Sinclair viewed the glistening point in much more detail. It appeared to be a circular pattern holding position in the sky about a mile above them. The pattern was a luminescent white, and its glow was a little like looking into a lightbulb, burning a brief afterimage on the retina. The circle was broken into sections and it spun continually as it held in place, the outer and inner circles rotating in opposite directions. Around its edge, symbols appeared to be written in the very air itself.

Sinclair whistled, handing her binocs to Cataman. "Looks like I don't know what," she said, shaking her head.

Cataman took the binoculars and held them briefly to his eyes before handing them back. Mariah was already busy setting up their computer equipment on a flat expanse of ground, using a blanket to protect the computer base. Cataman leaned down and tapped the screen, commanding it to run an analysis on the phenomenon in the sky. The distance was too great to get much info, he knew, but they had to do something—especially if this was the conclusion to whatever was happening out here.

While Cataman worked the computer, Mariah grabbed the field glasses and turned them to the sky. As she looked, she let out a gasp. "There's someone up there," she said.

"Yes," Edwards confirmed. He continued peering through the binoculars, but even without them the others could see the glowing circles fade from existence and the silhouette of a man plummet out of the sky, feet first.

"You told us not to jump to that parallax point without securing a landing platform," Sinclair reminded Cataman. "Whoever was up there could have done with your advice, no? That's one heck of a drop."

"Over a mile," Cataman agreed, thumbing through a plethora of screens on his computer terminal as he mentally processed the early data.

Mariah gasped again. "Then…they'll die," she said with evident concern.

Levelheaded and practical, Edwards was already engaging his Commtact to report what he could see. It took a moment for his communiqué to patch through to Cerberus, and the reply came through distorted.

"—ay again, Edw—?" Brewster Philboyd's voice stuttered. "—can't g—"

"I said we got something here appearing right out of that parallax point," Edwards repeated, speaking quickly to get the information across.

"Copy that," came Philboyd's reply, marred by the hiss of static. "We—ooking at same now."

Overhead, the figure in the sky was dropping to earth in a straight line, feet first as it fell.

"What if it's Domi?" Mariah asked. "Or Kane? Or…"

It was impossible to guess the plummeting figure's identity from this distance, but one thing was clear. This was not a controlled approach—the person was simply falling.

"It's not Kane," Sinclair said as she scrutinized the distant figure through the binoculars. "Not unless he's wearing a suit of armor."

"Ain't Domi, neither," Edwards confirmed, focusing his own binocs on the figure. He could see it now, as could Sinclair. The figure in the sky was masculine and it wore a radical suit of armor. The armor was a deep orange like the setting sun and included a towering headpiece that doubled the height of the man's head. And there was something else about the figure, too, Edwards realized as it plummeted toward them.

"That ain't a man," he said, whipping the binoculars from his face. "It's too darn big. Everybody clear the area. We need to get out of here, right now."

That was all the warning they needed. Professionals all, the group grabbed what they could and started to run, with Edwards bringing up the rear, the Beretta back in his hand from the shoulder rig he carried it in.

"What is it, Edwards?" Mariah asked between ragged breaths. "What did you see?"

"We made a mistake," Edwards told all of them. "Assumed

something 'cause of the distance. But that thing's a whole load bigger than a man. More like a ville tower."

A great shadow in human shape seemed to grow from nowhere behind the Cerberus survey team, darkening the foliage and ground like the ink of a tattoo. With every second, the shadow became larger still, until it was impossibly huge, stretching out across a vast acre of land. At the same time, the sound of the hurtling figure grew from an almost subliminal whine to a roar of rushing wind like a hurricane.

Mariah stumbled, and as she did she took a peek back over her shoulder to see the falling man properly for the first time. He was so large he obscured the sky, more like a toppling skyscraper than something human. It appeared to be a gigantic robot, a fixed expression cast on its face, glowing red eyes searing out from beneath a stylized brow.

Mariah gasped as the colossus sank beneath the tree line and out of her line of sight.

"Just keep running," Edwards instructed, shoving one hand between the geologist's shoulder blades and forcing her to move faster. "Cerberus, we have a problem!" he added, engaging his Commtact link.

Behind them, the enormous figure slammed through the highest branches of the trees, wrenching wood and leaves away as it plummeted to the ground. Birds cawed and took flight, other animals shrieked and ran, and the nocturnal creatures awoke with hideous yells of fear.

And then, for a single instant, everything seemed to fall utterly silent. Mariah, Edwards, Sinclair and Roy stopped and turned back, watching where the thing had fallen behind the line of trees.

The silence was followed by a noise like thunder, so close, so *loud* that it shook everyone in the vicinity right down to the core. The Cerberus field team was thrown to the ground by the aftershock, while uprooted trees toppled and fell. A massive flock of birds took flight and great lightning-shaped scars appeared across the earth, ripping holes in the ground with the power of the shock wave. The world armor had landed.

Bitterroot Mountains, Montana

THE SATELLITE IMAGERY was unambiguous. Lakesh stared at the live feed with a sinking feeling in his gut. There, standing in the midst of the forest, was a figure so tall it was almost impossible to picture.

Farrell sat at his desk, working back through the recorded footage of the event. "Damn thing appeared out of thin air," he confirmed with irritation. "One minute it's clear skies, next we have the dang Colossus of Rhodes on our doorstep. Relatively."

The satellite cameras had been poised when the figure had arrived, prompted by Roy Cataman's assertion that there was a parallax point up there in the sky. On screen now, Lakesh could see the circle of lights wink out as the figure itself materialized.

"Backtrack a little," Lakesh commanded, patting the top of Farrell's monitor with his fingers. "Let's look at the moments before the object appeared."

Farrell did so, rewinding the footage to just before the colossus began its descent. Lakesh leaned closer, scanning the twin circles of light that seemed to rotate in the air. The overhead camera of the satellite was looking directly at and through them.

"They must be a quarter mile across," Lakesh stated incredulously. "Freeze-frame and bring us closer."

Farrell tapped an instruction into the computer and the image froze on screen. Another tap and the circles magnified and recentered. They had lost some detail, but close up it was clear that there was some kind of patterning across the outer ring. Lakesh nodded slowly as realization dawned.

"Sumerian pictograms," Lakesh said. "Glyphs, icons, whatever you wish to call them."

Farrell looked up at Lakesh, brows raised in surprise. "Dr. Singh?" he asked.

"Just thinking aloud," Lakesh said, but he was clearly working something through in his mind. "If that portal is Annunaki controlled then it could mean…" He stopped, unable to finish as he realized the dark implications of what he was suggesting.

"Surely Enlil couldn't have risen from the dead," Farrell stated, recalling the most vicious Annunaki overlord who had been an ongoing thorn in the Cerberus operation's side until the recent God War.

Lakesh fixed him with a grim stare. "The Annunaki have ways of reviving themselves from even a deathlike scenario," he said bleakly. "If this parallax point leads to a hidden base of theirs, then our colleagues are in even more trouble than we assumed."

Even as Lakesh spoke, Brewster Philboyd was updating the ops room on what was occurring in Serra do Norte, care of the live satellite link. "Look alive, people," he said with trepidation. "That…thing, whatever it is, is moving."

On screen, the gigantic man-thing was walking through the forest, each stride covering over twenty yards, the feet trampling trees and flattening grass as they landed, crushing everything in its path.

"Forget Domi and Kane," Lakesh ordered. "We have a field team out there right now and they're directly in the path of that monster."

Serra do Norte, Brazil

MANIPULATING THE WORLD ARMOR via the mind rig, Wertham the Strange "tasted" Earth air for the first time in a millennium. Yes, the feeling was secondhand, relayed to him through the Titan suit's senses, but the sensation felt no less real for that. For all intents, Wertham *was* the suit now, towering over the lush green landscape of the Serra do Norte area. And tower he did.

The suit stood three hundred feet high, every inch constructed from gleaming metal. He strode forward, reveling in each step, feeling each thundering blow as the Titan suit's huge soles crashed down against the ground. Each stride took him sixty feet forward, two steps and he was at a river; three and he had crossed it.

Up ahead, people were running and screaming—four in all, scampering through the foliage like rats in a maze. Wertham focused the suit's powerful lenses toward the retreating forms, magnifying the image with a mental command. Their terrified faces washed across his mind's eye like projections on a theater screen, and Wertham felt a sense of joy at their fear. Surface men had killed Jack's son years ago. They were not to be trusted. They did well to be afraid of him—he was their new god. Soon the only word they would be able to scream would be his name, the only sound they would be able to make would be in tribute to him.

He lit the eyes, preparing to carve his name in fire across the landscape.

Cosmic Rift

ENTERING THE PALACE was easy. Kane and Grant followed King Jack as he used a back way, "Just to make sure we don't get busted," as he had phrased it.

The palace was dark, the lights flickering only occasionally, leaving ominous shadows to sprawl from the magnificent architecture. Equipped with the night-vision lenses, Kane and Grant barely noticed.

They came across several threats, Gene-agers who had been recruited into sentry duty, but they were slow moving and proved easy enough to avoid.

They heard voices as they passed the open doorway to a room that Jack identified as the ballroom, and peering inside they saw most of the royal retinue waiting there, watched over by grim-faced Gene-agers. Jack's people seemed to be taking the imprisonment well, by and large engaging in conversations that showed no sense of concern about their current situation.

"And these are the people you trust to advise you," Grant said with irony.

"A simpleton's advice is often the most incisive," Jack replied.

Leaving the captives, the group hurried on through the darkened corridors until they reached a door that appeared narrow by the proportions of the palace.

"Through here," Jack explained, pushing the door open. "This is a back way to the throne room. I used to access it sometimes when I had, um, business in the kitchens."

"The kind of business that fits between two slices of bread?" Grant asked.

"Or sometimes needs to be toasted," Jack replied, flashing his easy smile.

Kane and Grant followed the old man, and they found themselves in another corridor, this one lined with potted plants and featuring a fresco painted across the ceiling. An armored figure lay sprawled at the far end of the corridor, and it took Kane just a second to recognize her. It was Domi.

Kane hurried over to where the albino girl lay, calling her

name in an urgent whisper before crouching down to check her pulse. "Unconscious but alive," he told Grant.

"Guess this means we're on the right track," Grant said, nodding grimly.

Without another word, both men commanded their Sin Eaters from the hidden wrist holsters back into the palms of their hands. They had a feeling things were about to get worse before they got better.

Serra do Norte, Brazil

THE WORLD ARMOR loomed over the lush jungle like some fallen god. The Titan's eyes began to glow more fiercely, their ruby red turning a brighter orange-white like the heart of a fire. The change was accompanied by a hum that reverberated through the air.

Then the eyes took fire, twin beams blasting from them with sizzling heat. Ten feet from the Titan's nose, the beams combined and continued down toward the ground as one thick orange shaft before searing the forest in a six-foot-wide line of fire. The line continued, drawing a pattern across the ground.

Hiding amid the trees with his colleagues, Edwards looked up from where he had been checking the ammo in the M-16 rifle he carried and watched the Titan take another colossal step, covering sixty feet in a heartbeat.

"Cerberus," he said through the Commtact. "I'm going to need a bigger gun."

Chapter 31

Cosmic Rift

The concealed door brought them out behind the exit to the dining room, hidden in a quantum pocket, generating even more space in the impossibly large palace.

The court was quieter than Jack had ever known it, almost silent, in fact. Where once had sat the great lines of recorders, now it was empty, the goggle-wearing sub-men departed. Gone, too, were the birds that sang from the rafters, perhaps having sensed the change in the wind and leaving to nest elsewhere.

They entered behind the thrones, whose towering backs were thrust into the darkness like standing stones.

"Watch yourself," Kane whispered.

Jack led the way, pacing warily toward the raised dais in a wide circle that would bring them around to the thrones from the queen's side. Jack stifled a gasp as he passed the point where the back had obscured his view. Rosalind was sitting there in her usual place, her blue hair flickering with illumination even in the darkness, her robes as opulent as ever. She seemed unaware of the presence of these newcomers, and Jack continued making his way toward the thrones with Kane and Grant following.

Something glowed sickly between the thrones, colored like a plague sore. It was a God Rod, Jack realized, but markedly unlike the one he used.

Circling farther, Jack saw the figure sitting where his throne was. After everything they had said, he had expected it to be Wertham, and he was surprised to see his trusted aide Ronald sitting there instead, not on the throne but in the motion chair that compensated for his disability.

"Ronald," King Jack demanded. "What goes on here?"

Ronald looked around with surprise, but there was confidence in his expression. "I heard you were dead," was the first thing he said.

"Not quite," Jack replied, "though, heaven knows, those mindless brutes tried."

Ronald looked confused. "They reported that you had gone," he muttered to himself.

"Gone, yes, but not dead," King Jack replied. "Out of sight, out of mind. The way to trick the mindless."

"It doesn't matter," Ronald told him. "You've been replaced. I'm the king now."

Roz stood, hurrying over to where Jack approached. "My love, don't listen to him," she cried. "He's been turned mad by…"

"Wertham," Jack finished, his eyes narrowing in anger. "Yes, all the evidence pointed to it."

"You're not the king anymore," Ronald told him. "I am."

"You've recognized my authority for a thousand years, and you will recognize it now," Jack blustered, raising the God Rod in warning.

Ronald reached over and drew the Devil Rod from its hub between the thrones. It sparked angrily. "You gave up your authority the day you decided not to help me," he said. "The day you confined me to life as a cripple, despite all the wonders you have shared with your people."

"What is that?" Jack asked, indicating the Devil Rod.

"Your doom," Ronald replied, and he directed the end of

the Devil Rod toward King Jack and unleashed a cruel bolt of energy.

Jack raised his own rod just in time, and the dark energies played across its surface as it shielded him and his wife. Jack gritted his teeth as the forces were consumed by the golden baton. "Roz, get back," he ordered. "Don't get…"

Before he finished, Ronald unleashed a second bolt from the Devil Rod. It rocketed across the gulf between him and Jack, striking the old man's baton and racing up his armored sleeves. Jack held his ground, legs widely spaced as the dark energy blistered over him.

"I think that's our cue," Kane told Grant, and together the two Cerberus warriors pumped the triggers of their Sin Eaters, trapping Ronald in the crossfire. A flurry of 9 mm bullets whizzed over the red-and-green floor of the court, batting against Ronald where he sat in his chair. The bullets found their target but they failed to strike—instead, they were repelled by a shield of powerful energy that emerged from the Devil Rod, creating an oval plate between its wielder and his attackers.

"Dammit," Kane growled, adjusting his aim. "We can't hit him."

"I'm getting no joy here, either," Grant chipped in as he adjusted his Sin Eater and tried for a low angle. "Whatever's powering that God Rod of his is impervious to 9 mms. I'm going to try something bigger."

With that, Grant sent his Sin Eater back to its wrist holster and pulled free his Copperhead. The subgun blasted, the reports echoing loudly in the vast chamber of the throne room, but it did no good.

Ronald sent another bolt of dark energy at King Jack, knocking the old man off his feet.

"Anyone else got any bright ideas?" Grant shouted,

watching his bullets bounce harmlessly off the shield of energy surrounding their target.

BRIGID JOGGED ALONG the short, tunnel-like corridor and into the laboratory. She recognized Wertham immediately, waiting there in the gloom, the band of wires cinched to his skull.

"You're coming with me," Brigid said, raising her blaster.

Wertham's eyes seemed to flicker as if he was returning from a dream state, and then a cruel sneer appeared on his sallow features. "And why would I do that?" he asked.

Brigid stroked the TP-9's trigger and sent a single 9 mm bullet through a ruined file that stood on a shelf behind Wertham's head. "Because this here means I'm calling the shots," she informed him as he saw the damage she had caused.

Wertham smiled wider, his eyes fixing on the blaster. "That is an interesting device," he trilled. "Does it have a name?"

Brigid ignored him. "Get up," she said, gesturing with the semiautomatic.

Wertham seemed to think about it, his eyes glazing over for a moment. "Can't do that," he said. "Too many things still to do here."

And then he began to move, leaping from his position on the edge of the desk straight toward Brigid.

Surprised, Brigid stroked the trigger of the blaster, but her shot went wide. Wertham was moving like a whirlwind, the fight trance upon him once more, his consciousness split between his physical action, his mental concerns and the operation of the Titan suit.

Brigid was slammed off her feet as Wertham crashed into her, his arms outstretched to ensure he snagged her. She went reeling backward, falling heavily on her rump as she sailed back out into the corridor that led to the entrance.

Wertham stood over Brigid where she lay floundering,

drew back his foot and kicked. The kick struck her in the side of the head, making her jaw and cheek sing with pain. Her nose felt suddenly hollow and cavernous, her front teeth sensitive.

Brigid rolled as Wertham went in for a second kick, pulling her body out of his path and taking the blow to the top of her back instead. She shrieked as his foot struck, flopping back down to the floor when she had only just started to get up.

Wertham adjusted his position, fight mathematics working through his mind, figuring out the right angle to cripple his attacker with the minimum of effort. Brigid was faster this time—because she had to be. She whipped her gun around and fired blindly, sending a burst of slugs up into the ceiling and against the wall where they rattled like a woodpecker convention. Wertham staggered back as two of the bullets struck him, one burying itself in his left shoulder while the other passed right through, taking flesh with it like a trophy.

"You hit me," Wertham stated. He said it in the way a scientist might reveal a finding, dispassionate and clinical. His hand was against the wound where the bullet had passed, pressing at the blood that was forming there like a red flower.

"And I'll hit you again," Brigid said, drawing herself up into a crouch, the TP-9 thrust toward Wertham.

Wertham moved with lightning speed, jabbing his hand out over the gun's muzzle and shoving it away as Brigid fired. Five bullets cut through his hand. And then the weapon was wrenched from Brigid's grasp by Wertham, his blood flying across the corridor in a spray.

"You're…inhuman," Brigid uttered.

Wertham smiled grimly, his face and overalls patterned with his own red blood. "No," he said, "just better than them."

Brigid scrambled away as Wertham rushed at her, bounding down the corridor toward the door. He was behind her, running faster as she reached for the door handle. Brigid pulled it and slipped through, out onto a tiny ledge that had once been a walkway.

There was nowhere left to run.

IN THE ROYAL COURT, King Jack lay sprawled on his back, holding the God Rod out for protection as the blasting energy from Ronald's Devil Rod surged all around him. The dark energy formed a cone over the fallen monarch, washing through the air, closing him in its grasp.

"Ronald, you will stop this now," King Jack insisted, his voice firm despite the struggle he found himself in.

Ronald glided closer in his motion chair, his face locked in a cruel mask. "Why?" he asked. "Why would I do that, you old fool?"

"After the kindness we have shown you, Roz and I," Jack told him. As he said it his eyes flicked to Roz where she cowered behind one of the colossal pillars of the throne room. She was crying, something Jack had never known her to do.

"Kindness?" Ronald chided. "You call this kindness, leaving me locked in this blasted chair, unable to ever walk? You call it kindness when you leave me like this while the rest of your population can fly?"

"No, Ronald," Roz shouted, emerging from her hiding place. "It wasn't like that. We tried. Jack tried so hard to make you walk."

For a moment, Ronald flinched, his eyes flickering between King Jack and the queen. "How—?" he asked, unable to form the question he wanted to ask.

"Ronald," Jack said sorrowfully. "You were the best assistant we ever grew. You lasted a thousand years, where your Gene-ager brothers live for ten or twelve. You were the perfect aide, everything me or Roz could have asked for, but we couldn't stop the deterioration once it set it. Gene-agers have a shelf life, you know that."

"I…" Ronald began, trying to process what he was hearing. "I'm not…"

"Yes, you are," Jack told him. "The best gosh-darn assistant we ever grew. And if I could have made you walk again I would have. But it was better to have you like this than to lose you entirely…my loyal friend."

In the motion chair, Ronald's hand wavered until finally he let go of the Devil Rod sparking in his grip. The silver rod fell to the floor with a clatter, its beam of energy abruptly curtailed. "My king," he muttered, bowing his head. "What have I done?"

Standing to either side of the throne, Kane and Grant watched, their weapons poised. But they held off firing, merely watching as the scene played out.

King Jack lay on the floor, the God Rod smoldering in his hand.

Queen Rosalind hurried over to him, lines of concern etched on her face. "Husband? Are you hurt?"

"I'm old and tired," Jack replied with a pained smile. "Nothing the regen pool can't fix."

Ronald spoke up then, his head still bowed in shame. "Your Majesty, there's something else you need to know. Wertham has restarted the Doom Furnace. He plans to launch the World Armor and invade the surface. He's already there now, leading the charge."

"Wertham," the king spat as Roz helped her husband to his feet. "I always said that cat was strange."

With Roz's help, Jack made his way over to the throne and sat, while Ronald moved to his side. Kane and Grant followed, ascending the dais and standing before the king like loyal knights. They watched as Jack placed the God Rod—the real God Rod—back in the hub between the thrones and closed his eyes.

"I can divert the power away from the Doom Furnace,"

Jack explained. "But I can't stop what's already been launched. Kane, Grant—it looks like you boys are on call for some Earth-side action, if you think you're up for it."

"Saving the world," Grant said. "Gotta be a Thursday."

Chapter 32

Brigid stopped short, standing on the narrow ledge outside of the laboratory as a blood-spattered Wertham came barreling toward her.

"No! Don't!" Brigid cried. "You'll kill us bo—"

But it was too late. Absorbed in the fight trance and speckled in his own blood, Wertham had a mind for revenge. He slammed into Brigid as she teetered on the edge of the precipice, and both of them went flying from the ledge that had, just a few minutes earlier, been one end of a stone walkway stretching across the subterranean Doom Furnace.

Air rushed around them as they fell, Wertham atop Brigid, drawing back his fist and punching her in the face. He slammed the fist into her a second time, a third. And then something else hit her, and Brigid felt the cool wetness as she sank beneath the surface of the artificial lake.

For a moment, everything went quiet, the muffling effects of the water dulling all other noise. Brigid opened her eyes, searching the pool for her attacker. She had lost her gun, dropped it during the descent, and the night-vision lenses, too. She hadn't even noticed until now.

Wertham was recovering from the drop, waving arms and legs as he turned himself to come at her again. They must have been split when they hit the pool. There was still time, then.

Brigid stretched her arms out and began to swim, dragging her aching body forward in powerful strokes.

MOVING FAST, KING JACK organized everything. "I can be exhausted later," he told his wife as she urged him to slow down.

Roz smiled at that. Wasn't that just like her Jack—no wonder they called the man "King."

Kane and Grant were rapidly shuttled through the palace on the back of two high-speed conveyances called skycles, clinging behind the drivers who piloted the things through the corridors like birds of prey. The skycles traveled fast—faster even than the lightracer that the king had used to transport them back to the palace, and Grant closed his eyes against the rush that blurred past his eyes.

In no time at all, they arrived at the palace's hangar where two Mantas were being prepped for launch. King Jack had organized all of this; as soon as the God Rod was back in place he could commune with the smart-circuitry than ran through Authentiville and put all the pieces back where they belonged.

Jack's voice came over the room's hidden sound system as Kane was thanking the ground crew and pulling himself into the cockpit. This Manta wasn't much different from his own, maybe a little sleeker around the viewports. "It's going to be tight," Jack explained, "but I'm opening a quantum window remotely. You won't miss it. Soon as you lads pass through you'll be right where Wertham sent the Titan armor. The rest is down to you."

"Roger that," Grant said, drawing the hatch over the cockpit.

"Been good knowing you, Your Highness," Kane added as he placed a bulbous bronze flight helmet over his head. "In case we don't make it back, take care of Baptiste for me. She's…a heck of a girl."

"I hear ya, Kane," Jack said. "But you'll be back. Heroes don't get bad endings on my watch."

With those words echoing in their ears, Kane and Grant

launched the borrowed Mantas into the air, speeding through the open doors of the palace hangar and up into the rainbow sky overhead.

Serra do Norte, Brazil

WERTHAM WATCHED THROUGH the burning eyes of the world armor, taking another of those colossal strides. His mind was fractured across different worlds now, one part of him—the physical—controlled solely by the fight trance. At the same time, the sensor crown granted him a full report from the Titan suit as it strode through the forest of planet Earth. He watched, surprised and amused, as a figure emerged from close to his feet and turned some kind of weapon on him. The man was bald-headed with a bullet-bitten ear and his weapon looked like an elaborate long black stick on a leather strap. The stick spit tiny missiles that pinged hopelessly off the Titan's armored skin.

Wertham stood, bemused, as the man shouted something incomprehensible—outside of Authentiville, speech was no longer planed down to its component parts, which meant that out here he could not know the language without learning it. As if he would bother. Let them learn language from him. Let them speak only his name, soft or loud, in tribute to his greatness.

Then something came buzzing toward his body, cutting through the air like an angry insect until it struck his leg. It was a projectile of some sort, he realized—some kind of surface-man weapon he was not aware of.

STANDING IN THE PATH of the metal giant amid the flaming aisles of trees and grass, Edwards tossed a fragmentation grenade at the thing's legs, aiming for the knee joint. He was hoping it might be a weak spot. More importantly, he was trying to draw the thing's attention to give his ground crew colleagues a better chance to analyze it.

"Cerberus, do you read?" Edwards called over his Commtact. "I appear to be fighting some kind of…God, robot! Could do with your input here if you're not too busy."

Whatever the Cerberus comms desk came back with was lost in the sound of the explosion as the grenade went off. The robot shuddered momentarily, but it seemed to be more from surprise than any effect of the explosive.

Closing one eye, Edwards took careful aim with the M-16-style Colt rifle, targeting the monster's leg. "Let's see if I can make a dent, Too-tall-for-school," he muttered, rattling off a shot.

Cosmic Rift

BRIGID SWAM, HER BODY aching with exhaustion. This bowl of water was used as a cooling agent during the production process, and like everything in Authentiville it was massive. When she had seen it from above she'd mentally tagged it as a lake. Brigid could see the lip of the bowl now, or maybe she should call it the shore, but it was still some distance away.

Behind her, Wertham was moving with power but little grace, driving himself on in the chase across the water's surface, splashing great waves of spume behind him. The man looked demented, blood staining his soaking clothes, his right hand mangled where it had taken five bullets. Brigid peered over her shoulder again, confirming how near he was. Just a couple of body lengths behind her and gaining fast. She pushed herself on, drawing on reserves of energy she hardly believed she had. Without a gun, without any weapon, she would lose against this man. He was stronger, faster, possessed. The only way she could win was to outthink him.

Her mind tripped back to the conversation she had had

with Kane when he came upon her in the Cerberus swimming pool.

"It's always a competition with you, isn't it?" she had teased.

"It's kept me alive so far," Kane had responded.

Yeah, well, now Wertham was the competition and if she didn't outpace him she would end up dead, just like Kane said.

Have to keep moving, Brigid told herself, pushing the aches in her body to the back of her mind.

Brigid drew a deep breath and disappeared beneath the surface, carving a path there like a torpedo. She drove herself harder, eyeing the edge of the water as it shimmered closer, reaching harder and kicking out with all her strength.

ABOVE THE DOOM Furnace, Wertham's war fleet waited for the command to invade, like grim shadows of death hovering statically in the air.

Flying in formation, Kane and Grant powered their Mantas through the leading edge of the fleet. Kane wished their Commtacts would work here in the rift as he yearned to discuss tactics with his partner. But without that contact, all the friends could do was trust each other as they rocketed up past the fleet toward the quantum window that was opening in the sky above the city.

The quantum window was barely large enough to allow one Manta to pass, so Kane urged more power from his engines and sped ahead of Grant, taking the lead. In a moment he was through the window with Grant rushing to follow.

Chapter 33

Serra do Norte, Brazil

It was a second that lasted for eternity.

Then the lush forest and familiar snaking river material-ized in Kane's windshield like a vision from a dream. Some-thing else had changed, too, Kane realized as he felt the sun beating down on the Manta's cockpit. He was home, and he hadn't even realized how much he had missed it.

For a single perfect instant, Kane luxuriated in the feel of the sun on the craft's wingtips, the sight of the foliage spread beneath him like a painter's canvas.

"—ne buddy? Do you read me?" Grant's voice was loud in his ear after all this time.

"I read, over," Kane replied, engaging his Commtact, un-able to hide the joy in his voice.

"I'm right behind you," Grant explained. "What do we have?"

Kane turned back to business as he brought up the heads-up display and began scanning for the Titan suit. From what King Jack had said, Kane guessed it wouldn't be hard to spot. What the heck does a planet-invasion device look like anyway?

Up ahead, black smoke was billowing into the air from a portion of the forest. Kane had the sinking feeling that that was where they would find their quarry.

ON THE GROUND, Sinclair called to Edwards as he scrambled away from the Titan, foliage burning all around him. "Edwards, we have more company. Up there." She pointed.

Using what cover he could, Edwards halted and peered up into the sky. Beside Sinclair, Mariah Falk and Roy Cataman were doing the same, the latter peering through field glasses as an evergreen burned like a torch behind him. Edwards could see the two shapes swooping through the sky roughly a mile up and a little to the west, but it took him a moment to recognize them.

"Are those…? They're Mantas!" Edwards cried. "Dammit! Either we're in the middle of another Annunaki invasion or Kane and Grant just arrived to pull our fat out of the fire."

"Literally," Mariah added, trees and bushes burning all around her.

Sinclair looked at Edwards with alarm. "But which is it?" she asked.

Already, Edwards was engaging the subdermal implant of his Commtact, sending a query out. "Kane? Grant? Is that you up there, buddy?"

"I hear you, Edwards," Kane's voice responded an instant later. "Grant's behind me. Where are you?"

"About a half mile from the river below you and heading east," Edwards told him. "I got a field team out here—just follow the line of fire and you'll see us. And we have us a huge problem—big fella, armored, fell out of the sky about six minutes ago. Looks kind of like if Satan had mated with a cyborg. You can't miss him."

Bitterroot Mountains

KANE'S LAUGHTER BURST from the speaker at the comm desk as the conversation was relayed over an open frequency. "Hah! I guess not," he said.

Around the operations room, everyone was smiling and cheering. Several people shook hands in congratulations while others hugged, patting one another on the back. Lakesh stood poised over the comm desk, listening to every word of the conversation as he watched the satellite footage being relayed live from Serra do Norte.

"Kane, this is Lakesh," he began, adjusting the headset over his ear. "I need to know—are you all right?"

"I'm fine and Grant's with me," Kane said. "And when I last saw them, Baptiste and Domi were both still alive. No time to discuss right now—we've got a planet invasion to repel."

Lakesh watched the Mantas as they tracked across the satellite image, two bronze darts swooping over the green. "Good luck, my friends," he muttered. "Good luck."

In the skies above Serra do Norte, Kane and Grant angled the unfamiliar Mantas toward the colossal figure they saw looming above the tree line. As they approached, their heads-up displays brought the thing's head and torso into sharp focus where they poked over the tree cover as twin beams seared from the eyes to set great chunks of the forest alight.

Edwards's description was pretty much on the money, Kane thought—with its sunset-colored armor and burning eyes, the Titan suit looked darn satanic, truth be told.

"Now," Kane muttered, toggling switches on the dashboard, "let's see what kind of armaments we have."

A targeting reticle appeared over Kane's heads-up, twin circles adjusting and focusing as he eyed the colossal Titan.

"Launching Sidewinder missile," Kane said into the Commtact.

"Advised," Grant acknowledged, drawing his Manta away from Kane's before the missile launched to ensure he didn't get caught up in its path.

The missile blasted—a sleek shaft of gold ribbed with green—from a tube beneath the Manta's sloping right wing. It wasn't a Sidewinder—those were the missiles that their own Mantas were armed with—but at that moment Kane didn't have time to split hairs.

Cosmic Rift

THE WARSHIPS WAITED in the sky above the Doom Furnace, casting shadows on the vast body of cooling water. Two figures swam across that water, angling toward the side.

Head down, Brigid almost hit the edge, she was moving so fast. Her head bobbed from the water at the very last instant and she grabbed the side, yanking herself up and out of the water without missing a beat. Wertham was six body lengths behind her now, hurrying toward her, arm over arm, through the clear water of the tank.

Brigid turned and ran across the adjoining catwalk, eyes flicking left and right as she sought a path back up to the parked steed she had arrived in. She had an idea now—desperate, but it might work. It had to work. Otherwise she was dead. Maybe they all were.

Brigid ran.

Serra do Norte, Brazil

KANE'S MISSILE COVERED the distance between his Manta and the Titan in less than three seconds. Kane pulled up, bracing for impact as the missile detonated. There was a boom, and whatever was inside created a green explosion, like the film negative of a detonation.

When the blast cleared, Kane saw that the Titan armor looked unhurt, just a few wisps of white smoke trailed up from its chest where the missile had struck. The head turned, eyeing the Mantas with its sizzling orange gaze.

"Okay," Kane said. "We may need to rethink this."

To his starboard side, Grant was launching his own missile, patching through a warning via the Commtact as he did so. Kane watched Grant's missile draw a smoking trail in the air as it hurried toward the Titan. But before the missile could impact, the colossal head turned and the heat beam zeroed in, obliterating the missile into a million fragments.

"We definitely need to rethink this," Kane said as he pulled the Manta into a corkscrew turn, barreling past the Titan's shoulder at incredible speed. The Titan reached for him, one mighty hand grasping at the slope-winged aircraft.

Cosmic Rift

BRIGID SCRAMBLED UP an enclosed stairwell, her boots barely touching each step as she hurried back to the surface. Up above, Wertham's war fleet remained poised, darkening the rainbow sky like some insane mechanical construct, waiting for the final command to launch.

Brigid reached the top of the stairs and kept running, weaving between Gene-agers who stood dumbfounded as if caught in the path of an approaching hurricane. They had lost their impetus, Brigid guessed, though she had no time to fathom why. It seemed that somehow all of the Gene-agers had simply been placed on "pause," posed as if in a photograph.

Behind Brigid, Wertham was just reaching the top of the stairwell, his emerald jumpsuit dark with damp where he had been dunked in the lakelike pool. He still wore the sensor rig on his head like a crown, its wire frame glistening with droplets of water.

There was just one more staircase now, Brigid saw, a short flight of steps and she was at the parking bay where she had left the steed. She leaped up the steps, grabbing the handrail and taking them two at a time. Behind her, Wertham was almost near enough to touch, and Brigid could hear his breathing down below as she reached the topmost stair. She turned, one hand still gripping the handrail, and kicked out behind her, dipping her torso and head low and putting as much force as she could into the blow. It caught Wertham full in the chin as he ascended the staircase, and he went flying back with a satisfying yelp of pain.

There was no time to follow up. Instead, Brigid ran, leaping ahead like a runner from the starting blocks, arms and legs pumping as she hurried across the parking lot and back to her boxy steed.

The steed waited there, thankfully unmolested. Brigid willed the door hatch open, passing her hand across the space where she thought a sensor might be. She had never really thought about how the door operated, and now she could only hope that it worked, either feeling her need or responding to the touch of her hand. The door slid noiselessly back on its hidden track.

Then Brigid was inside, eyes focused on the thing she had come here for. This had better work, she told herself.

Behind Brigid, Wertham had reached the top of the short staircase and was making his way across the parking compound toward her.

Serra do Norte, Brazil

THE GIANT HAND reached for Kane's Manta, fingers grasping for him as he hopelessly tried to avoid it. The hand blocked the sun for a moment as it grabbed for the Manta's tail, and in that moment Kane thought it was all over. But then something happened, and the hand seemed to lock, drawing fractionally upward and missing Kane's Manta by the narrowest of margins.

Kane rolled the Manta through 360 degrees on its y-axis, slipping the wings out of the reach of the Titan's grasping hand. The massive fingers seized in position behind him, closing slowly on nothing but empty air.

"What happened?" Kane asked as he goosed more power from the air pulse engines.

"We've got company," Grant replied over the Commtact. "Looks like Bingo and Bongo came back to give us a hand."

Kane checked the sensors of the heads-up display, scanning the skies. Two familiar sky craft flew high above, close to where the parallax point had opened from Authentiville. They were the golden pebble-like vehicles that the Authentiville pilots had used to kidnap Grant's Manta during the sting operation. "Yahoo!" Kane cheered as he realized they were using their gravity beams to hold the Titan's hand in place.

Grant's voice relayed over the Commtact from where he was flying a parallel path to Kane. "That was a close one, pal," he said.

"Yeah," Kane agreed. "Don't be fooled by that thing's size—it's faster than you'd think."

Even as Kane spoke, twin beams of searing energy blasted from the Titan's eyes, joining and burning a single path toward one of the pebblelike ships. Kane watched as the beam blasted against the aircraft's armor, and in an instant the craft had been liquefied.

"We've lost Bingo," Kane muttered as he watched the superheated golden rain fall from the sky where moments before there had been an aircraft.

Freed from the triangulated gravity lock, the Titan's hand moved once more, reaching to swat Grant's Manta to the ground as it hurtled past its head.

Inside the cockpit, collision alarms were going crazy, alerting Grant to the very real possibility that he was about to get batted out of the sky by a three-hundred-foot man. Grant pushed the joystick forward as far as it would go, sending the Manta on a downward trajectory that brought it just barely beneath the swatting hand.

Grant's Manta continued on its new path, hurtling toward the ground at a vertical angle, engine protesting. Treetops came rushing toward the viewport at alarming speed, alarms singing in Grant's ears. Grant held the joystick in place, forcing the Manta to loop-the-loop in a forward roll. The wings cut through the highest branches of the trees and for a moment all Grant could see through the cockpit portholes was burning trees and ground as he was turned entirely upside down.

Above him, Kane flew an evasive pattern around the towering Titan, launching two more missiles in quick succession. The missiles slapped against the Titan's thick armor, exploding in great gouts of green fog, but the Titan merely stood there, absorbing the impacts without any effect.

"We're running out of options," Kane said over the linked Commtacts. "Anyone have any ideas? Cerberus? Edwards?"

INSIDE THE TITAN control grid, Wertham the Strange was having the time of his life. He had never been an air jockey, and being given this opportunity to knock the grins off these pilots' smug faces was one he could not resist passing up. There was no way that they could damage the World Armor, no way to penetrate its fabulous construction. It had been heat-sealed using the heart of a star dragged into the quantum rift—nothing could damage its skin. *Nothing.*

In his mind Wertham turned his head, bringing the Titan suit's head around before sending another burst of the heat ray at the retreating bronze vehicle.

"I could do this all day," he trilled.

Cosmic Rift

BRIGID REACHED FOR the static figure who waited in the steed exactly as she had left her. The woman's eyes were blank, and she took no notice when Brigid wrenched the mirrored headband from her head and pushed it down over her own. The headband was connected by a thin tube to the box at the woman's belt, and Brigid remained close as a bank of lights came to life across its surface.

Suddenly, Brigid could see the woman in a different way. She was standing there and yet there was an aura around her head, a series of overlays in different colors, each one an oval, new colors forming where they met. The colors were dull, like lightbulbs without power, only the color of the glass remaining.

Brigid spun as Wertham entered the steed, shoving back the door with his mangled right hand. His lips were peeled back, showing his teeth, and there was blood there. But there was something else, too, visible in the overlay that now appeared from the sensor rig's data feed playing straight into Brigid's ocular nerve.

The ovals around Wertham's head were bright and colorful, different shades of red and green clashing with one another as they vied for space. The largest of the ovals was huge, encompassing not just his head but almost the whole of the steed's buslike interior. Intelligence? Telepathic communion? Something else? Brigid could only speculate.

Behind Wertham, Brigid could see the Gene-agers where they waited for new commands, stock still and dead eyed. The ovals around them were small and washed out, made up of just three or four layers where Wertham's were a hundred or more.

Thoughts. The ovals were *thoughts.*

Kane had been right about that when they had arrived and

the two headband people had stopped and viewed them in the cockpit of the Manta. They had been scanning their thoughts, searching their minds for a hint of treachery. Brigid wondered what her mind had looked like to these people, what colors she thought in, but there wasn't time to consider that. Wertham was coming at her, a glowing line of fire visible around the headpiece he wore, his thoughts turning darker like a thunderstorm.

"I could do this all day," Wertham trilled as he reached out to grab Brigid's throat.

Chapter 34

As Wertham's hands reached for her throat, Brigid fired a thought at his mind. Via the sensors she wore, it seemed to rip like a spear through the ovals that surrounded his brain.

Wertham staggered, taking two steps away, his hands clenching and unclenching. "What…did you—?" he began, struggling to form the sentence.

Brigid thought again, sending her thought like a weapon at the dizzying pattern swirling around Wertham's head. It was his brain that she was looking at, she realized now, a visual representation of the processes, every thought he was having, conscious and subconscious. She recalled the parts of the human brain, plucking them from her eidetic memory. There was the medulla and the pons, the thalamus and the hypothalamus, the cerebellum, the cerebral cortex, the hippocampus and the ganglia. She ripped into each one, redefining it for Wertham's mental processes, those floating discs of red and green.

And Wertham—a genius, an inventor, a schemer—was unable to resist. He had entered the fight trance when Brigid had arrived in his laboratory, leaving his body to run on autopilot, a series of mathematical equations resulting in the perfect fighting maneuvers for any moment of combat.

Outside of his mind now, Wertham could only watch as the body he had been born in began to crumble at Brigid's mental onslaught. It sank to its knees, and the eyes lost their luster, gazing away into infinity while Wertham's mind stood to one side and watched.

Teeth gritted, Brigid took a single step forward, as far as the tube that connected her headband to the control box would allow, and sent another wave of emotion at the struggling figure in green. Wertham's face turned red, blood rushing to his brain and from it, and Brigid saw the veins throbbing there, fit to burst. She could feel the pressure, see it in the colored ovals that seemed to hover in the air around Wertham. Whatever that headpiece was that he wore, it sparkled like diamonds through the altered vision of her mind-tool, containing and constraining his mind as he tried to fight back.

Brigid did not expect what happened next. Wertham's head continued to redden and then suddenly the skin sank as the skull beneath cracked.

Wertham felt the blow to his mind like a kick to the head, and he retreated, running for the nearest vessel where he might yet be safe.

Serra do Norte, Brazil

SUDDENLY, WERTHAM'S MIND was entirely inside the Titan suit, searing a great line of fire across the landscape as the twin aircraft circled him, blasting with their pathetically inadequate weapons. There was a third vehicle up there, too, poised higher than the others and retaining its distance from the conflict now that its partner had been melted down to its component atoms.

Wertham reached forward, commanding the Titan suit to grab one of the irritating things that flew at his face. A missile impacted uselessly on his wrist, and then his fist snagged around the Manta, wrenching it from the sky as it hurtled toward him.

GRANT WATCHED IN horror as Kane's Manta was grabbed by the towering Titan. Kane's velocity was so great that the Titan was pulled the length of his arm as he strove to hang on.

"Eject!" Grant shouted, hoping Kane still could.

SEATED INSIDE HIS cockpit, Kane was yanked against the safety harness as the gigantic red hand plucked him from the sky. The Manta's internal compensators worked overtime as they fought to keep the pilot from careening through the windshield. Kane felt his breath wrenched out of him as the pressure wave slammed against his chest.

For a moment his vision went dark and Kane feared he was about to black out. But the voice in his ear wouldn't let him. Grant was shouting at him over their linked Commtacts, urging him to eject.

Blindly, Kane reached for the eject button, slapping his palm against it. The lid blew and Kane was suddenly climbing in the air, still seated in the pilot's chair, a gigantic hand beneath him holding his Manta like a child holding an insect.

Cosmic Rift

"NOT SO FAST," Brigid whispered, seeing the way that Wertham's mind was escaping from his body. Whether the man would last two minutes out of his physical form, Brigid didn't know—she only knew that she had to bring him back.

The mind web strained, reaching out to grab for Wertham where he had retreated into the World Armor. Brigid's mind reached for him, clawlike wisps grabbing his thoughts and pulling them back in fluttering tendrils that tore like cobwebs. She couldn't do it, couldn't pull him back. She could only grab bits of his mind and watch as they disintegrated before her eyes.

So Brigid did the only other thing she could think of. She reached forward and plucked the crown of wires from Wertham's head, wrenching it from him and tossing it into the corner of the steed.

She only hoped that it would be enough to stop him.

Serra do Norte, Brazil

MOVING THE MIGHTY arm of the Titan suit, Wertham reached for the fluttering figure of the Manta's pilot while his other hand clung to the straining aircraft like a trophy. His hand opened to snag Kane as he fell through the air strapped in the seat, and then…

The arm stopped moving, the hand locked in midreach.

Wertham tried again, but the body would not move. Something had happened; the connection had broken. The woman had done something and now he couldn't operate the Titan suit. He could only wear it, locked inside a suit designed never to degenerate. Locked inside forever.

Wertham's solitude had just begun again, imprisoned once more, as he had been for seven centuries. And this time, he could not even speak.

Cosmic Rift

WERTHAM'S BRAIN DIMMED before her eyes as Brigid watched him through the technology of the mind reader. The vibrant ovals had diminished in number and size, and slowly their color paled to a bland whiteness which, in turn, became clear before finally fading to nothingness. It was over.

Carefully, Brigid peeled off the headband. She was sweating, a slick line of saltwater over her forehead and running down her face. She was exhausted, too, mentally tired and physically shattered. Pacing over to the panoramic windows of the steed she stood there a moment and gazed out at the Doom Furnace. It was darkening, and the Gene-agers who had worked it were lined up solemnly, awaiting their next command. Above, Wertham's war fleet waited for an order that would never come.

Chapter 35

The quantum window opened one last time, disgorging two Mantas over the starlit forest of Serra do Norte.

"Clear skies," Grant said over the Commtact as he piloted the trailing aircraft.

Kane nodded where he sat in the pilot's seat of the lead vehicle. He knew how Grant felt—the comment wasn't a good luck motto or an observation of the, for once, lack of hostile activity in the vicinity; it was merely a greeting directed to familiar stars twinkling over their heads once more.

"We still have a couple of hours' flight time before we get home," Kane said, engaging his Commtact. "You and Domi going to be okay or you want to stop off somewhere and get a bite to eat?"

There was a brief pause while Grant discussed the options with his passenger. Then Domi's voice came over the Commtact, cheery as ever. "Let's just go home," she said. "I miss that place."

Kane heard Brigid laugh where she was seated behind him in the Manta's cockpit but he didn't know why. Only Brigid knew how taken Domi had been with Authentiville and how she had proclaimed her desire to stay there back when she and Brigid had been alone in the golden city. However, the attempted coup on King Jack's domain had rather put a damper on the woman's enthusiasm and she had elected to return home after all.

"Better the devil you know?" Brigid had suggested when Domi had told her.

"Better the friends you know," Domi had responded. And that was all that needed to be said.

King Jack had resumed his duties as monarch even before Brigid had defeated Wertham. Jack, it seemed, liked to keep things in order, and once he was in commune with the city's operating system, care of the God Rod in the palace hub, he could go about getting things back the way they had been before Wertham and his ally had mounted their attack.

The Gene-agers would be checked over individually and safeguards would be put in place to ensure they couldn't be turned on their rulers ever again. Dr. Ronald had been placed in charge of that task, and he proudly accepted, grateful to the king and queen for giving him another chance.

Jack had shut down the hidden broadcast signal that Wertham's Devil Rod had placed in the sound system, too, which meant people could start thinking for themselves again. Everyone agreed that Jack was a leader they would choose if it ever came down to it, which it wouldn't.

After the battle with the Titan, which had ended abruptly once the armored suit seized up where it stood, Grant had picked up Kane where he landed in the forest. Kane was a little shook up but, typical Kane, keen to get right back in the thick of things until they won. Hearing the World Armor had simply stopped operating came as something of a disappointment, but Kane did his best to hide it. After all, he figured, you take saving the world any way you can get it, even if you're not the guy who lands that decisive, knock-out punch.

Accompanied by the remaining scout, Kane and Grant had returned in Grant's Manta to Authentiville and the court of King Jack.

"The loss of Scout Alphred will be mourned," Jack assured the Cerberus men. "But it won't take away from what you two did for us. And, most of all, for me. You're heroes, both of you—don't let anyone ever tell you otherwise."

They figured that meant something coming from King Jack. He was a man who knew a hero when he saw one.

So, secure in their own Mantas once more, the Cerberus warriors returned home, passing through the quantum gateway one last time and seeing the stars of their own world waiting above the forest of Serra do Norte like favorite friends. Edwards and his field team had long since put out the fires and returned to Cerberus by interphaser by the time the Mantas re-emerged in the sky. Below them, Kane, Brigid, Grant and Domi saw the statuelike figure of the Titan looming above the treetops, one hand crushed around the remains of the Manta that Kane had piloted. It was an artifact now, just like the ones King Jack's people scoured Earth to salvage. Maybe they'd come back for it someday.

The Mantas banked in unison, turning northward, heading home.

* * * * *

The
Don Pendleton's
Executioner ®
HARD TARGETS

A missing-persons case escalates into Mafia war…

While investigating a missing-persons case, Mack Bolan's brother Johnny uncovers a link between the Buffalo police department and the Mafia. But when he's forced to kill one of the cops moonlighting for the mob, the stakes suddenly go through the roof. Both sides want him to pay—in blood. But they're not the only ones looking for payback. The Mafia don is about to get a lethal message—delivered personally by the Executioner.

JAMES AXLER

DEATH LANDS®

SIREN SONG

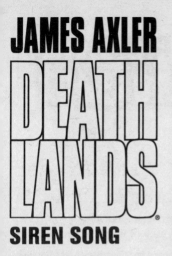
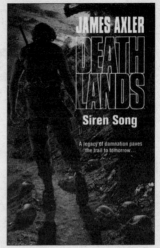

A legacy of damnation paves the trail to tomorrow

If utopia exists in post-apocalyptic America, Ryan and his companions have yet to greet it. But in the mountains of Virginia, their quest may find its reward. Heaven Falls is an idyll of thriving humanity harnessing powerful feminine energy and the medicinal qualities of honey. Bountiful and serene, this agrarian community is the closest thing to sanctuary the companions have ever encountered. But as they are seduced by a life they have only envisioned, they discover Heaven has a trapdoor that opens straight to hell....

Available January wherever books and ebooks are sold.

AleX Archer
TREASURE OF LIMA

A myth of the past holds the promise of wealth...and death.

Costa Rica's white beaches and coral reefs should have been adventure-proof. But naturally, archaeologist and TV show host Annja Creed's peace is interrupted by a mysterious woman with a strange tale. Her husband has disappeared after leading an expedition in search of the "Lost Loot of Lima." The treasure was lost in the late nineteenth century, when a Peruvian ship captain had gone mad with greed. Now Annja has been asked to lead a fateful sojourn for the lost loot. But where treasures are lost, danger will always be found....

Available January wherever books and ebooks are sold.

GRA46